One Final Request

"Dusty . . . ?"

Spurr grimaced as he placed a hand on the sheriff's left shoulder. He was shot up bad. He might have been dead. He wasn't moving. Spurr jerked the man's shoulder slightly and was surprised when Mason stiffened and lifted his head a little.

The man grunted, tried straightening his back, but cursed softly and rested his chest back down against the grulla's neck. His hat was gone, and his thin, sweat-matted hair was mussed.

"Easy, Dusty," Spurr said. "I'll get you down."

Mason turned to him. Even the man's face was splattered with blood—likely from the many wounds in his chest and belly. Blood slithered down from both nostrils, matting his mustache. He ground his jaws. His eyes were dark and flat with pain.

"Spurr . . . ?" His voice was a wheeze that barely made it through his lips.

Spurr squeezed the man's bloody arm, his own knees threatening to buckle. "I'm here, Dusty." He blinked hard as tears oozed out of his eyes to roll down his cheeks.

"Spurr," Mason said again, only slightly louder this time. His eyes bored into Spurr's for a full ten seconds, his jaws quivering as he ground them together. And then he said between quick, shallow breaths, "Kill 'em. . . ."

THE LAST LAWMAN

A RUSTY SPURR NOVEL

PETER BRANDVOLD

BERKLEY BOOKS, NEW YORK

THE BERKLEY PUBLISHING GROUP
Published by the Penguin Group
Penguin Group (USA) Inc.
375 Hudson Street, New York, New York 10014, USA
Penguin Group (Canada), 90 Eglinton Avenue East, Suite 700, Toronto, Ontario M4P 2Y3, Canada
(a division of Pearson Penguin Canada Inc.) • Penguin Books Ltd., 80 Strand, London WC2R 0RL,
England • Penguin Group Ireland, 25 St. Stephen's Green, Dublin 2, Ireland (a division of Penguin
Books Ltd.) • Penguin Group (Australia), 250 Camberwell Road, Camberwell, Victoria 3124, Australia
(a division of Pearson Australia Group Pty. Ltd.) • Penguin Books India Pvt. Ltd., 11 Community
Centre, Panchsheel Park, New Delhi—110 017, India • Penguin Group (NZ), 67 Apollo Drive,
Rosedale, Auckland 0632, New Zealand (a division of Pearson New Zealand Ltd.) • Penguin Books
(South Africa) (Pty.) Ltd., 24 Sturdee Avenue, Rosebank, Johannesburg 2196, South Africa

Penguin Books Ltd., Registered Offices: 80 Strand, London WC2R 0RL, England

This is a work of fiction. Names, characters, places, and incidents either are the product of the author's imagination or are used fictitiously, and any resemblance to actual persons, living or dead, business establishments, events, or locales is entirely coincidental. The publisher does not have any control over and does not assume any responsibility for author or third-party websites or their content.

THE LAST LAWMAN

A Berkley Book / published by arrangement with the author

PUBLISHING HISTORY
Berkley edition / October 2012

Copyright © 2012 by Peter Brandvold.
Cover illustration by Bruce Emmett.
Cover design by Edwin Tse.
Interior text design by Laura K. Corless.

ISBN: 978-0-425-25050-1

BERKLEY®
Berkley Books are published by The Berkley Publishing Group,
a division of Penguin Group (USA) Inc.,
375 Hudson Street, New York, New York 10014.
BERKLEY® is a registered trademark of Penguin Group (USA) Inc.
The "B" design is a trademark of Penguin Group (USA) Inc.

PRINTED IN THE UNITED STATES OF AMERICA

10 9 8 7 6 5 4 3 2 1

ALWAYS LEARNING   PEARSON

ONE

The kid cried, "Spurr, you whoremongerin' ole devil—I'm all shot up over here!"

"I told you to stay to ground, you worthless pup!"

Guns blasted from the three front windows of the outlaw shack. Chunks of hot lead screeched through the air, thumped into the ground near where Deputy Sheriff Kenny Potter lay writhing, his rifle in the dirt beside him. He had both hands cupped to his bloody left side, holding his guts in.

"Spurr, I can't get up!" the kid cried as a bullet blew up sand and gravel two feet beside his curly head. He whipped his face away from where the bullet had hit, screaming, *"Spurr!"*

Deputy United States Marshal Spurr Morgan chewed out a frustrated curse, brushed the back of his buckskin glove across his patch-bearded cheek, and raised his '66 Winchester to his bowed, old shoulder. He fired once, twice, three times, the rifle thundering and stabbing smoke and flames toward the brush-roofed, adobe-brick cabin.

The echoes sounded like shrill witches' squeals as they chased each other around the New Mexico canyon.

The sun-washed outlaw shack fronted a lumpy stone escarpment about sixty yards away from the dry wash that Spurr was hunkered in. Two of his bullets hammered the gray wooden casing around two windows with loud, wooden *whumps!* The third slug winged through the window right of the Z-frame door, evoking a clipped scream from inside.

"Goddamn you, Spurr!" shouted one of the train robbers holed up in the shack. "You just blew one of my ears off!"

"Come on out of there peaceable-like!" the old lawman shouted, "or I'm gonna shoot off a helluva lot more than that, Philpot!"

Spurr, Sheriff Ralph Adams, and Adams's deputy, Kenny Potter, had tracked the outlaw gang, known far and wide as Philpot's Dogs, out of Jicarilla, New Mexico Territory, and into the nearby Jicarilla Mountains. Adams had been shot in the left leg the day before when Hector Philpot's bunch had bushwhacked the three lawmen. Spurr had patched up the sheriff as well as he could and sent him back home for tending.

Spurr and the young deputy, Potter, whom Spurr doubted was a day past twenty and was as green as willow bark, had continued to the shack here along Turkey Gulch, in one of the range's dry canyons. The gang of five was holed up inside with the eight thousand dollars they'd stolen from a payroll shipment belonging to a mine in southern Colorado. The mine had been contracted by the federal government, which had made looting it a federal offense.

Thus, Chief Marshal Henry Brackett had sent his most experienced, also oldest, deputy, Spurr Morgan, down from his headquarters in Denver to run the dogs to ground. Since Philpot's gang had shot up Jicarilla on their southern dash to the border, Adams had insisted that he and his wet-behind-the-ears deputy throw in with the federal lawdog.

Spurr had welcomed Adams's help, but he didn't cotton

to younguns tracking experienced killers. Now, as young Potter continued to scream and curse and roll his guts out into his bloody hands, the federal lawman remembered why.

Spurr had told the kid to remain in the wash, but since there'd been no horses in the corral flanking the cabin, and they'd seen no signs of life around the place, Potter had insisted the shack was vacant. Against Spurr's orders, he'd risen up out of the wash, calling Spurr an old woman, and walked toward the cabin, whistling.

That's when the gang had thrown the shack's shutters wide and opened up with their rifles.

Now, Hector Philpot showed his hatless head in the window, his left hand covering his left ear, holding a Spencer .56 in his other hand. "You got more sand than brains, old man! You're one against five, and my gang's just like me"— the long-faced outlaw flashed a silver-toothed grin—*"poison mean!"*

Spurr pumped a fresh shell into his Winchester's chamber and fired. Philpot gave a taunting whoop and slid his head back behind the window frame as Spurr's slug sliced the air where the sneering face had been a wink before. Inside the cabin, a bottle broke with a hollow bark of shattering glass.

Judging by the sound, the bottle had been at least half full. Spurr smiled.

"Shit!" yelled another outlaw with a raspy Texas twang— Nordecker Riley, most likely. "That there was our last bottle o' red-eye!"

A rifle snaked out the window left of the door, and Spurr jerked his head back behind his covering boulder as the gun roared. The slug hammered the front of Spurr's boulder with a crashing squeal, spraying rock dust and shards in all directions.

"Throw that old cannon of yours out here, Spurr!" shouted Philpot. "Then the hogleg. You don't got a chance against us. If you don't, the boy dies—understand?"

Hunkered low behind the boulder on the bank of the wash, Spurr chewed his lip as he held his cocked rifle straight up and down against his shoulder. He cast his blue-eyed gaze out from beneath the brim of his tan Stetson till he could see Kenny Potter lying about thirty yards out from the cabin. He was thirty yards to Spurr's right, where the dry wash curved around to the south side of the cactus- and yucca-stippled yard.

A covered stone well lay within five yards of him.

"Kenny, crawl behind that well!" Spurr called. "Can you do that, son?"

The outlaws had stopped shooting. An eerie silence hovered over the yard blasted with brilliant mountain sunshine raining out of a cobalt sky. Kenny rolled onto his right shoulder, his deputy sheriff's badge glinting on his brown wool vest, and lifted his hatless head. His curly auburn hair bounced around his ears and neck. The boy's face was a mask of pain and horror.

He shook his head and clamped his hands tighter against his bloody side. "I can't, goddamnit, Spurr. My insides is fallin' out!"

Just then a rifle roared from a cabin window. Out of the corner of his left eye, Spurr saw the bright red-orange flash and the streak of powder smoke. Kenny screamed and jerked his head down, pressing his forehead against the sand and gravel as he moved one hand up from his belly to his left ear.

"That's for my ear, Spurr!" Philpot shouted above the metallic rasp of a rifle's cocking lever. "An ear for an ear. That's fair, ain't it?"

Spurr looked at Kenny. The young deputy was twisted around with his face in the dirt, shoulders jerking as he sobbed and clutched the far side of his shaggy head. A good-looking kid. The kind that no doubt drew many a young woman's eye back home in Jicarilla.

But he'd be considerably less attractive without that ear, though the belly wound would likely be the end of him.

Rage burned through Spurr like a glowing war lance.

"Goddamnit, Philpot—he's just a kid. Can't you see he's down?"

The only reply was ribald laughter and the loud rasp of another shell being jacked into Philpot's .56.

Spurr snaked his rifle around the rock and cut loose with three more shots before return fire pushed him back behind cover. Several slugs spanged off the boulder. A few more blew up clumps of dirt and gravel around him. One large-caliber bullet tore up a yucca plant and hurled it back into the wash behind him.

Amidst the din, Spurr heard the distinctive roar of Philpot's Spencer. Kenny shrieked. As the gunfire died, Spurr edged another look around the rock to see Kenny arching his back and awkwardly reaching for his bloody left knee. The young man's mouth formed a perfect *O* as he lifted his head and loosed a horrific scream.

The gunfire died.

Silence like a held breath descended.

Spurr could hear the boy sobbing against the ground as the blood ran out of him. The cries were like razor-edged daggers raked across every nerve in the old lawman's big, sinewy body. He pushed his hat off his head, raked a hand down his patchy, light-brown beard streaked with gray, cursing under his breath. His weak ticker heaved like a foundering horse in his chest.

Part of him wanted to throw his guns down and walk out from behind the rock. But the experienced lawman in him knew that that wouldn't save Kenny. It would only get them both killed. And Philpot would ride free, laughing, him and the rest of his wolves heading off to whore away the winter in Las Cruces.

"Kenny," Spurr said, hearing the anguish in his own voice. "Hold on, son."

Philpot called, "What do you say, Spurr? You gonna come out with your hands wide, or we gonna have to go on killin' this poor pup . . . *slow*?"

Spurr raised the Winchester to his shoulder, keeping it low and back where no one from the cabin could see its dusty, octagonal, blue-steel barrel. He stared out over the sights at Kenny's slumped, prone figure, the boy mewling now like a gut-shot coyote. His head lolled slowly from side to side, and he was digging the toes of his spurred boots into the gravel, as though feebly trying to push himself forward.

Spurr cleared the emotion from his throat as he pressed his cheek up against the Winchester's worn walnut stock. "Ya done good, Kenny!" he shouted, though it came out cracked and shrill. "Ya done real good!"

The Winchester roared, bucking against Spurr's brittle shoulder.

The old lawman sobbed and sniffed, a single tear rolling down his weathered face and tracking into his scraggly beard as he ejected the spent cartridge from the Winchester's breech. It clinked off a rock behind him.

"You'd have made a damn good lawman one day," he added tightly, not looking at the deputy's spasming figure beyond the rifle's smoking barrel, blood blossoming from the hole in his left temple.

"Jesus Christ, Spurr!" Philpot yelled from the cabin, chuckling in disbelief. "What'd you *do*?"

"I killed him," Spurr said softly, weakly, ramming a fresh cartridge into the Winchester's chamber, then brushing the tear from his cheek with the back of his gloved hand. "And now, if it's the last thing I do, by thunder, I'm gonna kill you."

TWO

Spurr pressed the back of his head against his covering boulder, his heart thudding heavily but slowly, skipping a beat now and then. He'd let the outlaws wonder for a few seconds what his next move would be, let them start wondering what theirs should be.

When enough time had passed that they were likely letting their guards down just a little, he turned sharply to his left and pressed his cheek tight against his Winchester's stock. A target presented itself in a cabin window—the vague shape of a man's hatted head as he stared toward Spurr. The old lawman saw the man's eyes snap wide as Spurr's Winchester spoke.

Before the man could jerk his head back behind the cabin wall, his right eye disappeared. Spurr caught a brief glimpse of red as the bullet hammered through the man's head and out the back of his skull before Spurr pulled his own head and his rifle back behind the boulder. Sucking a sharp breath, the lawman pushed off the boulder and slid down the bank and into the sandy-bottomed wash.

Spurr had always worn high-topped moccasins instead of stockmen's boots with spurs and jinglebobs—had started the practice just after he'd left his horse-trading family's shotgun farm in western Kansas to hunt buffalo nigh on forty years ago—and he was especially glad to be wearing them now. The soft-soled, low-heeled moccasins fairly propelled him—as much as anything could propel his tired, broken-down carcass—down the gravelly wash. He was able to move quietly, and the willows and cottonwoods lining the wash hid him from view of the cabin.

When he'd run thirty yards, his wizened lungs heaving in his chest, his heart tattooing a manic rhythm against his breastbone, he followed a game path up the bank. It was only about a six-foot climb, and not a steep one, but Spurr had to pause at the top and bend forward, placing a hand on his knee, to catch his breath. His chest felt as though a hundred little black spiders were crawling around in it. A trap was sinking its steel jaws into his heart. His temples throbbed.

Letting his rifle hang down in his right hand, he stretched his lips back from his teeth. "Come on, goddamnit. Don't give out on me now, ticker. One more job to do. Just one more."

He pressed his left hand against his chest and straightened, sucking a deep draught of air. The trap loosened its jaws a little, and the ground stopped pitching around him.

"All right. That wasn't so damn hard now, was it?"

He looked toward the cabin, hidden from view by willows and a couple of wagon-sized boulders that had been spit out by whatever river had carved this canyon a million years ago. Good. He ran forward, dropped down into another wash, and followed it north along the west side of the cabin.

Philpot's gang was shouting now, though Spurr couldn't make out what they were saying. He was breathing too hard, though his moccasins moved along nearly soundlessly. He'd traded an old Sioux woman up in Dakota a bag of Arbuckles and a Schofield .44 for the pair he currently wore. He'd have to look her up—Little Crow Feather was her name—when he was up that way again, as the old woman knew her salt.

If he ever made it out of here, that was.

As the dry wash's right bank lowered, the cabin appeared about fifty yards away. Spurr dropped to his knees, crabbed over to the bank, and peered over it. One of the outlaw gang had left the cabin and was now crouched behind an over-turned handcart about twenty feet in front of it, a rifle in his hands. The men were shouting back and forth, but Spurr still couldn't make out what they were saying, though it was obvious they were looking for him.

He gave a grim smile. He had them confused. Maybe a little scared. Spurr wasn't half the lawman he once was—at least not physically—but if he could still make as ring-tailed a crew as Philpot's streak their drawers, maybe he still had a year or two left in him.

He lowered his head and ran crouching along the wash. When he was north of the cabin, he followed a right-forking branch of the wash into a broader draw that ran generally northeast to southwest and skirted the knobby escarpment. He couldn't see the cabin because of the six-foot-high right bank and screening brush, but it was probably about fifty yards away.

The outlaws had stopped shouting. That was a good sign. It meant they had no idea what Spurr was up to, and they were growing more and more nervous about that.

Spurr strode around a bend in the wash. Something moved ahead of him, and he stopped, crouching and raising the Winchester. He removed his thumb from the hammer. Ahead was a string of horses tied to a long picket rope threaded through some cedars growing along the draw's bottom. Spurr moved forward until he could see all five of the mounts—two paints, a brown-and-white pinto, an Appaloosa, and a Morgan-cross. They were all saddled and ready to ride, though their bits were slipped and their latigo straps hung free beneath their bellies.

Buckets of water had been set out for the small remuda. The Appaloosa and the Morgan were snorting up whatever oats remained of a recent feeding. The pinto had lifted its head high and was staring toward Spurr, the sunlight glinting in its soft brown eyes. Its ears were slightly back, and its nostrils were working like a miniature bellows.

The air around the remuda smelled richly of horses and cedars.

The Morgan jerked its own head up as Spurr approached. The Appaloosa whinnied shrilly and lurched back against the bridle reins tied to the picket line, kicking a pile of fresh apples and causing the picket rope to bow and squawk.

"Easy, easy," Spurr rasped, sucking air through his open mouth as he moved out in front of the horses.

They were real beauties. Fiery-eyed. All five built for bottom as well as speed. Philpot knew horses. The old lawman would give him that.

That and a bullet.

Chuckling to himself, Spurr pulled his bowie knife out of the sheath sewn into his right moccasin, and quickly went down the picket line, cutting the horses free.

The horses backed away, rearing, from the picket line and the crusty old stranger whose smell they were not familiar with. Their manes buffeted in the hot, dry breeze. Sand-colored dust lifted.

"All right—move your mangy asses!" Spurr shouted, throwing his arms up high above his head.

A couple of the mounts whinnied as they galloped on down the draw and along the base of the escarpment and out of sight, the rataplan of their hooves dwindling quickly.

Spurr wheeled and ran south. The draw's southern bank was little more than a gradual incline studded with cedars, rocks, and yucca. There were many large, pale boulders that had likely tumbled down from the main escarpment on Spurr's left, offering cover.

He'd heard the outlaws begin shouting again just after

the Appaloosa had loosed its warning whinny. Now the shouts were growing louder, and as Spurr crouched behind a boulder and stretched a look around it toward the cabin, he saw why.

The outlaws were running toward him, strung out to either side in a shaggy line, brightly colored neckerchiefs billowing, bandoliers winking, broad-brimmed hats shading their faces. All four.

Philpot was the second man from the left. They were about halfway between Spurr and the cabin, about sixty yards away and closing fast. The frantic looks on their faces betrayed their worry about the horses. Men on foot out here in the remote Jicarillas were coyote bait. If thirst or rattle-snakes didn't get them, the wolflike Jicarilla Apaches would.

"Stop and throw down your guns!" Spurr shouted as he rose up from behind his cover.

Not giving the killers time to stop or throw down their guns—they hadn't given Kenny Potter time to crawl for cover—he pumped a round through Philpot's right knee. The outlaw ran another two yards, stretching a look of anguish across his face while reaching for his leg. He hit the ground and rolled, howling, losing his hat and his rifle. He came up on his ass, clutching his knee with both hands, red-faced with fury, eyes nearly popping out of his hairless head.

The others ran to skidding stops, kicking gravel up around their knees and raising their rifles. Spurr had ejected the spent cartridge from his Winchester's breech. He aimed quickly, and the Winchester roared like near thunder. Vernon Drake stumbled backward and twisted as he fell a half second after his own shot had sliced through the slack of Spurr's deerskin vest and carved a hot line along his left side.

Spurr cocked and fired again, again, and again, until all four of the outlaws were down and howling. Through his own wafting powder smoke, the old lawman saw Philpot crawling back toward the cabin, sort of leapfrogging while clutching his bloody knee. Spurr was about to draw a bead on the killer, but then he saw one of the other three—the man farthest to Spurr's right—leap to his feet and dash toward a boulder at the edge of the yard.

Spurr fired hastily, his shot plunking into the ground several yards behind and beyond the big man in a black-and-white checked shirt, red bandanna, and patched denims, whom he recognized as the half-Comanche Alvin Silva. Silva dove behind a large rock. As he lifted his head, Spurr levered another shell into his Winchester's breech, aimed more by instinct than sight, and fired.

Silva's head jerked back sharply, as though he'd been punched hard in the face. His head wobbled forward, and the sun glinted off the ragged hole that Spurr's .44 round had punched through his face, just to the right of his long, hooked nose. Silva had not hit the ground before Spurr swung his Winchester back toward the cabin to which Philpot was approaching like a giant, wounded frog.

As the gang leader ran to within ten yards of the open back door, Spurr fired twice, empty cartridges winking over his shoulder. His first shot plunked into the back of Philpot's left thigh, evoking another shrill scream. His second bullet slammed against the adobe-brick wall left of the door with an angry crack.

Philpot threw himself through the open door, mewling. As the outlaw twisted around, reaching for the door, wide-eyed and red-faced, Spurr triggered his Winchester and cursed as the hammer pinged on an empty chamber.

He caught another glimpse of Philpot's bald head and bearded face as the outlaw slammed the door closed in its frame.

"Fuck you, old man!" The indictment was muffled by the closed door.

"I may be old," Spurr said, striding forward while plucking .44 cartridges from his shell belt and sliding them through the gate in the Winchester's receiver, "but I ain't fixin' to meet my maker like you are, you cold-blooded son of a bitch."

As Spurr continued striding toward the cabin and loading his long gun, Philpot slid his head into the open window right of the door, so that Spurr could see half of his face. "What if I give up?" the outlaw leader cried, his blue eyes flashing his fear.

Spurr shook his head. "I'd like to help you there. Too late. When you killed that boy, you killed your chances of seein' what tomorrow looks like."

Philpot angled a long-barreled pistol out the window. It flashed and thundered, smoke wafting from its maw. Spurr ignored the bullet spanging off the ground ten yards behind him. The old, bandy-legged deputy U.S. marshal kept walking, shoving an eighth shell into the Winchester's breech, pumping one into the chamber, then shoving a ninth through the loading gate.

"Spurr!" Philpot cried. "I'm wounded bad! I'm givin' myself up, ya hear?"

Spurr stopped. Philpot's entire face was in the window's lower right corner, as though he were kneeling on the floor. His eyes were bright, mouth stretched wide, showing his two silver-capped front teeth. Tears dribbled down his brown-bearded cheeks.

"A few years ago, I'd have honored that request," Spurr said. "And I'd likely have shunned any lawman who'd do otherwise. Now, as old and stove up as a thirty-year-old whore, I am one of them that's gonna do otherwise." Spurr chuckled wryly and shook his head. "Ain't that just a bitch, Philpot?"

"Spurr!" the outlaw screamed, poking his pistol out the window again.

Spurr raised his rifle and fired a quarter second before Philpot's revolver belched, blowing up sand and gravel five feet in front of Spurr's moccasins. The gun dropped to the ground in front of the window as Philpot screamed still louder and flew back into the cabin, clutching the bloody hole in his right shoulder.

Spurr could no longer see the outlaw, but he could hear him scrambling around inside and sobbing, his boots thumping, spurs trilling on the earthen floor. Spurr walked up to the closed door and rammed his rifle butt against it twice near the steel-and-leather latch before the locking bolt broke and the door swung wide on its creaky hinges.

As the door banged against the wall, Spurr raised his rifle to his shoulder. Philpot had just staggered out the front door and into the yard, stumbling over his boot toes.

Spurr lowered the Winchester slightly and walked through the cabin that reeked like an old goat in late August. Philpot continued staggering into the front yard, both his wounded legs stiffening up on him.

"Turn around or take it in the back, Philpot!"

Philpot dropped to his left knee, the other leg stretched out behind him. He rolled onto a hip and looked up at Spurr, his eyes pinched with pain and terror. He threw up his hands in supplication.

"You can't shoot an unarmed man, Spurr."

The old lawman ambled on through the cabin and out the front door. As he lowered the rifle to his side, Philpot's bearded cheeks slacked in a slight show of relief.

Spurr stopped six feet away from the kneeling outlaw. He glanced over to where Kenny Potter lay dead near the well, his curly hair crusted with dried blood. Rage boiled anew in the old man's veins, and he raised the rifle, aiming down from his right cheek.

"Wanna lay odds on that?"

Philpot's lower jaw dropped, and his eyes widened.

Boom!

THREE

"Please don't kill me, Sheriff. Oh, god . . . please don't kill me! I've had a change of heart—I really have!"

The killer's plea echoed around the Laramie County courthouse—at least that wing which housed the Brule County sheriff's office and jail. Sheriff Dusty Mason sat kicked back in his chair, spurred boots crossed on his rolltop desk. A wry half smile shaped itself on his broad mouth mantled by a brushy, dark-brown mustache as he slowly, methodically rolled a quirley and stared out the dusty window before him.

On Willow City's dusty main street, Cheyenne Street, the workmen were putting the finishing touches on the gallows that would hang the man whose false pleas Mason had been enduring for the past half hour.

"Give it a rest, Clell," the sheriff said, twisting the quirley closed. "Your caterwaulin's fallin' on deaf ears. In a few minutes . . ." He glanced at the old regulator clock ticking on the pine-paneled wall behind him, beside a large, framed, government survey map of Wyoming Territory. "Twelve minutes and thirty-two seconds to be more precise. The hangman, Luther LaForge, likes things precise, don't ya know. We mustn't be late!"

From the jail block on the open balcony above Mason, the notorious bank robber and pistoleer Clell Stanhope shook the door of his barred cage and screamed, "Please, Sheriff. I really *mean* it! Ahh, lordy, I do!"

He sobbed and snorted, sort of mewling like a trapped coyote trying to chew its leg off. "I've had a change of heart. I don't wanna die. Please fetch the judge back and tell him I'll confess all my past evil doin's, and I'll tell you both where the rest of my gang's holed up so's you can go out and fetch 'em in!"

Mason chuckled as he leaned forward and scraped a sulfur-tipped match to life on his desktop.

"Come on, Mason—hear me out! Ya'll think we're in Wyoming. But you got another think comin'. We're down in Colorado. *Southern* Colorado!"

"*Southern* Colorado's big country." Mason blew a smoke plume at the dusty, sunlit window beyond which the hangman, Luther LaForge, dressed in a bow tie and black claw-hammer coat with a Lincoln-style opera hat on his coyote-like head, was strolling around the gallows, pointing details out to the three workmen giving the platform its finishing touches.

One man stood atop the gallows, adjusting the hangman's knot that would soon encircle Clell Stanhope's thick neck. Another was testing the trapdoor lever bristling from the platform's near side, opening and closing the door beneath a sandbag weighing the same as Stanhope himself.

A sizeable crowd had already gathered around the gallows—men, women, children, and dogs. Even a few chickens and someone's pet coyote. A Mexican woman and her son were hawking burritos while Burt Givens had set his beer keg on the broad porch of his establishment, the Brule House Saloon and Pleasure Parlor. He was filling

mugs with his frothy ale while men crowded around, handing nickels to his best whore, the voluptuous and scantily
clad Trixie Tate.

Trixie was really working the crowd, laughing, rattling
the coins in her beer glass, funning with the men, and ruf-
fling the hair of several lucky patrons while leaning forward
to show her bosoms bulging up like small, pale mountains
from her deep purple corset.

"You fetch the judge and have him change my sentence
to life in the pen, Mason, and I'll tell you exactly where the
hideout is. Oh, Jesus, god, look how they're funnin' out
there, gettin' ready to see me hang!" Stanhope mewled some
more and sniffed and snorted before adding, "You fetch him
and have him throw me in the pen. Hell, I'll work the rock
quarries for the rest of my days. I'll blow railroad tunnels!
I just don't wanna die, Mason. Please! You gotta listen to
me, Mason. You gotta understand."

"Be tough, Clell. Be tough as the hombre who rode in
with his gang and robbed the Bank and Trust a month ago
and shot Dave Tully and Homer Simms dead in the street."

Mason had led a posse out after the gang who called
themselves the Vultures. They'd split up somewhere in the
southeastern corner of Wyoming, though it might have been
western Dakota; it was hard to tell just where a fellow was
in those brutally hot, dry, rattlesnake-infested buttes north
of the Platte.

Mason and the posse had run Stanhope and two other
Vultures down after a long, hard chase. They hadn't been
hard to capture, however, as all three, including Stanhope,
had been wounded in their getaway from Willow City and
were more like cornered coyotes than angry wolves. They'd
stopped to have their wounds tended by an old Hunkpapa
woman at a trading post on some nearly dry creek that
Mason hadn't learned the name of, and that's where his
posse had found them.

The rest of the gang, though, had gotten away. Mason

figured they'd headed on back out to western Wyoming, where, according to a string of consistent rumors, the curly wolves had a hideout, likely somewhere in the badlands along the Green River or up in the Wind River Range.

"Yeah, I was tough," Stanhope said. "You got that right. I'm a cold-blooded killer. But I reckon I'm one o' those killers who, when I'm gettin' ready to cash in my chips, I start squirtin' down my leg. Sure, I'm ashamed of it. But, *damnit, Mason—I'm scared o' dyin', and I'm offerin' you an option here*!"

Mason glanced up to see the big outlaw in a red bandanna and with two black vultures tattooed on his cheeks, above a thick, dark brown beard, press his ugly face against the cell and rattle it until Mason could feel the vibration throughout the entire two-story office. The desperado's right arm was trussed up in a burlap shoulder sling. Stanhope had been taking a midnight crap in the outhouse flanking the trading post, groaning from the pain of his wound, and Mason had simply shoved his rifle barrel between two of the structure's brittle boards and pressed it hard against the back of Stanhope's neck.

Mason chuckled at the remembered image from that hot, starry night along the creek that smelled as bad as the privy, and said, "Your only option, Clell, is to hang from the neck until you shit your pants and die. Besides, look at that crowd out there. You wouldn't want me to go out and disappoint 'em with the news you're bein' hauled off to the territorial pen when they've been waitin' over a month to watch you stretch hemp! Look at them kids laughin' an' cavortin' and runnin' around that gallows like they was waitin' for the Fourth of July rodeo parade!"

Before Stanhope could retort, the office's front door opened and a stocky figure stepped in, removing his black, bullet-crowned hat, his white clerical collar showing against his thick neck and the ropes of flesh sagging from his chin. "Good morning, Sheriff."

Mason gave a cordial nod as he blew out another smoke plume. "Padre."

Father H. Charles Connagher stood just inside the open door, holding his Bible in both hands before his prominent paunch, and raised his eyes to the cell block in the balcony over the main office. "I guess it's about time for the . . . the, uh . . . execution."

"We'll be out in a minute, Father." Mason dropped his boots to the floor and stubbed his cigarette out in a peach tin on his desk.

"Perhaps the prisoner would care to make a confession?"

Mason was about to tell the preacher to forget it when Stanhope said in an eerie little boy's voice, "I'm awful scared, Father. Could you come up here please and hear my confession?"

Mason stood. "Go on outside, Father. We'll be out in a minute. You can say a prayer over him before he drops."

Connagher looked at Mason, the preacher's eyes hidden by the twin reflections in his round-rimmed spectacles. His voice was soft, resonate, officious. "The prisoner has asked for a confession, Sheriff. It's only right that I hear it."

"All right, all right," Mason said, giving an impatient wave. "Go on up and hear it." Mason lifted his voice. "Finn?"

One of Mason's two deputies, who'd been standing on guard just outside the office, stepped into the doorway, nearly filling it. Mark Finn was a big man who shaved only every three or four days. He was dressed like a cowhand, though he had an extra cartridge belt slanting across his broad chest. In his hands was a brass-cased Henry rifle.

"Ready, Dusty?" Finn said. "Want me to fetch him?"

"I want you to escort the preacher up to his cell while the pious Clell gives his confession."

The reverend gave a patient smile. "Confessions are a private matter, Sheriff."

"Not around here they ain't." Mason glanced at Finn and jerked his head to indicate Stanhope.

Finn shouldered his rifle and walked over to the stairs rising to the second-floor cell block. "Right this way, Father."

"Hold on," Mason said, extending his hand to Finn. "Rifle, Mark."

The big deputy's fleshy, unshaven face broke in a sheepish grin. "Whoops—forgot." He handed his rifle over to Mason. The sheriff didn't have a problem with the man approaching the cell with the Colt on his hip, but a rifle was too easy to snatch through the bars.

Finn started up the stairs with the preacher, and Mason leaned the deputy's rifle against his desk. As the two were still clomping up the stairs, their footfalls echoing hollowly around the office, Mason rose and walked over to the window right of the door.

A few horsebackers rode along the street, men from area ranches in town on business, and there were a few farm supply wagons, as well. Most everyone else was on foot, some dressed in their Sunday best though this was only Wednesday, and gathered in jovial expectation around the gallows. A collie dog was following the hangman and giving him holy hell, tail up, while several in the surrounding crowd as well as the buxom blond whore, Trixie Tate, pointed out the barking dog to others, laughing.

For his part, LaForge ignored the dog that kept just out of kicking range and continued supervising the finishing touches being applied to his gallows.

Mason hooked his thumbs behind his cartridge belt and chuckled.

"Good lord—what's going on here?" the preacher said behind and above him.

At the same time, there was a squeal of hinges. Mason spun and frowned up at the jail block atop the stairs, where Finn was opening the door of Clell Stanhope's cell while the preacher stood to his left, scowling at Stanhope, who appeared to be moving toward the opening.

"Mark, what the hell are you doing?" Mason said. "I didn't tell you to let him *out*!"

Stanhope rammed his shoulder against the door, and in a blur of motion, the outlaw leader grabbed the preacher around the neck and spun him around so that he faced the sheriff. The preacher made a face, gasping.

Sunlight glinted off something in Stanhope's right hand, and Mason reached for the Colt Army .44 jutting from the holster tied to his right thigh.

"Mark, he's got a gun!"

"Hold it, Mason!" Stanhope shouted, pressing his pistol's barrel against the preacher's right temple and loudly ratcheting the hammer back. "Skin that hogleg and the preacher's as dead as Christ on the cross!"

Mason froze with his hand wrapped around the .44's walnut grips. Finn laughed loudly, blue eyes flashing in the light from the windows. "I know he's got a gun. Hell, I gave it to him!"

The deputy leaned forward over the balcony's pine rail, roaring and slapping his thigh. He had his own Colt in his hand, and he was aiming it down at Mason. "Slide your popper out slow, Dusty, and we'll let you and the preacher live."

"We?" Mason stared in shock at the big deputy he'd known for at least two years and had come to trust like a brother. "What the hell happened to you, Mark?"

"Well, you see, Stanhope here pays a little more than you, Dusty. That's really about all there is to it."

Finn laughed again devilishly.

"You heard your boy, Sheriff," Stanhope said, pressing his gun barrel hard against the preacher's head. Connagher's glasses were sagging low on his face, and his eyes were bright with sheer terror, lips stretched back from his teeth against the pain of the gun barrel grinding into his temple. "Toss that pistol over there by your desk and get your hands up. You got two seconds, then I give this sky pilot a third eye!"

"Hold on, hold on. I don't know how you figure you're gonna make it through that crowd out yonder, but . . ." Mason slowly lifted his Colt from its holster with his thumb and index finger and tossed it onto the wooden floor by his desk. It skidded up against a filing cabinet.

"Oh, I'll think of somethin'," the leader of the Vultures said, his broad, dark face brightening with a psychotic grin beneath the bandanna wrapped around the top of his head. When he grinned, the wings of the vultures on his cheeks rose as though the carrion eaters were taking flight.

That Stanhope had one brown and one bright blue-gray eye did little to temper his crazy aspect. He hadn't shaved since he'd been locked up, and he'd grown nearly a full beard. His hair was long, dark, and curly. Around his neck he wore a tight choker of vulture talons.

He brusquely pushed the preacher over to the top of the stairs. Connagher stumbled forward and nearly fell down the stairs before grabbing the rail with both hands.

Mason stretched his hands out and lurched forward. "Easy!"

Stanhope laughed, then crooked his right elbow around the preacher's neck, jerking the man's head back against Stanhope's chest. His big arm hid nearly the preacher's entire face. The priest gave a startled cry. Stanhope jerked Connagher's head back and to one side sharply.

Mason's knees turned to jelly when he heard the sharp crack.

Connagher flung his arms out to both sides, and they and his legs began quivering as though he'd been hit by lightning. Stanhope released the man. The preacher's head wobbled, broken, on his shoulders.

Then his knees buckled and he went tumbling down the stairs to pile up at Mason's feet.

FOUR

The shock, horror, and rage that Sheriff Dusty Mason was feeling did not show on his face. He was good at holding his emotions close to his vest. Having been a lawman for the past ten years had taught him the value of remaining calm in any situation and to give away nothing to his opponents.

When he'd crouched over the dead preacher and then straightened his back to stare up the stairs at Clell Stanhope and Mark Finn, who were walking down toward him, keeping their cocked pistols aimed at his head, he merely said, "You had no call to do that, Clell."

"How many times you think you can hang me, Mason?"

Stanhope dropped down the stairs to stand two feet in front of Mason, on the other side of the dead Connagher. He was a huge man, standing a good three inches over Mason's rangy six feet, and he was grinning with one side of his mouth. Outside, Mason could hear the crowd getting louder, impatient for him to lead Stanhope outside and up onto the gallows.

Stanhope jerked his pistol to one side. "Get those hands raised. And step back, Mason."

Vaguely surprised that he was still alive, Mason raised his hands to his shoulders and stepped away from Stanhope and Finn, who'd followed the leader of the Vultures down the stairs.

"Keep your gun on him, Mark," Stanhope ordered as he crossed the room to where his gun belt and hat and his long, dirty cream duster hung from pegs in the wall near Mason's desk. His sawed-off, double-barreled shotgun hung there, as well—a mean little weapon with a hand-carved stock. "And cuff his hands behind his back."

As the outlaw strapped his black, two-gun rig around his waist, Finn kept his eyes and gun on Mason while reaching around behind his own thick body and removing a set of handcuffs from the back of his cartridge belt. "What're we gonna do with him? We let him live, he'll follow us."

He tossed the cuffs to Mason. "Put 'em on, Dusty. Nice an' tight."

Stanhope said, "You mean, he'll follow us like him . . . and you . . . followed us before?"

"Sure." Finn frowned as he glanced at the outlaw, who was making sure both his Peacemakers showed brass. "I was part o' the posse, but that was before I threw in with you, Clell." The big deputy laughed nervously. "You can't fault me for that. I was just doin' my job!"

"Nope. Can't fault you at all." Stanhope dropped his shotgun's lanyard over his neck, letting the popper hang down over his belly, and set his hat on his head. It was an opera hat sort of like that which the hangman, LaForge, wore. Only Stanhope's wasn't as tall, and it was a sun-faded, brassy brown, with what Mason assumed was a vulture plume poking up from the braided rawhide band. He wore it snugged down over the red bandanna.

"Whatever he paid you, Mark," Mason said, a grim smile curving his mouth beneath his thick mustache as he snaked his hands around behind his back and cuffed himself. "It wasn't enough. It wasn't *near* enough."

"Shut up." Clell drilled Mason with his weird brown-and-gray gaze, then spun the cylinder of his second Colt and poked it into the holster he wore for the cross draw on his left hip. To Finn, he barked, "Let's go—get him outside!"

Finn prodded Mason out the door with his pistol barrel, and the lawman walked out onto the street, his heart thudding in his chest. With the cuffs, he was defenseless, but he'd had no choice but to put them on. His only hope was that he could signal his only other deputy, Regus Bone, before Stanhope and Finn got the drop on him.

As the two walked out of the sheriff's office behind him, his own pale blue eyes searched the crowd milling around the gallows. No one had yet seen him and the other two emerge from the office, though it looked as though LaForge and his gallows were ready.

The tall, gray-haired executioner, who looked like a vulture himself dressed in his black suit with clawhammer coat and tails, was standing in front of the platform, hands behind his back, looking up at the single rope shunting a little in the hot, dry breeze. He wore a devilishly proud smile on his face.

Mason saw Regus Bone at the same time Bone saw him. The middle-aged deputy was standing where Mason had expected he'd be—near Trixie Tate, a beer in his hand. He held the butt of his double-barreled shotgun in the crook of his other arm. Catching Mason's eye, his bug-eyed face acquired a sheepish cast, and he quickly polished off his beer, gave the glass to the whore, then hitched his wash-worn, checked wool trousers higher on his lean hips and began walking around the front of the gallows toward Mason. He obviously hadn't yet seen anything odd in the fact that Stanhope was not only clad in trail duds and that he and Finn were flanking Mason, holding pistols on him.

Or maybe he hadn't yet seen them or recognized Stanhope in his opera hat and duster.

Mason glowered at the slouch-shouldered deputy, grinding his teeth in a silent, desperate plea that Bone make eye contact with him and get the message that trouble was boiling over for both of them.

But as the older deputy approached the sheriff's office, he kept his shotgun in the crook of his arm and didn't even lift his eyes from the street.

When Bone ran the back of his right hand across his mouth, likely wiping the remains of the beer away, the words fairly burst from Mason's lungs. "Goddamnit, Bone—*shoot* these sons o' bitches!"

Mason thew himself sidways and hit the street on his left shoulder and hip, exposing Stanhope and Finn to Bone's double-barrel greener. Mason looked up to see Bone stopping dead in his tracks, staring down at Mason and beetling the gray-brown brows mantling his close-set eyes.

"Shoot 'em!" Mason shouted, futilely trying to pull his hands out of the cuffs and kicking his legs in frustration.

Just then, one of the crowd near Bone—a tall, slender, long-haired man in a black bowler, shabby black suit, and red vest faded to nearly pink, swung around toward Bone. It was the Vulture known as Magpie Quint. Mason didn't see the sawed-off shotgun that the man extended from beneath his shabby suit jacket until a loud boom went rocketing around between the false facades on both sides of the street.

Bone was picked two feet up in the air and thrown six feet back before hitting the street with a yelp. His shotgun landed another fifteen feet behind him. He moved his arms and legs, groaning feebly. The man in the shabby suit and red vest walked over to Bone, extended his shotgun out and down, and triggered his second load of buckshot into his already bloody chest and belly.

Two women in the crowd screamed at nearly the same

time. The collie dog stopped barking, yelped, and ran toward an alley mouth, warily glancing back over its shoulder.

Bone ground his heels into the dirt, arched his back slightly, then collapsed and lay still.

A baby on the other side of the street from Mason started crying.

Mason felt all the air leave his lungs as he said, "Ah, Christ!"

Stanhope laughed as he looked down at the county lawman. "Sheriff, what in the hell are you doin' down there?" He laughed again, then canted his head toward Finn, who was staring a little regretfully at old Bone. "Stand him up."

Finn aimed his pistol at Mason. The big deputy wasn't smiling anymore, however. "Get up, Dusty."

Mason climbed heavily, wearily to his feet as he watched several men separate by ones and twos from the crowd and step out away from its perimeter. A hush had fallen over the street. All faces, slack-jawed with awe, were staring toward the jailhouse.

Trixie Tate and the barman, Burt Givens, both stood as slack-jawed as the rest of the crowd. Only a few beer drinkers were around them now, most of the others having moved down into the street to await the hanging.

Only now, it seemed to be occurring to the entire crowd collectively that there wouldn't be any festivities today.

Mason stood in front of the jailhouse, his hands cuffed behind his back, feeling a hot frustration rippling across every fiber of his being. He looked around at the hard men who'd separated themselves from the crowd and were now forming a rough circle around it.

They all carried rifles or shotguns, and they were bearing down on the crowd. One by one, cold stones dropped in Mason's belly as he recognized the unshaven, sneering faces of Ed Crow, Doc Plowright, Magpie Quint, Red Ryan, Clell's brother Lester Stanhope, Hector Debo, "Quiet" Boone Coffey, and Santos Estrada.

All members of the Vultures.

Somehow, they'd infiltrated the town without being recognized. Or maybe there was no one else around who would recognize them excepting Mason, who'd seen their likenesses all gracing wanted circulars, several of which adorned his bulletin board. Mason had been preoccupied, guarding his prisoner—the most notoriously deadly killer he'd ever jailed.

Only to have him taken out of his hands by a man he'd come to trust, his own hands cuffed behind his back.

What a goddamn fool he was! Why in hell didn't they go ahead and shoot him? Or hang him? Either would be better than he deserved, having imperiled his town like this.

"Crow!" Stanhope said as he walked toward the gallows.

The outlaw nearest him—a stocky, bearded gent with an eye patch—tossed the gang leader a carbine. Then Ed Crow slid his two Colts out of their sheaths and cocked them, holding them on the crowd on Mason's side of the street. Mason looked stonily on as Stanhope approached the hangman, who still stood in front of his gallows. LaForge let his hands drop to his sides. He scowled out from his long horsey face and deep-set eyes under heavy, grizzled brows as the man he'd been sent to Willow City to execute approached him.

Stanhope grabbed the man's arm and swung him around to face the gallows. LaForge grunted and looked indignantly over his shoulder at the tall Vulture in the dirty cream duster behind him. A collective gasp rose from the crowd as Stanhope shoved LaForge toward the gallows steps. He shoved the elderly, tall, and skinny hangman too hard, and LaForge fell onto the steps.

"Leave me, damn you! What do you think you're doing?" the executioner shouted in his stentorian southern drawl. His face was sunset red, the bulbous tip of his nose turning deep purple.

Stanhope cocked his right boot and rammed it hard against the executioner's ass. "Get up there, hangman. Time to test your hemp!"

"No!" yelped LaForge as the outlaw's kick propelled him up the steps, long arms and skinny legs flopping like those of a ragdoll, his hat tumbling off his shoulder.

He continued to yell, his voice cracking desperately, as Stanhope kicked him up onto the platform. Near the noose dangling from its beam, LaForge dropped to his knees and raised his long arms and opened his hands in supplication. *"Please! I beg you! Don't do this!"*

His voice turned shrill as a rusty saw, and he began sobbing, his craggy face crumpling, thin lips quivering.

Stanhope laughed. "You're crow bait, hangman!"

He set his carbine on the platform, then crouched over LaForge, wrapping an arm around his lean waist and hauling the hysterical man to his feet. When he had him standing on his skinny legs, he pushed him over to the noose and, while the hangman continued to plead for his life, sobbing, cords of sinew stretching beneath his chin, tears dribbling down his paper-pale cheeks, Stanhope drew the noose down over his gray head and tightened the knot around his skinny neck.

LaForge howled and mewled and danced atop the trapdoor, clawing at the noose with his long spidery fingers.

Mason stared in disbelief, as did the rest of the crowd. A few of the mothers, clad in sunbonnets and Mother Hubbards, were ushering their children off down alleys and away from the scene of the hangman's imminent demise. Most everyone else, including several women, held their ground, staring up in eerie fascination as the hangman bawled and danced, his coarse gray hair blowing in the breeze. Piss darkened his trousers as it oozed down his legs and darkened the door leaping in its frame around his black, thumping half boots.

"Don't do it, Clell!" Mason's shout was too low to be

heard above the hangman's cries, so he raised it several decibels. "Clell . . . let him go! LaForge was just doin' his job! I'm the one you oughta hang—not him!"

Stanhope turned toward Mason, grinning. "I'm savin' you fer later, Sheriff!"

He glanced at one of the other Vultures, a big, red-bearded man called Red Ryan, who stood with one hand on the brake-like handle rigged to the trapdoor. Stanhope nodded. Red Ryan grinned, showing his yellow teeth inside his heavy beard, and a collective gasp rose like a distant thunder peal from the crowd.

Red Ryan threw the lever.

The trapdoor opened with a wooden rasp.

LaForge dropped straight down to the end of the rope and jerked back up with a crack like the report of a small-caliber pistol. His hands that had continued to claw at the rope now dropped to his sides. His long, lean body stiffened as it swung from side to side on the creaking rope.

His feet continued to dance. His fingers twitched. His eyes bulged in his skull and he worked his thin lips as though he were trying to say something but couldn't get the words out.

Then his body slackened. The light left his eyes over which his papery lids drooped halfway down.

Mason's knees buckled. He dropped to the street. "Ah, Christ."

Stanhope, standing alone on the gallows now, holding his carbine in one hand, his sawed-off gut shredder in the other, turned back to him. "Don't pass out, Sheriff. We ain't done yet. Nope. We ain't done by a *long shot*!"

The next half-hour passed as though in an excruciatingly drawn-out nightmare while Mason watched from his knees, hands cuffed behind his back. Stanhope ordered each man who'd ridden in the posse that had hunted him down to step out away from the crowd or Stanhope and his men would rape all the women and shoot all the children in town, then burn Willow City to the ground.

There was much crying and yelling, but finally the six innocent townsmen who'd ridden with Mason were lined up in front of the gallows and shot by the Vultures, who in turn had lined up ten feet away to form a firing squad. While the posse men's wives and children ran to where the men lay quivering with death spasms, one of the Vultures led a small horse herd out of an alley, and the gang members, including Mark Finn, all mounted, firing their guns in the air in celebration.

While cries of terror continued to rise from the dispersing, wildly shifting crowd, Clell Stanhope rode over to where Trixie Tate knelt near Burt Givens's beer keg, sobbing. Givens himself had taken cover inside the saloon. The leader of the Vultures grabbed the stricken whore's arm and pulled her, kicking and screaming, over the pommels of his saddle.

While the rest of the gang galloped on out of town to the north, Stanhope trotted his grulla gelding over to Mason. Trixie screamed and kicked her legs down one side of the horse while trying to pound her fists against Stanhope's right leg with the other, her long blond hair brushing across the ground.

The vultures on Stanhope's cheeks spread their wings as the outlaw leader extended his sawed-off popper toward Mason and ratcheted back one of the two hammers. "Been nice palaverin' with you, Sheriff. Hope ya don't take none of this personal!"

He laughed. Mason watched the man's thick, red-brown finger with its dirt-encrusted nail tighten inside the shotgun's trigger guard. The lawman slowly closed his eyes. His shoulders jerked when the blast came. It hadn't sounded as loud as Mason would have expected from a double-bore shotgun loaded with ten-gauge buck.

It came again, and finding himself oddly still alive, Mason opened his eyes to see dust puff ten feet in front of him. Stanhope was galloping away, glaring back over his shoulder but not at Mason. He was looking up toward the rooftops somewhere to Mason's left, one eye narrowed, the shotgun half extended in his right hand, the hammer still cocked.

A rifle cracked again. The bullet plunked into the street to the right of Stanhope's grulla. The outlaw flinched, spat a curse, then turned forward, let the popper hang against his belly, took his reins in both hands, and booted the horse on up the street toward the north edge of town.

Trixie continued to scream and kick and flail her fists as she lay draped across his saddle.

Mason turned to stare in the direction from which the rifle had spoken. He ran his gaze across a couple of peaked roofs until he spied a silhouetted figure crouched atop the roof of the Laramie House Hotel, half hidden by the tall false facade.

It was a long-haired figure with a low-crowned, flat-brimmed hat. A claw necklace hung around the man's neck. He was too far away for Mason to tell for sure, but the rifle in his hands looked like a brass-cased Yellowboy repeater. From what Mason could see, the man looked Indian. Maybe a half-breed.

Holding his rifle barrel-up in both hands, the man held Mason's gaze for about three seconds, then pulled his head back behind the facade and was gone.

Mason looked away from his unknown benefactor, saw the women screaming over the bodies of their dead husbands in front of the gallows. He saw LaForge twisting at the end of his own rope. Regus Bone lay sprawled in the street to his right, blood glistening across every inch of the old deputy's upper body and dribbling down his gray-bristled cheeks.

Shock lay like a heavy yoke on Mason's shoulders. Shaking it off, he rose to his feet, trying to jerk his hands free of the steel bracelets and raging, and yelled, *"Someone get me out of these goddamn cuffs!"*

He looked once more toward where the rifleman who'd saved him from Stanhope's bullet had shown himself briefly and disappeared.

FIVE

"Come on, Cochise," Spurr said to his horse. "Let's rustle us up a drink."

The old lawman started down the stock car's ramp in his high-topped Indian moccasins, and the big roan's shod hooves clomped on the worn boards behind him, its bridle bit dangling below its long snout. At the bottom of the ramp, Spurr stopped and looked toward the little jerkwater town sitting along a two-track trail that paralleled the recently laid rails of the spur line about a hundred yards north of the tracks and the depot building that appeared little larger than a chicken coop.

A wooden sign nailed to a cottonwood post in front of the hovel announced the name of the town as ALKALI FLATS.

The shake-shingled building sat on a sun-bleached bed of graded gravel to Spurr's left. On the far side of it stood a water tank, and at the moment the train's engineer and fireman were swinging the tank's canvas spigot toward the Baldwin locomotive that sat panting like some exhausted, parched beast in dire need of a long, cold drink. There were no other disembarking passengers except for Spurr and a young, sullen saddle tramp, who had already ridden off with his horse probably in search of work on one of the area ranches in this big, empty, grassy country south of Willow City—a vast sage-stippled bowl hemmed in by high, misty blue mountains in all directions.

At least, that was Spurr's guess about the youngster's business. He didn't know for certain-sure, because while he and the lad had ridden the Burlington Flyer up from Denver, and then the spur line west from Chugwater, the kid had re-buffed any and all of Spurr's attempts at friendly, boredom-relieving conversation. He'd merely gazed out the stock car's open door and yawned and grunted or chewed his fingernails or sat dangling his legs toward the tracks and staring at his big right toe sticking out of the hole in his boot as though it were some complicated problem he was forever trying to solve.

That was a cowpuncher, for you. Too stupid to talk. Prob-ably an east Texan. Spurr had known horses smarter than most of the cowpunchers he'd known, and he'd known many, having been one himself back in his younger days down in the Texas *brasada* country and on the Oklahoma panhandle.

Spurr stared after the cowboy loping off into the western distance along the rails. Coal smoke and briefly glowing cinders puffed from the engine's diamond-shaped stack, obscuring Spurr's view for a moment before billowing toward Wyoming's high-arching, faultless blue sky.

Since the train carried so few passengers on this leg, the depot master had time to gas with the two trainsmen, rising up and down on the toes of his black brogans, jingling the change in his pockets and chuckling and shaking his head— likely a poor, lonely soul this far out in the tall and uncut.

The town beyond the depot appeared to have a total of eight buildings—three business establishments and five cot-tonwood log cabins that had turned the silver of a newly minted nickel in the unforgiving Wyoming summer sun.

Spurr hoped at least one of those establishments had a drink in it. Intending to find out, he pushed Cochise's bit into the horse's mouth, tightened the latigo strap beneath his belly, then toed a stirrup, grabbed the apple, and pushed and pulled his old, withered carcass into the leather.

He'd just gotten seated when his breath grew short and the dun prairie and blue sky began to pitch and swirl around him.

"Shit!" he rasped through gritted teeth, his heart hiccupping in his ears. "Goddamn, you old . . . !"

Spurr quickly wrapped his reins around his saddlehorn. That steel crab had closed a pincher over his pumper again. His left arm grew heavy, so he used his right hand to dig into an inside pocket of his elkskin vest for a small leather sack.

One-handed, he pulled the sack open, plucked out a small, gold tablet that his sawbones called a "heart starter" but that Spurr knew was nitroglycerin, and popped it into his mouth. He threw his head back and swallowed hard before leaning forward against the saddle horn to wait for the nitro pill to give his old ticker the kick in the pants it needed and to shrug off the crab's assault.

"You all right over there, mister?"

Spurr looked to his left. The depot agent had turned away from the men busy filling the locomotive's boiler to give his concerned gaze to the old lawman sitting crouched atop the big roan. The agent wavered drunkenly from side to side, only Spurr knew that it wasn't the man himself staggering but Spurr's oxygen-starved image of him. The blue-uniformed man shifted around a few more times before he gradually steadied, standing where he was off the far front corner of the shack, his hands in his pockets.

Then the lawman's old heart stopped buck kicking like a broomtail bronc in his chest. It settled down and started beating more slowly, regularly, and without the ache stretching across his chest and into his left shoulder and arm.

One time, likely soon, he knew, it would kick him right on out of here and off to storied Glory, wherever in hell that was. But for now, once more, the pill had done its job. Spurr straightened in his saddle, extended his left arm before him, flexed his fingers, and drew a long, refreshing breath. His throat opened to welcome the life-sustaining substance into his chest.

Air never tasted as wonderful as on the heels of one of his "colicky pumper spells."

"Sir?" the agent said, frowning beneath the leather bill of his uniform cap.

Spurr looked at him. He appeared around thirty, half Spurr's age. He had a big, open, clear-eyed face. The face of a midwestern farmboy, most likely. A juniper. A hayseed. There was no touch of gray in his blond sideburns or blond mustache. He had a paunch, but his shoulders were straight and strong.

Spurr didn't recognize him. Once, he'd known all the railroaders in this neck of the West. Now, most of the men with whom he'd drifted to the wild and wooly frontier in the years preceding the war, and then again *after* the war, were either dead or holed up in a rooming house somewhere, playing checkers, filing their dentures, or sneaking off to the nearest saloon for a proscribed shot of red-eye to dull the pain of their syphilis.

Spurr chuckled at the thought. He raised his gloved hand to the depot agent. "Son," Spurr said, "it was just the devil reachin' up to tickle my toes there for a minute. He'll do that just to remind me what's comin'."

"You're lookin' a little pale, mister."

"Will I find a drink over yonder?"

The depot agent canted his head toward the small collection of buildings to the north. "The Bighorn Saloon will set you up right nicely."

"That'll bring the color back to these old cheeks. Much obliged." Spurr slanted a stiff finger against his tan hat brim and touched his heels to Cochise's flanks.

As the horse sauntered off toward the single-track trail

leading away from the rails and the depot toward the buildings beyond, the agent called behind him, "Hey, wait a minute, mister."

Spurr drew back on Cochise's reins, curveted the horse, and looked back at the depot agent.

The man frowned more curiously than before and gave a wry, disbelieving chuckle. "Ain't you Spurr Morgan? The lawman?"

Spurr touched his fingers to the thin gray-brown beard hanging off his wart-studded chin and looked off. "Am I?" He returned his blue-eyed gaze to the agent regarding him with a half-skeptical grin. "You know—I might just be. When you get to be my age, you're lucky if you remember to wear your underwear."

He reined Cochise up the trail and threw up a parting hand. "Word to the wise, young man—don't ever get old!"

Cochise clomped slowly along the trail toward the collection of mismatched buildings comprising the jerkwater stop of Alkali Flats. Some of the log buildings were obviously older, probably built well before the spur line had been laid. A couple, including a large, white, Victorian-style hotel, looked far newer.

Spurr was in no hurry. It was one o'clock in the afternoon, and he wasn't due to meet Sheriff Dusty Mason here for another hour. He'd returned to Denver from New Mexico three days ago, having polished off Hector Philpot's bunch and buried poor Kenny Potter near the cabin where he'd been shot. He'd no sooner written his report, sort of fudging the details of how Philpot himself had died just a tad, and turned it in to Chief Marshal Henry Brackett's office than the old chief marshal had laid this new assignment on his most veteran deputy.

Funny, Spurr thought, how the chief marshal always prefaced each assignment with the obligatory recommendation that Spurr retire down in Mexico. Brackett never pushed the matter, however. It seemed to please him just to mention it and have Spurr snort and chuckle and brush his fist across his warty nose.

Spurr might have been the oldest lawdog in Brackett's stable, but Brackett, no spring chicken himself, knew the value of a keeping a lawman of Spurr's experience in his cavvy of commissioned deputy marshals. A pious man, Brackett knew Spurr's reputation for strong drink and whoremongering. Spurr thought the wise old Civil War veteran, once an adjutant for Grant himself, probably suspected that Spurr occasionally blurred the lines between what was lawful and what was unlawful in running evildoers to ground.

Even so, the chief marshal always reserved the trickiest, nastiest assignments for the long-toothed veteran, who'd had his federal commission for over ten years but who'd worn several other badges, including county sheriff and town marshal before that. He'd even spent some time in western Dakota as a range detective. Anything to make a living without having to punch cattle who were only marginally more stupid than the men who punched them.

This current assignment looked no different.

It involved a gang known as the Vultures for one, led by the notorious killer Clell Stanhope. Stanhope's gang had busted their kill-crazy leader out of jail before hanging the executioner who'd been sent to play cat's cradle with Stanhope's own neck. They'd executed every man in the posse of the sheriff who'd run him to ground, and they'd kidnapped a whore.

That sheriff was Dusty Mason of Willow City, a small county seat situated about eighty miles north of Alkali Flats. Spurr had dusted trail with the sheriff a year ago when they'd both been tracking a young firebrand who'd broken out of a federal pen in southern Colorado—Cuno Massey. Spurr and Mason had been partnered up for several weeks, and while Spurr had eventually warmed to the taciturn, steely-eyed lawman a good twenty years Spurr's junior, Mason wasn't exactly Spurr's brand of hombre.

Spurr appreciated a good joke and a soft whore now and then, whereas he'd found Mason relatively humorless and guarded. If he enjoyed a mattress dance on occasion, the sheriff sure hadn't chinned about it.

Spurr wasn't comfortable with a man who didn't admit to a few frivolities, a man who couldn't bust out with a hearty laugh now and then. The old federal deputy had little time for a man who took himself and life too seriously, for life sure as hell didn't return the favor, given how the winds of fate blew fickle and rampant, toying with each and every one of us willy-nilly.

Come to think of it, Spurr pondered now as he approached the buildings clustered along the trail ahead of him, he didn't recollect Mason mentioning if he was even married.

No, sir—there were other men Spurr would rather ride the owlhoot trail with. But the dice had rolled, and he'd been given the assignment of tracking the gang that had all but sacked Mason's town.

Spurr made a quick appraisal of the buildings around him, most with smoke skeining from their chimneys. He swung left onto the main trail and angled toward the Bighorn Saloon. The watering hole appeared Spurr's kind of place—a long, low building of splintery logs, with a large sign over its porch roof announcing "cheap women, bubbly beer, a hoedown with fiddles every Saturday night, and free tooth extractions for patrons only!"

Spurr didn't have a sore tooth at the moment. Only a powerful thirst. But he'd ridden only a dozen yards before voices rose on his right. He glanced toward the large, white, Victorian-style hotel that he'd given only a passing appraisal, as such an obviously "civilized" establishment held little allure for Spurr, and saw a leather two-seater buggy with high red wheels sitting in front of the place. A handsome

Morgan lazed in the traces. A man and a woman—both extremely well tailored—stood on the broad front porch, in front of the door, facing each other.

The man was facing Spurr while the woman was facing the man. Spurr couldn't see much of the woman except the shape of her head and the set of her shoulders beneath her white straw picture hat plumed with ostrich feathers. But there seemed something familiar about what he could see, as well as in the timbre of her voice, which he could barely hear from fifty or sixty yards away, though there wasn't a breath of breeze or any other sound around the little town whatever.

Spurr reined Cochise back the other way along the street, staring with unabashed curiosity at the pair atop the porch. He clomped past the buggy, then reined Cochise to another stop at the hotel's far front corner. The woman was saying, ". . . Not at all, Olden. You go ahead. Really. I'll start with coffee, and later, when you get hungry . . ."

"Are you sure, Martha?"

"Of course I'm sure. Your friends obviously don't want to meet here." The woman gave a wry, throaty chuckle as she glanced over her left shoulder, in the direction of the Bighorn Saloon before which three saddled horses stood tied to the hitchrack, one drawing water from the stock trough. "Go on and have your meeting. I'll sit inside here where it's cool, and you can come over later for a bite to eat."

"All right," Olden said, leaning toward the woman, removing his high-crowned, broad-brimmed, gray-felt Stetson to peck her cheek. He was dressed entirely in gray—a good-quality gray wool—except for his shirt, the white collar of which could be seen just above the lapels of his expensive wool jacket. "I won't be long."

"Don't hurry on my account. I know how Norman enjoys his poker!"

She said that last to the man's back as he descended the porch steps and headed up the street toward the saloon, slanting two stiff fingers toward his hat brim to the woman in parting. Digging a cigar out of the breast pocket of his jacket, he quickened his pace.

The hair falling to his collar was snow white, his neck pink as a western sunset behind it, as was the clean-shaven face that Spurr had glimpsed when he'd descended the steps. He was as old as Spurr, most likely. Or nearly so. The woman was younger by fifteen or twenty years, Spurr judged, as he stared at her in open appreciation of her beauty, though he still couldn't see much of her.

She'd swung full around to stare after the old gent—a successful rancher, judging by his clothes and the buggy and the man's slightly stiff walk. But the woman's hair, gathered into a chignon behind her head, was dark brown. Nearly black. Maybe a few stray strands of gray hid amongst the rich, twisted tresses. Her body in her white taffeta dress with its long pleated skirt was straight and fine. Full in all the right places.

Spurr felt a twinge of sadness as well as old regret. The man had called her Martha. Spurr did not recollect any Marthas in his past, but his body was telling him he knew this woman staring rather pensively, maybe a bit longingly at the older gent walking away from her toward his friends in the rough-hewn saloon. Leaving her to entertain herself at the hotel.

No, not Martha . . .

"Why, Abilene!"

SIX

The woman whipped around with a gasp, her fine, high cheeks coloring, brown eyes wide and curiously staring. Recognition sparked in them, and she said, "Well, I'll be hanged!"

She slapped a hand to her mouth and rolled her eyes around as if to see if anyone had heard. Her cheeks dimpling devilishly, she said more properly but also with a touch of irony, "I mean . . . what a surprise to see you here, Marshal Spurr."

"I reckon the surprise is half mine."

Spurr swung down from Cochise's back and tossed his reins over the nearest hitching post—a pretentious, wrought-iron affair with a wrought-iron horse figure at either end. Whoever owned the hotel had some mighty high aspirations for it and the railroad. He doffed his hat as he walked up the porch steps a little more heavily than he would have liked to in front of the woman he knew as Abilene, his breath rasping in and out of his still-painful chest.

"Good lord, lady," he said, approaching her, "what the

devil are you doin' way out here?" He extended his hat in the direction in which the older gent had disappeared. "Who was that? And who in the hell is *Martha*?"

"Shh!" Again, she looked around secretively, though humor flashed in her eyes as she stepped back away from him when he moved in to hug her. "That's . . . my husband, Olden Chandler."

"*Husband?* Abilene, the last time I saw you, you was workin' up in Buffaloville, workin' at the—"

"Shh! No one knows me by that name . . . nor by that reputation, Spurr, you old fool!" She chuckled in spite of herself, staring up at him fondly, her eyes reaching out to him as his reached out to her. His hands hung, tingling, at his sides. He wanted very badly to hold her in his arms.

He hadn't seen her for a couple of years, but they'd once had a grand old time together, having first met when she'd been plying the "trade" down in Texas and then running into each other infrequently later across the frontier. He'd seen her more recently in Laramie and then, about two years ago, he'd found her over in Buffaloville, on the eastern edge of the Big Horn Mountains.

Abilene was the only name he'd ever known her by. Sometimes, just for fun, when they'd been lounging around in some lumpy bed together, naked as jaybirds, he'd called her "Texas." Though she was a good twenty, maybe twenty-five years younger than him—he did not know her age for sure but guessed she was around thirty-five by now—there'd been a spark between them from the very first time they'd met.

Kindred spirits, they were—she, a whore; Spurr, a whoremongering old frontier lawman. They'd both seen the elephant a time or two. They had similarly wry senses of humor, a taste for tanglefoot, and a cynicism that shielded their hearts against the ravages of time and the mercurial nature of the frontier gods.

"Please," she said, "call me Mrs. Chandler."

Spurr's lower jaw dropped, and he shook his head. "That handle sure don't roll easy off this ole child's tongue."

"Try it out a few times"—she canted her head toward the front door of the hotel—"over pie and a cup of coffee?"

"You sure that'd be proper . . . Mrs. Chandler?"

"Put your badge on, and no one will question our morals."

"Unless they think you're wanted." He gave a snort as he dug into his vest pocket for his nickel-washed moon-and-star badge of the deputy U.S. marshal and pinned it to his hickory shirt. "How's that?"

Abilene's warm, brown gaze rose from the badge to his craggy face. "Right handsome."

"Now, that's somethin' I ain't been accused of in a long time."

"Come on."

Abilene opened the front door and stepped inside, and Spurr followed her through the hotel's small but immaculate lobby and into a dining room tricked out with cloth-covered tables, potted palms, and a ticking grandfather clock. There were no other patrons, and the matronly woman in a black gown and frilly white apron who filled their coffee cups said they were the first business she'd had in a week.

"Mrs. Anderson," Abilene said, "this is an old, dear friend of mine—Deputy United States Marshal Spurr Morgan. Spurr, meet Mrs. Anderson. She and her husband built this place, home of some of the finest dining in all of south-central Wyoming Territory."

"Oh, please, Mrs. Chandler," the jowly but stately old woman intoned, holding her silver pot in a pudgy, beringed hand. She had a heavy eastern accent. "We're the *only* dining within a hundred square miles!" She gave a falsetto laugh and favored Spurr with a bemused glance behind her round-rimmed spectacles. "And if the spur line's business doesn't pick up soon, we're going to have to return to Philadelphia, though the dry air out here is so much better for Malcolm's cough!"

Humming nervously under her breath, she returned to the kitchen through a swinging door. When she'd brought out two pieces of peach cobbler topped with rich plops of buttery whipped cream, she topped off her only two customers' coffee cups and retreated to the silent kitchen.

Spurr sat back in his chair, staring in wonder at the woman he knew as Abilene, who held his gaze with a wry, faintly sad look of her own. "Mrs. Chandler . . ." he said, absently caressing his spoon handle with his thumb. "How did that happen?"

"I answered a newspaper ad."

Spurr arched a brow.

"Olden was looking for a wife. His first one died two winters ago of a lung fever, and he was lonely. Not too many women out here as you can imagine. Lots of cattle, a few horses. Not many women."

"Where's the ranch?"

"Twelve miles north of here, in the foothills of the Bighorns. Pretty place along a creek."

"Must be a lonely place along a creek."

"Not half as lonely as Buffaloville, Spurr . . . when you never came back." She stared at him pointedly through the steam rising from her coffee.

Spurr arched his other brow. "And do what—marry you?"

"Take me with you down to Mexico. That's where you were going, were't you?" She frowned at the badge on his shirt. "Why did you change your mind?"

"About what—Mexico or retirement?"

"Both."

Spurr leaned forward and lifted his coffee cup to his mouth. He blew on the hot liquid and sipped. "When old bulls get put out to a back pasture, they're soon found with their bones strewn by coyotes along some draw."

"Not if they have a nice, fat heifer to entertain them." Abilene smiled, then slid her eyes to one side, making sure they were still alone.

"Come on, now," Spurr said, smearing the cream around on his pie with his fork, "we done talked through all that foolishness."

"So we did. Still, Spurr, I'd hoped to see you again."

"I got a job to do, Abilene. Besides, you and I both know we had our best times in Laramie—at the Lady's Hole Card."

She laughed in her customarily sexy, husky way. "Yes. And, as you pointed out, if we tried to stretch the game any farther or longer, we'd end up dealing from the bottom of the deck. You'd either shoot me or I'd shoot you. It's just our way."

Spurr laughed. "There you go."

She cut into her pie and said over the piece she held atop her fork, "I'm glad you didn't go to Mexico before I could see you again, Spurr. But . . . I wish . . ." She studied the cream-topped chunk of pie on her fork.

"If wishes were wings, pigs would fly," Spurr said around the pie in his mouth, before she could finish her sentence. He swallowed, sipped his coffee. "Is he good to you? I mean, aside from leavin' you here to drift over to the Bighorn with his pards . . . ?"

"He's likely a hell of a lot more honest with me than I've been with him. He thinks I'm a widow." She sipped her coffee, wrinkling the skin above the bridge of her nose. She set her cup down in its saucer, then dabbed at her lips with her napkin and looked past him toward the front window and the street. "He's very good to me. Better than anyone's been to me before, except for you, for the short times we were together. But it's all . . . it's . . . a little . . . boring. Do you know what I mean, Spurr?"

"Hell, there's nothin' wrong with boring, Abilene."

"Easy for you to say, livin' the life you've lived." She

glanced around, then leaned forward to whisper, "On the back of a horse and not on your back."

"Abilene!"

They both laughed quietly and at considerable length, hunkered over their plates. When their mirth finally dwindled to snickers, then died altogether, a silence fell over the table.

Then Spurr said, "Nah, but it's worn me—this life o' mine."

Chewing, she canted her head to one side and regarded him quizzically for a time before saying, "Your heart?"

"My heart, my pecker, everything." The laughter boiled up again in his chest, and he covered his mouth like an abashed schoolboy funning with his favorite girl at school, hoping the old schoolmarm wasn't overhearing.

"Spurr!" Abilene choked on her coffee, tears glistening in her eyes. "You haven't changed." She patted her chest and swallowed and regarded him tenderly from beneath her brows. "I always loved that about you."

"No wife would."

"Of course not."

"That's why it's best things turned out the way they did, I reckon."

"Oh, hell," she said, whispering. "How would we ever know if the other way wouldn't have worked just as well, after it's all tallied up?"

"Your wisdom is equaled only by your beauty, Mrs. Chandler." He frowned. "Who's Martha?"

"No one you'd care to know," she said. "Whose trail are you on, Spurr?"

He looked up from the plate he was cleaning with his last bit of pie, a little surprised by her abrupt change of subject. His brows beetled. "Let's stay on this awhile longer. Damn, how I've missed you!"

She sat still in her chair, only half her pie eaten. The

corners of her mouth rose slightly, and she said softly, "I'd love nothing better than to go upstairs with you, Spurr. Bring us a bottle, toil away the afternoon, listen to your jokes. Just like old times. You're not going to believe this, but I miss the way you always sighed into my neck when we finished and tugged on my ear."

Spurr tipped his head back and loosed a loud guffaw before catching himself and covering his mouth with a napkin. He felt the wetness of tears dribbling down his cheeks. Looking across the table, he saw her mouth straighten. The humor faded from her eyes.

He cleared his throat. "But those times is through—is that what you're sayin'?"

"I'll die out there at the ranch, and I'll be buried near Olden and his first wife, May, and his boy, James, who died three days after he was born. And these last years may be a little dull, and I'll always remember you with a smile, but I have it good now—better than I deserve." She looked down at her lap. "And this is the last time I'm likely to see you, Spurr."

He stared at her, his joyful nostalgia turning to a lonely ache behind his belt buckle.

She stared back at him, this time tears of sadness glistening in those large, brown eyes of hers. "You oughta go on down to Mexico like you planned once before."

"I look that bad?"

"Spurr, you burned it from both ends. You deserve a rest."

"Or a proper grave?"

"Not some ravine somewhere, dyin' slow with a bullet in your belly."

She stared those words home for a time.

He found himself feeling rankled by them, defiant. "Listen, goddamnit, like I done told you once before, I'm gonna live to a hundred and twenty, and I'll gallop out to that ranch to lay lilacs on your grave, Abilene."

Her eyes brightened. She brushed one hand and then the other across each cheek. "I'd like that, Spurr." Her gaze drifted, and she frowned out the window behind him.

"What is it?" he asked.

"Your friends are here."

SEVEN

At roughly the same time but about twenty-five miles as the crow flies to the west, Erin Wilde looked up from the open account book in the second-floor office of her mercantile. She swept her thick, curly chestnut hair back from her face with one slender hand and plucked her steel-rimmed reading glasses off her nose.

She slid her swivel chair back away from her desk and lowered her hazel gaze to the floor. She'd dropped a pencil a few minutes ago but had been too immersed in the futile attempt at balancing her accounts, trying to keep her business running smoothly in these months after the death of her husband, to bother retrieving it. She'd simply picked up another one.

Now the pencil that was still on the floor quivered and bounced ever so slightly, turning a slow circle on the scarred floorboards. She could feel the vibration through the soles of her low-heeled leather boots.

Riders coming hard toward Sweetwater. A good many of them, too.

Erin's heart quickened slightly. More business, perhaps? She could certainly use it. She had more credit customers than those who paid, and, as more than one of her fellow businessmen had told her, her generous heart would not continue indefinitely to provide food for herself and her young son, Jim. Maybe the thuds she began hearing now were the hoofbeats of ranch riders heading to town for supplies.

If so, they'd better have more in their pockets than lint and tobacco flakes.

Erin—a tall, slender, clear-eyed woman of twenty-six—rose from her chair and strode to the window overlooking the street. She wore a brown-and-cream-plaid Mother Hubbard dress to conceal the lush curves of her body and to forestall the advances of the men of Sweetwater, whom she sensed were waiting for the proper amount of time to pass after Daniel's death from cancer to begin knocking on her door after business hours.

She was only half consciously aware that the dress did little to scuttle the lusty glances directed her way. And she had no idea that many of the single as well as the married men of the town were covertly licking their proverbial chops and fantasizing about how the widow of Daniel Wilde would look with her clothes scattered about their bedroom floors.

Erin was lushly pretty. Her full hips and bust, olive-hued skin, passionate eyes, and thick chestnut hair, which often defied her attempts at containing it in a conservative bun atop her head—all betrayed the heritage of her Irish mother. Her pragmatic, hardworking nature hailed from her Norwegian father. It was those practical, ever-hopeful eyes that she directed out the sashed window and into the wide, dusty street of Sweetwater just as the riders appeared on her right.

Led by a tall man in a top hat and cream duster riding a mouse-brown gelding and with a short, stout shotgun dangling against his belly, the group slowed their mounts and then walked them along the street toward the mercantile.

They were a hard-looking, dusty, unshaven lot. The leader appeared to have grease or something—possibly tattoos—on his broad, ruddy cheeks above a thick, scraggly beard.

Something about the gang made Erin uneasy. But she was a businesswoman, and that part of her hoped they patronized her store. Turning away from the window and nervously pressing her dress tight across her thighs with her hands, she left the office that still smelled of her late husband's cigar smoke and descended the stairs to the main store below. She walked between the aisles of dry goods to the front of the store and looked through the glass upper panel of the door on which WILDE MERCANTILE—DRY GOODS AND SUNDRIES was stenciled in gold-leaf lettering.

The gang had stopped in the street fronting the store. They milled now, holding their sweat-lathered horses on tight reins as they looked around. Their dust was catching up to them, and the sunlight touched it, making it glow an ethereal gold-brown.

Several townsfolk had stopped on both sides of the street to regard the strangers with wary curiosity. One of the gang members (and that's what they looked like, Erin decided now, as well-armed as they were—a gang) rode double with a young, sour-faced woman with long blond hair and very little on her body save for a skimpy, torn dress that revealed nearly all of her heavy breasts. Her pale legs were bare. She wore no shoes.

Erin stood frozen in place before the mercantile's front door, staring out, her heart quickening dreadfully, palms tingling. The gang leader in the feathered top hat sat his horse straight out before her, about fifty feet off the mercantile's loading dock. As more people gathered on the boardwalks around him, he lifted his chin and flared his nostrils and shouted, "I am Clell Stanhope and we are the gang known far and wide as the Vultures!"

The townsmen all looked at each other fearfully and shifted their feet on the boardwalks.

Their reaction apparently pleased Stanhope. He shaped a grin that made the two vultures tattooed on his cheeks spread their wings, and said, "Heard of us, have ye? Well, don't fret. We're just here to pack on some trail supplies and git on our way. Won't pay for 'em, of course. If that's a problem for any of you, please step out and say so now or forever hold your peace!"

A man had been walking along the far side of the street, heading toward the gang. Erin recognized town marshal Jake Mercer, saw the five-pointed tin star pinned to his blue shirt. The mule ears of his boots flapped as he walked, and the brim of his floppy felt hat bent in the breeze, flickering shade across his freckled, clean-shaven face.

Erin's insides coiled when she saw Mercer approach the group, stop, and point a finger at Stanhope. "You, sir, are not wanted here. You're outlaws. Common trail wolves. And if you think you're going to loot my town, you have another think comin'!"

"That a fact?" Stanhope leaned forward on his saddle horn, regarding the lawman amusedly.

Mercer's hard, authoritative look softened. His eyes flicked across the gang before him, gradually acquiring a fearful cast. His throat moved as he swallowed.

Stanhope's right hand whipped across his belly. He brought up the savage-looking shotgun hanging from his neck by a wide leather lanyard. The gun exploded in his hand. It sounded like three sticks of dynamite going off.

Mercer jerked as though he'd been hit by lightning. He flew straight back into a water trough. The water splashed out of the trough, then closed over his lolling, lifeless body, arms and legs dangling down the trough's wooden sides, his hat riding the surface above his forehead and squeezed-shut eyes.

"*Ohh!*" Erin heard the exclamation explode from her throat as she opened the door and fairly bounded outside, fury and exasperation boiling through her.

As she marched across the loading dock toward the front steps, Stanhope jerked his head and shotgun toward her, narrowing one eye as he stared down the barrel at her.

"Ma!"

Erin froze, then whipped her head to the left. Her son, Jim, stood across the near side street, under the porch awning fronting Burnside's Harness Shop. Earlier, she'd sent the ten-year-old out running errands, and he must have been heading back to the mercantile when the gang had ridden into town. Jim was a small, wiry lad with straight brown bangs cropped just above his eyebrows, beneath the brim of his floppy felt hat. His horrified eyes bored into those of his equally horrified mother.

"Stay there, son!" she yelled, throwing out a waylaying hand and turning back to Stanhope.

The outlaw slid his gaze to the boy, then returned it to Erin. He was still holding the cocked shotgun on her, his gloved hand steady. His evil, faintly sneering eyes flicked down her body and back up again, acquiring a cast of lusty approval.

His eyes glinted, and then he swung the pistol around at the other townsfolk, mostly men but also a few ladies in sunbonnets who'd been out shopping, standing around in hushed awe.

Bean Wilson and Edgar Longbow, who owned shops near where the sheriff flopped in the stock trough, walked meekly over to the lawman, casting their terror-racked gazes from Mercer to the Vultures sitting their horses in the middle of the broad street. Bean held a broom in one hand. Edgar Longbow, short and paunchy, stretched his pink cheeks back from his teeth in revulsion. Neither man was armed. In fact, she knew of few citizens in Sweetwater who went around with a pistol lashed to his hip. The only men she usually saw wearing pistols around here were cowpunchers from area ranches, in town for fun or business, or the occasional market hunters who visited Sweetwater for ammunition and trail supplies.

Erin could tell by the druggist's expression as he peered down at Mercer that the town's only lawman, the only man here who routinely carried a gun, was dead.

"Anyone got anything they wanna get off their chests?" Stanhope said, looking around at the fearful faces staring back at him.

An eerie hush had fallen over the town. There was only Stanhope's voice, echoing around the false fronts of the main street. His cream duster blew out around him. His savage gun smoked in his hand.

"All right, then." The gang leader let the gun dangle freely down his chest. "We'll just be doin' our business and be on our way."

He rode back through the gang, yelling orders that Erin could only hear pieces of, when Stanhope turned his head toward her as his grulla clomped along the street. She turned to Jim, her heart racing, wanting only to get the boy out of harm's way. She beckoned him off down the side street, then turned back toward the main street when she heard hooves clomping loudly.

Stanhope rode toward her, the man's ugly face hard, his eyes—one brown, one gray—bright and leering as they roamed over her, more slowly this time. The men around him were yelling and howling and galloping off toward the various shops, a couple triggering pistols into the air. The men of Sweetwater yelled and the women screamed, scattering, some ducking into shops, others running off down the breaks between buildings.

"While you fellas are gettin' whiskey and guns an' ammo an' such," Stanhope shouted as he put his horse up to the hitchrack fronting Erin's store, "I do believe I'll lay in a few dry goods over here at the mercantile!"

Erin stared at the man. Her heart drummed a war rhythm in her chest. She wrung her hands against her belly and backed away, hating her fear. She had several rifles inside—none loaded, all for sale—but she should make a break for one of the new Winchesters and at least try to shove some shells into its breech. She, like all the others in Sweetwater, should at least *try* to defend themselves.

What were they, sheep helpless against this pack of bloodthirsty wolves they'd all heard so much about—the Vultures?

Stanhope tossed his horse's reins over the hitchrack, then, staring at her with that horrible, hard, ugly face with the vulture tattoos on his cheeks, with those pitiless, flintlike, mismatched eyes boring into her, raking her like invisible hands, he mounted the steps of the loading dock. His boots drummed a staccato rhythm on the boards, his large-roweled spurs ringing raucously.

Rage trickled over her fear. She hardened her jaws and her eyes and held his gaze with a cold, stubborn one of her own.

"Everything I have is for sale. I don't give handouts to cutthroats."

He stopped before her, towering over her, and stared brashly down at her heaving breasts. He smiled, showing the ends of his sharp eyeteeth beneath his thick, dusty, sweat-damp mustache, as he returned his gaze to her face. "How 'bout you? You for sale?"

Erin said nothing. He waited, his eyes mocking her. Around her she could hear the gang shooting their pistols and yelling like wolves as they sacked the other stores. Vaguely, she recognized the pleas of several shop owners, but these were drowned by the echoing reports of the guns and the screeching of breaking glass.

"Nah," Stanhope said finally. "You're as much a handout as anything else in this town."

His big, gloved hand lashed toward her like a striking snake, grabbing the front of her dress over her breasts.

"No!" she shouted, fighting him.

He was too strong for her. He swung her around and pulled her so brusquely toward the mercantile's door that she nearly lost her footing. She heard the soft gasp of tearing fabric, felt the dress across her bosom slacken.

"*Ma!*" Jim cried.

Horror rippled through her as she heard footsteps running toward her from the side street. She'd hoped that Jim had run off as she'd ordered, but now she turned to see the boy mounting the loading dock from the direction of the side street.

"*No, Jim—go!*" she shouted, hysterical now.

Stanhope stopped in front of the door. Erin's momentum sent her stumbling past him and into the closed door itself as Stanhope turned toward Jim, the sawed-off shotgun coming up in another blur of quick motion. Erin had just glimpsed the movement, her brain having no time to digest it, before the gun was up and out.

Somewhere amidst the movement she heard the click of the shotgun's hammer being ratcheted back.

"*Leave my ma alone, damn you!*"

Jim's screeching shout was punctuated by what sounded like a boulder falling on a cabin. The explosion was a giant fist punching Erin's head back against the door.

Her vision swam. Whistles blew in her ears. Her knees turned to liquid. They struck the loading dock with a solid thump that she could distantly hear beneath the ringing in her ears. She glanced toward where Jim had been running toward her, and again she felt as though a stout fist was hammered against her face.

There was a splotch of blood just above the steps on the north side of the loading dock, the side facing the street. She could see the underside of the sole of Jim's right boot at the top of the steps. It was moving slightly.

Twitching.

"Ah, Christ," she heard a man's disgusted voice behind her.

In the periphery of her vision, the outlaw leader pushed

the mercantile's door open and disappeared inside, leaving
her alone on the dock and staring at her son's twitching boot.

His name exploded out of her on a geyser of suddenly
released horror. "Jim! *Jimmeeee!*"

Erin scrambled to her feet and ran over to the steps and
gasped when she saw her young son lying sprawled down
them, his head brushing the ground at the base of the dock.

Again, she screamed his name and ran down the steps.
She sat on the bottom one and cradled his head in both her
arms, rocking him gently. The blood pumping from the
large, ragged hole in his chest was a savage, merciless fist
hammering her again and again, knocking her senseless.

"Oh, Jim," she said. "Oh, Jim. Oh, Jim. Please don't die.
Please don't be *dead!*"

Then she started screaming for help—for someone, anyone to help her. She screamed for the town doctor, but as
she continued to rake her gaze between her son's inert face
with its closed eyelids and growing pallor, she saw no one
on the street except for the outlaws hauling goods of one
kind or another out of the shops in burlap sacks that they
lashed to their saddle horns.

She jerked her terror-stricken gaze toward where the
town marshal lolled dead in the stock trough, the ground
around the trough darkly muddy. In the window just beyond
the marshal was the face of Edgar Longbow staring out the
front window of his drugstore. He looked like a ghost hovering there.

"Edgar!" Erin screamed. "Help me!"

The druggist shook his head, then reached up and pulled
the shade down over his window.

"Edgarrrr!" the woman screamed, clutching her boy to
her chest, squeezing him, feeling him growing cold, a dead-
weight in her arms.

Time seemed to stop. She cried and rocked the dead child
as she'd once rocked him to get him to sleep at night. The

world around her became a blur. The whooping and holler-
ing and sporadic gunshots grew distant, like some storm
drifting off toward the next valley.

Suddenly, she was aware of a strong smell of horse and
man sweat. Hooves clomped. The heavy, unyielding body
of a horse pushed against her. She turned her head to look
up and behind her. Clell Stanhope sat his tall grulla, reaching toward her with those cold, faintly leering eyes.

"Leave me," Erin said, her voice sounding like someone
else's.

"Uh-uh," the outlaw leader grunted as he wrapped his
hand around her arm.

Before she could stand and fight him, he'd jerked her
away from the loading dock. She tried to hold on to Jim, but
when Stanhope drew her closer to his horse, she dropped
the child in the dirt.

She became hysterical. She swung around and pounded
her fists against the outlaw's knees and thighs, though most
of her punches landed on the stirrup fender or on the grulla's
whither or on the barrel of the shotgun that had killed Jim.
Despite her screams and her fighting, she felt her right arm
being pulled out of its socket until she found herself lying
belly down across Stanhope's saddle.

Then the horse was galloping up the street. Each lunge
was like a punch to her belly, the saddlebows digging into
her middle while the horn raked her left hip raw.

The ground pocked with hoofprints swept past her. She
could see her hair hanging toward it, the ends barely brushing the finely churned dirt and bits of straw. She passed a
body lying dead in the street. Idly, staring beyond the grulla's lunging legs, she recognized the banker, Earl Thornberg,
a hole in his forehead, his open eyes glassy.

Then the town slid back behind her and she was carried
off into the country to the west, screaming, *"Jimmy!"*

EIGHT

Feeling old and grumpy, Spurr walked out of the Laramie House Hotel, drawing the door closed behind him and setting his battered tan hat on his head. The five riders who Abilene had spied from the dining room window sat their horses around Spurr's big roan, who stood tied to the hitchrack, thrashing his thick tail in guarded greeting.

One of the newcomer's horses was kind enough to pluck a bug of some kind from Cochise's hindquarters, just behind Spurr's blanket roll. Spurr did not recognize the man astraddle the thoughtful steeldust. He recognized only three of the five: Sheriff Dusty Mason of Willow City and two longtime Wyoming territorial marshals, Bill Stockton and Ed Gentry. The latter two were only a few years Spurr's junior, warty oldsters in their own right.

They were all looking at Spurr, though it was Mason himself who said, "I'd recognize this old cayuse of yours anywhere, but I couldn't believe he was standing here and not over *there*. What happened—you get kicked out of the Bighorn?"

"Hell, no," Spurr said, walking down the porch steps. "I had me a civilized piece of cobbler and a cup of coffee." He didn't mention Abilene. He wasn't sure why he didn't.

Mason scrutinized him from the saddle of his buckskin. "Don't tell me you've given up drinkin'. Can you track sober?"

"I can track standin' on my head."

Mason gave a quick glance to the others. "Ed and Bill here tell me they've ridden a few trails with you before.

"Hidy, Bill," Spurr said, nodding. "Ed, you old ramshagger."

"Spurr, ya plug-ugly peckerwood. Figured some jealous jake would've gut-shot you by now."

Mason said, "These two's Web Mitchell and Calico Strang. Wells Fargo detectives. Boys, this is Spurr Morgan."

"You don't say," said one of the Pinkertons, Calico Strang. Despite being clean-shaven, he had a greasy look that Spurr didn't like, though he was properly attired in a wool vest, white silk shirt, and bowler hat. He might have been thirty, but his eyes were young and brash. He had buckteeth. Long copper hair dangled from his crisp, brown bowler. "I beg your pardon, Marshal, but I thought you were dead!"

He looked at his partner, the taller and mustachioed and also properly attired Web Mitchell. Mitchell, appearing older, maybe thirty, smiled but not as brashly as his young partner.

Spurr had grabbed Cochise's reins off the hitchrack, and now he narrowed an eye up at the two Pinkertons. Before he could grumble a proper reply to the younger man's greasy hoorawing, Mason said, "Strang, do me a favor. Do us all a favor, and shut your fuckin' trapdoor before I drive the butt of my hogleg through it. You men are here only as my personal favor to the Pinkerton agency. No one said you could track or even shoot, and I'm still not convinced you can ride. So don't push me."

The sheriff, all business as usual, looked at Spurr. "You ready for a hard pull?"

Spurr swung into the leather and turned Cochise away from the hitchrack. "What do you think I came out here for—pie and coffee?" He was surprised—no, stunned—at Mason's having stuck up for him. Not that he needed the sheriff's help with these two Pinkerton tinhorns. He could have pistol-whipped the pair till their brains dribbled out their ears. It just wasn't like Mason to come to the aid of a man whom Mason saw as old and washed up.

At least, that's how Spurr had figured the younger sheriff regarded him after their testy, often outright argumentative partnership during their long ride to the Mexican border a year ago. Mason, who Spurr saw as an unproven lawman often blinded by his distrust of federals and too pigheaded to take direction from a far more experienced badge toter, had fared little better in Spurr's eyes.

The Pinkertons were flushed, their eyes indignant.

Spurr looked all the men over. "Your horses need a rest, water?"

"We gave 'em a blow and water at the Mud Creek Stage Station," said Ed Gentry. "But me—I could use a bottle." He was eyeing the saloon yonder with interest.

"No time for that," Mason said.

Gentry, a skinny oldster about ten years Mason's senior and Spurr's junior, a good lawman from what Spurr remembered, spat a thick wad of chew onto a fresh horse apple. "Maybe no time to sit and play cards, but I'll be damned if I'm ridin' dry. Spurr, your holds got slosh?"

"I ain't no juniper, Ed." Spurr reached back to pat one of his saddlebag pouches, then offered the man a brotherly smile.

"You boys go on ahead," Gentry said. "I'll be along shortly."

As the territorial marshal trotted his claybank off toward the saloon, Mason cursed, then tipped his cream Stetson down low over his high forehead as he swung his buckskin out into the street and touched its flanks with his spurs. Spurr pulled Cochise up beside the sheriff's mount. Stockton rode to Mason's other side, rolling chew behind his lower lip. The two Pinkertons, looking ornery after Mason's verbal assault, fell in behind.

As they rode past the saloon before which old Ed Gentry was just now dismounting, Spurr scrutinized the young sheriff riding on his left. Mason looked even more grim and serious than Spurr remembered. Spurr figured the man had a right. The worst that could happen to any lawman had happened to Mason. His jail and his town had been sacked. His prisoner, a notorious killer, had been freed by his equally notorious gang. They'd killed several innocent bystanders and kidnapped another.

Those were all the details that Chief Marshal Brackett had shared with Spurr. They were all he'd needed to know on the front end of the assignment. He knew the Vultures' reputation, had even tracked them, in vain, twice before. He figured Mason would eventually fill him in on the rest of their most recent depradations.

"Go easy, Dusty," Spurr said, staring straight ahead over his horse's ears as they trotted on out of the fledgling town.

Mason glowered at him. "What'd you say?"

"I said go easy. Bring them beans in your pot back to a simmer. You goin' off on a full boil like this ain't the way to track killers of Clell Stanhope's ilk."

"You know about Stanhope?"

"Hell, Stanhope's been runnin' off his leash for nigh on ten years now. I once took down two members of his gang, but never did get close to the rest." Spurr looked at Mason, who was still glowering at him. "I know his reputation." He paused. "I also know what he did to your town."

Mason looked straight off over the old horse trail they were following through a long valley hemmed in by ridges in all directions. They'd ridden nearly a quarter mile before the sheriff turned back to Spurr, his pale blue eyes brightly anguished beneath his hat brim. "They shot down a whole posse, Spurr. Men—citizens of *my town*—who helped me run Stanhope down."

His lips quivered a little as he spoke through gritted teeth. "They shot 'em down in front of their wives and children. I was on my knees. Handcuffed. I watched the whole goddamn thing and couldn't do nothin' about it. Nothin'."

The sheriff stretched his lips, showing more of his teeth. "So don't tell me you know his reputation. And please spare me all your sage advice. I didn't request you for that. I requested you because, though you're older than them mountains yonder and you'll likely die on me tomorrow, you can track. And that's what I need—a tracker."

Mason turned his head forward, pulled his hat brim still lower on his forehead, and rammed his heels into his buckskin's loins. The horse gave a whinny as it put its head down and stretched its stride into a full gallop. Spurr squinted against Mason's dust, shaking his head.

The surly sheriff had amazed him once again.

"You requested me, didja?" he muttered. "Well, if that don't beat all."

Spurr held Cochise to a trot, knowing they had a long trail to fog. The Pinkertons passed him, Calico Strang glancing back, his long, dark red hair bouncing over his collar as he sneered. "What's the matter, old man—can't you keep up?"

Spurr only grinned and shook his head as the two Pinkertons booted their own mounts into gallops after Mason. Bill Stockton held his horse back to a more reasonable pace. He met Spurr's gaze, then shook his head in defeat and continued on up the trail.

After a time, when all four had disappeared over the far side of a hill a good half mile away, Spurr followed the trail halfway up a low hill, then stopped Cochise and curveted the horse so that he was facing south. He glanced behind, saw Ed Gentry loping along Spurr's back trail, about a half mile away.

Out of long habit, Spurr scrutinized the broad valley rolling between high, dark mountains. As Gentry and his dapple gray meandered toward Spurr along the curving trail, growing gradually larger so that Spurr could begin making out the man's features, including his black wool coat that whipped out behind him in the wind, and his checked wool shirt and brown leather vest, Spurr spied movement behind the man.

Spurr's eyes weren't what they once were, but as he narrowed the blue orbs beneath his grizzled brows, he thought he could make out a dust plume along Gentry's back trail. Gradually, as Gentry continued toward Spurr, who could now begin hearing the dapple gray's footfalls, Spurr saw the two indistinct figures of what were most likely horseback riders.

He reached into one of his saddlebag pouches and pulled out his spyglass sheathed in elk hide worn soft as mountain ferns. He removed the old, brass-chased glass from the leather, brushed the lens across his neckerchief, and telescoped it. Holding it to his right eye, following the growing dust plume on Gentry's back trail, he heard Gentry say dryly beneath the clomps of his horse, "You waitin' on me or the busthead?"

Spurr lowered the spyglass slightly to the old, gray-bearded lawman coming up the hill, holding his reins loosely in his black-gloved hands above his saddle horn. Spurr was glad Gentry and Stockton were included in Mason's posse. They were old, familiar faces, and there were getting to be fewer and fewer men he knew on this younger man's frontier.

Spurr snorted. "What do you think, Ed?"

"I'm thinkin' you look like you need a drink, you old mossyhorn."

"Don't normally imbibe this time of the day, but I'd take

a snort to be sociable. Since you got a fresh new bottle an' all."

Grinning, Gentry pulled the dapple gray up beside Spurr, on the downside of the hill, and reached back with a grunt into his left saddlebag pouch. "Where's the others?"

"Lightin' a shuck like there's a passel of high-priced whores givin' free pokes in the Wind Rivers."

Gentry wrapped his reins around his saddle horn and pried the cork out of the bottle labeled Old Kentucky, with a low hill and a lone oak etched just beneath the words. "He won't slow down till his horse throws a shoe or comes up lame."

"No, he won't."

"Bill said he'd stay as close as he could, to keep him from gettin' dry-gulched."

Spurr was still staring through his spyglass, smiling with concentration.

"What you see back there?" Gentry asked him, holding out the bottle.

"You grew two extra shadows, Ed."

The territorial marshal was indignant. "The hell I did."

Spurr traded Gentry's bottle for his spyglass. While Spurr tipped the bottle back, enjoying the burn as the southern bourbon washed down his throat and over his tonsils, instantly quelling his sundry and customary aches and pains in his rickety body, Gentry held the spyglass to his eye with both hands, adjusting it.

"I'll be goddamned."

Spurr took another drink, then wiped his mouth with the back of his hand. "You didn't stir up any trouble in the saloon back there, did ya, partner?"

"Hell, no. Weren't nobody in there but some paper collars off the local ranches."

Spurr thought of the paper collar that Abilene had married. Abilene . . . or Martha? He preferred to think of her as Abilene, however, and he would forevermore.

"Probably just a couple of punchers headin' back to their spreads." Spurr gave the bottle back to Gentry and replaced his spyglass in its sheath, then returned it to its saddlebag pouch. "We'd best get to bobbasheelyin' after Mason."

When they'd ridden up the trail a ways, Spurr said, "How'd you an' Bill get involved in this mess, Ed?"

"Mason sent us a telegram over to Buffaloville, where we been tryin' to rustle us up some long loopers who been twistin' the panties of some ranchers over there. We rode over to Willow City the next day, picked up Mason, and started trackin' them Vultures west through the Stony Butte country. That's where the two Pinkertons were waitin' on us. Mason had sent a telegram to their office up in Thunder City, and ole Bryan Rand sent them two—Strang and Mitchell—because the Vultures been puttin' a nice dent in their business, don't ya know."

"I do know."

"Web ain't so bad for a Pinkerton, but you can take that Calico Strang and hang him from the nearest tree."

"I'd like to take Strang."

Gentry chuckled, then he shook his head. "Willow City's a damn mess, I tall ya, Spurr. Them Vultures killed Mason's entire posse. Hanged the hangman."

"So I heard."

"He didn't even ask any of the citizens up there to posse up this time. I don't reckon it woulda done any good. Shit, you ride through there, you can still hear the women cryin' and the little ones squallin'. Awful damn mess. Never see the like since you and me put the kibosh on that land war up in Dakota—what was it, three, four years ago?"

Spurr laughed as he and Gentry angled around the base of a flat-topped butte. "More like eight or nine, you old wildcat!"

"Can't be that long!" Gentry said, rolling his brown eyes toward Spurr in expasperation.

Spurr just laughed and changed the subject. "Is Mason

on the Vultures' trail? I sure ain't pickin' up any fresh sign this way."

"We lost it yesterday. Came on down this way to meet you, but we're thinkin' they swung west just north of where we picked you up. They'll probably come out where the Cottonwood Valley meets the North Fork of Dead Woman Creek. We're only two, maybe three days behind 'em. Sure is lucky you was able to get up from Denver so fast. Mason—he seems to fancy your trackin' skills, though I done informed him I taught you everything you know."

Gentry maintained an expression of exaggerated seriousness for about five seconds. Then he turned toward Spurr and stretched his lips back from his large, yellow teeth. One of his front teeth was capped, and it sparkled in the westering sun.

"You're still so full of shit your eyes are brown," Spurr noted. "But I'm obliged for that bourbon. I don't know what it is, but a good label of busthead just invigorates this old devil!"

"Probably that and your visit with Mrs. Chandler."

Spurr jerked a surprised look at his gray-bearded partner, who said, "I seen you through the window."

"You know Mr. Chandler, do you?"

"This here is my stompin' ground. Chandler was one of the paper collars in the Bighorn."

"Is he a good man, Ed?"

"He's got a closetful of silver-headed walkin' sticks—I'll give him that." Gentry held Spurr's gaze with a serious one of his own. "But I doubt he'd ever hit her with one of 'em."

"Well, hell," Spurr said, frowning pensively, pooching out his lips as he booted Cochise into a lope across a broad flat between rock-rimmed mesas. "I reckon he'll do, then."

NINE

White smoke curled up from a grove of cottonwoods along a creek about a hundred yards off the trail's right side. Sandstone walls had risen along the trail, forming a canyon about a half a mile wide. It was dusk here in the canyon though the sky above it was still blue. The tops of the canyon walls shone golden with the waning rays of the west-falling sun.

Spurr scrutinized the ground. Mason's gang of four had left the trail here, and the prints of the shod hooves angled off through the rock and sage toward the smoke.

"Well, he finally stopped," Gentry said. "I thought he was gonna ride all night."

"I tell you one thing, Ed, ole Sheriff Dusty might have a giant burr under his blanket, but he won't be pullin' this kind of shit no more. Not if he wants me trackin' for him he won't."

"If you say so, Spurr."

"I say so!"

Spurr cursed and booted Cochise off the trail and along the tracks of the four shod horses. There was a small escarpment off to the right, and from here came the sudden, loud metallic rasp of a rifle being cocked. Spurr turned to see Calico Strang grinning at him and Gentry as he lifted his bowler-hatted head from his nest near the top of the scarp.

"Show off," Gentry muttered.

Spurr swung Cochise over to the escarpment and stopped, staring up at Strang still grinning down at him from his night guard position. "You might find yourself a better spot from which to keep watch," Spurr suggested.

The smile faded from the young Pinkerton's face. "What's wrong with this one?"

"If you look to your right, you'll see what."

Strang turned his head to see the diamondback dropping straight down out of a hole in the scarp about even with the Pinkerton's position. The snake's head and about a foot of its stone-gray body were visible. In the faint pink light of the sunset, it flicked its forked tongue hungrily.

Strang jerked with a start. "Shit!"

"Likely a nest of 'em in there," Spurr said.

Gentry chuckled.

Spurr said, "Keep your eyes peeled on our back trail. Two fellas been shadowin' us. Don't get excited when you see 'em, just make sure they know you see 'em."

"Yeah . . . yeah, all right," Strang said, still staring, hang-jawed, at the snake still slithering out of its hole.

As the young Pinkerton began scrambling around, look-ing for another night watch position, Spurr and Gentry gigged their horses toward the cottonwoods. Spurr could smell the smoke of cedar and cottonwood and the aroma of boiling beans.

"Hello, the camp," he called when he saw the low flames dancing amongst the trunks, and the figures of Mason, Bill Stockton, and Web Mitchell hunkered around the cookfire. A pot was bubbling on a flat rock inside the fire ring.

The men's horses were tied to a picket line off to the left

of the fire, just inside the cottonwood grove and near a shallow ravine that angled along the backside of the grove toward the creek. The creek muttered in the distance—a cool, pleasant sound. The air was cooling now, too, as the sun quickly fell.

Spurr did not feel cool, though. He was hot with anger at Mason's way of going after the Vultures. When he saw the state of Mason's horse—the beast was obviously blown, standing hang-headed and droopy-eyed at the picket line to which it was tied—he was even angrier. Mason was not a tinhorn. Spurr knew that from having ridden with the man. The sheriff took himself too seriously most of the time, and he had little sense of humor whatever, but he was too good a lawman to let himself get goaded into a bear trap like this.

Spurr and Gentry tended their horses, letting them cool and rubbing them down before leading them over to the creek to draw water. When both horses had had their fill, the two men grained them and tied them to the picket line with the other four, where grama and bluestem grew around the cottonwoods. Then they hauled their gear including their sheathed rifles over to the fire.

Mason sat on a rock, his hat on the ground beside him, his cup in his hands. He did not look up as Spurr and Gentry approached and threw down their gear. The others— Stockton and Mitchell—nodded as they smoked or sipped their coffee, but no one said anything. It was a grim crew.

Spurr consciously cooled himself. When dealing with a prideful son of a bitch like Dusty Mason, whose icy demeanor had a fiery flipside that Spurr had seen explode a time or two down in Colorado and New Mexico, it was wise to carefully choose one's words.

He didn't say anything until he and Gentry each had a cup of coffee and were sitting on a log on the creek side of the fire from Mason and Web. Stockton lay back against a tree, hat off, ankles crossed, a long, thin black cheroot smoldering between his long, knob-knuckled brown fingers.

"Well, I'll tell you one thing," Spurr said over the rim of his smoking cup to Mason, "if this was a horse race, you'd have won you a new saddle and the first dance at the do-si-do with the mayor's plain-faced daughter."

Mason was like a scolded but stubborn child. Fidgeting uncomfortably, he glanced up at the sky that was spruce green and then at the creek beyond Spurr and Gentry, and then he said, "I should have brought a spare. We all should've."

"Well, we all didn't." Spurr saw he wasn't getting anywhere trying to be subtle. Still he kept his voice low, reasonable. "You blow out your horse, you're on foot out here all by your lonesome. None of us is gonna ride double with you, Dusty."

"I realize I been foggin' a little hard, but those are killers we're after. A horse is a horse."

"Not out here it ain't, and you know it. It's all that stands between you and the grave."

Now Mason let his gaze stray to Spurr, who held it. An uncomfortable silence fell over the bivouac. The fire crackled and popped and the bean pot bubbled, juice dribbling down over the sides and sizzling on the hot coals beneath it.

Web finally dismissed himself, saying he had to take a piss. He drifted off over to the creek. Stockton said he was going to check on the horses. Gentry merely sat back against a log and rolled a smoke. He knew both Mason and Spurr and didn't feel he had to go anywhere while the old bull and the young bull locked horns.

In fact, a referee might be necessary.

He drew a deep, fateful sigh as he rolled his quirley closed.

Spurr finally said, "I know what's eatin' you about this, Dusty."

"What's that?"

"You're alive."

Mason stared at him. The hardness of his eyes softened just a little, and he swallowed.

Spurr nodded.

Mason turned to stare off to his left, then lowered his head and ran his hand through his thin brown hair that was swept back from his sharp widow's peak pale as flour compared to the redness lower where the sun had reddened his face.

"Don't make sense," Mason said, keeping his head down and massaging his neck. "They killed Bone and all the posse members, left their women wailin', and they hanged poor ole LaForge. Clell was about to pop a cap on me when someone shot at him from a rooftop." He looked up now, shuttling his openly befuddled gaze between the two older lawdogs on the other side of the fire from him. "For the life of me, I don't know who that was. I got no idea who saved my hide. Or why."

"A townsman with a rifle," Spurr said.

"I don't think so. I couldn't see much of the man, but from what I could see, I don't think I'd ever seen him before."

"What'd he look like?" Gentry asked.

"I don't know."

Spurr glanced at Gentry. The territorial lawman glanced back at him, a gray brow faintly, skeptically arched.

"Ah, hell," Mason said, growing impatient with the conversation. "Don't matter who he was. He saved my bacon, that's all. Maybe I do know him. He was a long ways away. Maybe he just didn't want anyone to know who he was should Stanhope find out and do to him what they done to the posse."

"That's probably it," Spurr said.

"Shit, I'm hungry," Mason said, his disgruntlement over the whole affair aggravated by the fact that he owed his life to some stranger. He set his cup aside and dug a tin plate and a spoon out of his saddlebags. "I don't care if these beans is done or not. I'm eating."

After Spurr, Mason, Gentry, Stockton, and Mitchell had all eaten, the dark night settled like a black glove though stars were smeared like flour across the sky. A high-country chill laced the air. The creek seemed to murmur a little louder than before in the cooler, denser air, muffling the distant yammering of coyotes.

When Spurr had come back from washing his plate and fork in the creek, he stowed the utensils in his saddlebags, then slid his rifle out of its elkhide sheath.

"I reckon I'll go relieve Calico," he said.

Calico himself replied with a yell from somewhere out beyond the fire: "Two riders ridin' in!"

Spurr glanced at Gentry, then stepped wide of the fire and leaned his left shoulder with feigned casualness against a tree. He levered a live round into his Winchester's chamber, then slowly lowered the hammer to half cock.

Mason rose from where he sat by the fire, as did the others, Gentry unholstering his pistol, Web and Stockton grabbing their rifles. They all spread out to the edges of the firelight, so they could see better into the darkness out by the trail they'd ridden in on.

An anxious hush fell over the camp, the fire snapping, an occasional spur chinging. Stockton puffed his cheroot. Hoof clomps sounded. They grew louder, the slow plodding of walking horses, until Spurr could see the two riders moving toward him slowly. Doubtless, these were the two men he'd spied on their back trail.

"That's far enough," Mason said, keeping his voice low.

The riders lifted their hands to their shoulders, drawing back on their horses' reins. The horses blew and snorted. One of the tied horses whinnied and the horse of the newcomer on the right answered in kind.

Keeping his voice friendly but knowing that trouble could

be brewing, Spurr said, "A little dark out here. Name yourselves."

The man on the left said, "Homer Willoughby and Tate Beauchamp from over Dakota way. Smelled the fire. We're a little light, as the ranchers ain't hirin' in these parts till fall." The voice sounded dull, depressed. His horse snorted again, shook its head, the bridle bit rattling in its teeth.

Knowing that if anyone of the group knew them, Spurr would, Mason gave the federal lawman a deferential glance.

"Sure, sure," Spurr said. "We got some beans. Not many, and one of us ain't eaten yet, but you can have you a couple o' spoonfuls. Picket your horses over yonder. The creek's got good water in it."

"Obliged," said the man on the right as they both swung down from their saddles, making the leather squawk.

Spurr didn't get a good look at either man but saw only their silhouettes as they led their horses wide around the fire and through the trees toward the picket line. The other horses stomped and generally lifted a fuss in guarded greeting of the newcomers.

Cochise whinnied raucously, drawing back on his picket line, and Spurr walked over to calm the horse. The two newcomers tended their own mounts in silence. Neither looked toward Spurr. When they'd led their horses off to the creek, Spurr returned to the fire, and that's where he was sitting, smoking on a log, when Willoughby and Beauchamp moved toward him through the trees.

They were both medium-tall men. They looked like typical drovers in work shirts, battered hats, and leather chaps over faded denims. Their eyes were dull. Their jaws were dark with beard stubble. Willoughby had a mustache and a stylish pinch of fur under his lower lip. Beauchamp walked with a slight hitch in his step—an old hip injury, most likely.

They both had gaunt, hungry looks, though neither really looked as though they'd missed a meal. They also both wore sheathed pistols tied to their thighs.

Willoughby's eyes dropped to the badge pinned to Spurr's vest. He stopped suddenly, as did his partner, who glanced at him curiously. Willoughby looked at the other men spread out around the fire, all holding guns though none actually aiming them at the newcomers. The guns were a precaution, not a threat.

Willoughby smiled in surprise, his eyes sparking in the firelight. "Well, I'll be damned. Y'all are lawmen!"

Spurr studied him, trying to place him. He thought he and Beauchamp looked vaguely familiar, but he'd run into a lot of men across the West, not all of them bad.

"That a problem for you?" Spurr asked.

"No, hell," Willoughby said, still grinning as he looked around at the other badge toters. "We got nothin' against the law. Ain't ridin' crossways of it, anyways—if that's what you mean."

"No, hell," echoed Beauchamp nervously, hooking his thumbs behind his cartridge belt. "I reckon we know we're safe here amongst these fellas—huh, Homer? Out here, you never know. We'd just as soon steer wide of most folks, but since we done lost our pokes to some cardsharp in Cisco up in the Mummy Range two days ago, I reckon we're a little desperate."

"Desperate for what?" Mason asked them pointedly.

"Why, food, of course!" Beauchamp said with a laugh.

Bill Stockton dropped his fist-sized chin and growled, "You ever hear of shooting your own?"

"Sure, sure, we heard of it," said Willoughby. "Only neither of us can shoot fer shit." He chuckled, rolling his eyes toward his partner standing beside him, just inside the sphere of flickering firelight. "Can we, Tate? No, sir. We're cowpunchers, not market hunters. I for one carry a carbine but mostly just for show, so's road agents'll leave us alone. And my six-shooter—hell, I ain't fired it in weeks and then it was only at a sidewinder slithering up to my hoss. Mostly, I just use it to pound coffee beans."

Both men were grinning, showing chipped, yellow teeth.

"Help yourself to the beans, boys," said Spurr, depressing his Winchester's off-cocked hammer and leaning the rifle against a tree. "Just leave enough for that Pinkerton out guarding the trail, or he'll likely start caterwaulin' like a trapped polecat."

Feeling more at ease, and understanding how these two had likely just stumbled onto some bad luck—hell, he'd done the same a time or two—he sat down on his log near the fire. The other lawmen all put up their guns and slacked back down into their previous places around the fire. Stockton and Gentry tossed the newcomers a couple of plates and three-tined, wood-handled forks and made room for them around the fire.

As the two walked past Spurr, Spurr caught a brief glimpse of Willoughby rolling a quick, shrewd glance toward him. It was so fleeting as to be damn near unnoticeable.

To anyone but a seasoned lawdog.

"Sure do appreciate this, fellas," Willoughby said, instantly stretching his previous grin across his face.

"De nada," Spurr said.

At the same time, he snaked his right hand across his belly and unsnapped the keeper thong from over the hammer of the Starr .44 he wore for the cross draw just left of his shell belt's square buckle. He slid the popper from its sheath at the same time he saw Willoughby wheel toward him, hardening his jaws and steeling his eyes as he clamped a big, brown hand over the wooden grips of the Schofield .44 thonged on his right thigh.

Spurr bounded up off his log, raised the Starr like a club, and smashed it down hard across the side of Willhoughby's head. The man screamed and dropped his gun and ran staggering across the fire. At the same time, Beauchamp twisted around quickly, a cocked Smith & Wesson in his hand.

Spurr's pistol leapt and roared. Flames lapped from the maw. Beauchamp grunted and triggered his Smithy into the log near where Ed Gentry was still sitting, the lawman's lower jaw hanging. He'd managed to clamp his hand over his holstered pistol by the time Beauchamp had stumbled across the fire, kicking burning branches every which way, and fell in a heap with his pants on fire, screaming, blood oozing from the hole in his chest.

Willhouby had dropped to his knees at the base of a tree.

"Goddamn, you miserable sons o' lawdoggin' bitches!" he wailed as he reached inside his denim jacket and hauled out an over-and-under derringer.

Spurr swung his Starr toward the raging would-be dry-gulcher but slackened his trigger finger when Dusty Mason's Colt Army thundered twice, drilling one shot through Willoughby's forehead, the other through his chest, punching him back against the tree and silencing his caterwauling forever. The derringer dropped in the dirt.

All the lawmen were standing now, boots spread, staring in awe at the two dead men. Beauchamp had knocked over the beans. The scattered branches burned. Flames licked up both of the screaming brigand's legs and he kicked at them as though they were dogs that had grabbed ahold of his ankles. At the same time, he clamped a hand over the ragged, bloody hole in his chest.

"Help me!" he cried. "Please, god—someone get some water. Don't let me burn, you bastards!"

Web Mitchell plucked the empty bean pot off the ground and yelled, "I'll fetch some water!"

"Forget it." Spurr extended his Starr and put the howling bushwhacker out of his misery with a well-placed shot to his forehead, just above the bridge of his nose.

Silence save for the cracking of the several small fires settled over the lawmen's camp. The others looked at the two dead men, then at Spurr, scowling curiously. Running foot thuds sounded from the direction of the trail, and Spurr turned to see Calico Strang run into the trees and stop suddenly, mouth agape, chest rising and falling sharply, his cocked rifle in both his slender, black-gloved hands.

"What the hell . . . ?"

"That's what we'd all like to know," said Bill Stockton, straight-faced but chuckling incredulously.

"Horse thieves," Spurr said. "Didn't recognize 'em 'cause they used their own true names. Willoughby and Beauchamp. They was a part of a horse-stealin' ring down in the Nations some years ago. I killed Beauchamp's brother, Lyle, but couldn't pin nothin' on him or his cousin, Willoughby, so I had to let 'em go. Didn't recognize either one till Willoughby gave me that little look of the devil just before they was about to help themselves to our beans."

Mason shoved his Colt down into its holster with a snick of iron against leather. "They see you at the hotel yonder?"

"If they did, I didn't see them. Most likely, they seen us from a distance and got after our horses but recognized me just now and decided to go ahead and bushwhack us all and get it over with before I recognized them."

"I'll be damned," Gentry said, chuckling and staring down at the burning Beauchamp. "Can't take you anywhere, can we, you old whore banger?"

Mitchell bounced the bean pot in his hand. "You mind if I fetch that water now?"

"Yeah, go ahead," said Spurr.

When Mitchell had put the fires out and Mason and Gentry had built up their own cookfire again in its stone ring, Spurr threw back a long slug of Gentry's tanglefoot and smacked his lips. "Shit, I was gonna take the first watch after young Strang here. But I reckon this miserable episode just frazzled my old, tender nerves like lightnin' streakin' along telegraph wires." The craggy-faced federal lawman popped a nitro tablet into his mouth and washed it down with another pull from Gentry's bottle. "I'm gonna have to sit here awhile, get myself settled down."

With that, he lay back against his saddle and pulled his hat brim down over his eyes. He was snoring inside of a minute.

Mason, Gentry, and Stockton snorted.

TEN

Clell Stanhope's Colt revolver was so close to Erin Wilde's right hand that it made her hair tingle and her heart flutter.

She looked down at it now as she rode on the back of Stanhope's grulla, behind Stanhope himself, as they trotted across the flat top of a dusty mesa. She held on to the back of his cartridge belt to keep her purchase. The man himself repulsed her, and she only clutched him around his waist when they broke into a lope or a gallop or headed up a steep hill, when she was in danger of being thrown.

She stared at the gun, then at her hands. She needed only to slide her right hand a few inches across the small of the rawhider's sweaty back to grab the revolver's wooden handle and draw it from where it rested in the holster lashed to his thigh.

Erin's heart quickened. It skipped a beat. She lifted her gaze to the man's upper back; his black-and-red calico shirt was stretched taut across his shoulders. He'd lashed his duster behind his saddle. She'd grab the gun, his own gun, and shoot him in the back with it. She wanted very much to watch him die slowly as payback for shooting her boy, Jim, as well as for the abuse he'd visited on her last night, her first night on the trail with the passel of snakes known as the Vultures.

But she'd settle for blowing out his heart through his back with his own sidearm.

She didn't care what happened to her after that. The rest of the gang riding to each side and behind her and Stanhope would doubtless shoot her. She'd kill him and then she'd kill herself to deny the other brutes in the wolf pack the satisfaction of abusing her further before they slit her throat.

Erin couldn't bear her racing heart any longer. She removed her right hand from Stanhope's cartridge belt. Quickly, she flicked it down around his side to where the handle jutted from his thigh, the butt quivering in its holster with each pitch of the trotting horse. She'd rather shoot him with the shotgun, the same gun he'd used to blow that terrible hole in Jim, but it was out of her reach in front of him. She closed her hands around the pistol's handle and, gritting her teeth harder, pulled.

It wouldn't budge.

Just as she remembered that it was probably held in place by a strip of leather across the hammer and fastened to the holster itself, Stanhope closed his gloved hand over hers. He held her hand there atop the butt of his gun, pressing down hard until she groaned from the pain shooting up into her wrist and arm.

"Whoa!" the leader of the Vultures yelled, drawing back on the grulla's reins.

He continued to press down harder on Erin's hand as he stopped the horse in the trail. The others in the gang checked their mounts down, as well, as the dust wafted around Erin and Stanhope, stinging her eyes.

"Let me go!" she cried.

The man looked over his shoulder at her. His lips were

pursed. His eyes were coldly smiling. He curled his lip slightly as he pressed down harder.

"No!" Erin said, using her other hand now to try to pry his big, powerful, merciless hand off of her right one.

Suddenly, he lifted his hand from hers. She had no time to register relief before his elbow came up and smacked her face so hard that it snapped her head back. She found herself flying off the side of the horse. The trail came up to smack her hard on her left shoulder and hip.

She groaned from the dull pain of the blow in her eye, cheek, and jaw, and from the sharper pain in her shoulder and hip and ribs from her violent meeting with the ground. She sort of lay on her side, her left leg bent up under her hip, that shoulder pressed against the ground. Her dress was in tatters, and her legs were bare. Stanhope had taken her underwear and her shoes last night, when he'd forced himself on her. He'd torn her dress down the front almost to her belly. The dirt of the wagon trail they were following burned her legs and her feet.

She sobbed from the pain and the burning and the utter fury and disappointment of not having been able to kill the man who'd killed her son so pointlessly. So offhandedly, as though he'd merely been swatting a pesky fly.

Stanhope gave a patient sigh as he swung down from the grulla's back. He glanced around at the others, his gaze holding on the only Mexican in his gang. "Santos, you keepin' careful watch on our back trail?"

"*Si, si, jefe.* No one back there. If I didn't know better, I'd say we had all of Wyoming to ourselves."

"No one's gonna come after us after what we done to that posse up in Willow City," said the black-clad Magpie Quint.

Doc Plowright nodded at Erin sobbing on the ground near a patch of Spanish bayonet. "What's that all about? You figurin' on turnin' her over to us finally, Boss? About time. She's a real lulu."

"Not yet. You fellas rest your horses in that shade over

yonder." Stanhope glanced toward a small copse of box elders and cottonwoods offering thin shade about seventy yards off the trail's south side. Then he turned toward a lone cottonwood another fifty yards to the north. "Me an' the mercantile lady are gonna go over to that cottonwood and have us another go round."

"No," Erin said, feeling a shudder wrack her. She looked up at Stanhope. "Please . . . no. Just kill me."

"Oh, I wouldn't kill a looker like you," Stanhope said. "Now, Miss Trixie Tate—I might kill her."

Erin followed the gang leader's hard, sneering gaze toward the blond whore riding behind Red Ryan. "She ain't as good-lookin' as you, and besides, when you've banged one whore you've banged 'em all."

Trixie Tate, who was sporting one black eye, shrank back a little behind the big redhead with the red beard and soiled tan sombrero.

Former deputy sheriff of Willow City, Mark Finn, spoke up. "No point in killin' Trixie, Clell. Hell, she takes the edge off all this hard ridin'." The big, fleshy-faced, potbellied man grinned at the woman, who looked away from him in disgust. "At least, she did for me last night."

"I don't think she likes you, Mark," Clell said. "And to tell you the truth, I don't, either."

Finn looked exasperated, hurt. "Huh? After how I helped you out in Willow Springs?"

"You're a turncoat, Mark." Clell raised the double-bore shotgun hanging from the lanyard around his neck. "I wouldn't trust you as far as I could throw you and your fat ass uphill in a steep wind."

"Oh, now, Clell," Finn said, raising his hands to his thick shoulders, palms out. "You can't do me like that! Why . . ."

The popper thundered. The ten-gauge buck blew Finn straight off his saddle, as though he'd been lassoed from behind. He hit the ground with a loud thud and a heavy groan, blood pumping from the pumpkin-sized hole in his chest and frayed shirt. His horse whinnied and pranced off the side of the trail.

Finn groaned again, tried to stand, and collapsed, dead.

The Vultures all stared down at him stonily. Trixie Tate stared at Stanhope's shotgun. Gray smoke curled from the left barrel.

Composing herself as well as she could in her tattered dress, she batted her lashes and manufactured an alluring expression. "Oh, you wouldn't want to kill me, Clell," she said, shuttling her gaze from the smoking cannon to Erin, sprawled in the dust and staring in awe at the dead deputy. "All she'll do is lay there. Me . . . now, I know how to please a man." She glanced around at the seven other sweaty, dusty, sunburned riders. "Just ask any of your partners here."

Clell's scrawny brother, Lester, who had a ferret face and a thin, patchy beard, grinned. "She ain't bad, Clell. Why don't you give her a try while I teach the mercantile lady a thing or two about pleasin' fellas like ourselves." He rose up in his saddle a little and cupped his crotch.

"Go ahead—shoot her," said Trixie Tate, staring around Red Ryan at Erin still half lying in the trail, now silent and staring somewhere off beyond Stanhope, resigning herself to the further abuse she knew she was about to endure. "That woman's trouble. She'll hold us up. Now, me—I'm *easy*! I'm *fun* to have around. Finn had that much right!"

As the words penetrated Erin's consciousness, she turned her bewildered gaze to the blonde. Trixie Tate looked away quickly, flushing a little, sheepish, then manufactured another of her desperate, truckling smiles at Stanhope.

"Git goin', fellas," Stanhope said. "I'll be the one teachin' the purty mercantiler her man-pleasin' lessons till further notice." Holding his horse's reins, he walked over and jerked Erin up by an arm. "Let's go, purty lady," he grumbled, grabbing her wrist and leading both her and the grulla off toward the cottonwood.

Stanhope walked too fast, faster than Erin could manage

in her beaten and battered condition, tripping over the torn hem of her dress. When she fell, Stanhope dragged her, and she fought desperately to regain her footing only to fall again and to have Stanhope drag her as he kept up his long, merciless stride.

When they got to the cottonwood, he dropped the grulla's reins, and threw Erin down in the shade. She tried desperately to get away from him, even managed to crawl several yards away on her hands and bare knees, but he dragged her back to the tree by her hair.

He held her down with one foot as he tossed away his gun belt and shotgun and dropped his trousers and underwear to his knees. He jerked her dress up around her waist, spread her knees wide with his hands, and took her savagely and brutally, grunting like a goat and staring with cold taunting into her eyes—just as he had the night before. Those mismatched eyes were demon's eyes riding above the black vultures tattooed on his cheeks.

Halfway through, she stopped fighting and just lay there, staring up through the fluttering leaves of the cottonwood at a lone, white cloud hovering low in the deep blue sky. When he finished grunting and stood and pulled his pants and balbriggans up, strapped his gun belt around his waist, and dropped the shotgun back down over his head, he said, "Try somethin' like that again—goin' fer a gun or tryin' to flee—I'll do this again before I throw you to the others. I'll make Lester go last. When he's done, he'll likely gut you and leave you to die screaming while the buzzards pick at your eyes."

Erin stared up at him. She felt as hollow and dried up as an old gourd. She wanted only to die, to be released of this physical torment from which there appeared no other escape, and to join Jim and his father in heaven. "You will anyway," she said, closing her knees.

"Maybe," Stanhope said, pulling her dress down and then jerking her to her feet once more. "Maybe not." He squeezed her chin and thrust his big, ugly face up close to hers, jutting his lower jaw. "You're too damn purty to kill before I've wrung you dry."

"I'll do it again," she said, staring back at him. "First chance I get."

"Fair enough."

Chuckling, Stanhope pushed her ahead of him and his horse, heading back toward where his gang milled around the blond whore, who was down on her knees amongst them.

ELEVEN

Stanhope threw Erin up onto the back of his horse as though she weighed little more than a sack of flour. When he'd climbed aboard the horse himself, he glanced over his shoulder at her, grinned, and slid his Colt from its holster. He held it up in front of her face, taunting her, then wedged it somewhere in front of him, likely behind his belt buckle.

Out of her reach.

She didn't care. She didn't have the energy to try to kill him again so soon after her first attempt had gone awry and he'd taught her another lesson. She was sore deep in her womb. Fatigue lay heavy in every fiber of her being.

Still, behind the pain and fatigue, rage smoldered like the ominous, unseen heat that remained in the wake of a deadly wildfire. Threatening a blowup and an even worse firestorm than that which had come before.

The gang rode out across the mesa and then down a switchback trail along its western side. Erin leaned forward against the broad, sweaty, smelly back of the man who'd

killed her son and raped her and beat her, and she fell not
so much asleep as into a semi-awake trance.

She was only vaguely aware of the rugged country sliding
around her. She was more aware of her half-waking dream
of somehow slitting Stanhope's throat from ear to ear with
a sharp knife as he stared up at her, screaming, pleading for
his life, and squealing his regret over taking that of her boy.

The waking dream caused her upper lip to curl slightly
as her head bounced against Stanhope's back. It was a very
faint hope buried deep in her soul, but a hope just the same—
similar to that heat festering beneath the forest-like duff of
her nearly unbearable torment, threatening a blowup.

The ride seemed everlasting.

The gang stopped a few times to rest their horses, but
mostly they continued heading straight west—walking, trotting, galloping. Walking, trotting, galloping. Stopping for
another short time, passing a bottle around, laughing and
cajoling each other, then climbing back into the leather and
walking, trotting, and galloping their horses by turns. Saving
them for the long pull they still had ahead of them.

Erin gritted her teeth and endured, her dream of Stanhope's death the only thing keeping her soul even halfway
intact.

The sun dropped. Cool darkness came, a relief from the
searing sun.

Erin lifted her head when she felt Stanhope's grulla slow-
ing. Lights lay ahead, sort of shifting back and forth along
the wagon trail they were on. Then she made out a log ranch
portal adorned with elk antlers and a board across the top
into which WAYLON HUMPHREYS BOX BAR B RANCH—COOL
SPRING CREEK had been burned.

Stanhope and Erin passed beneath the portal and rode
on into the ranch yard. The gang followed, hooves drum-
ming. There were a couple of barns and several corrals and
small log buildings whose windows were dark. The main

house sat on a small rise, lamplight glowing behind most of its sashed, first-floor windows.

It was a small ranch, Erin saw. The buildings, including what appeared to be the main house, were crude, mud-chinked log affairs. There was no bunkhouse. She could smell wood smoke and the smell of cattle and pine resin from the dark forest that pushed up all around the buildings. There was the faint murmur of a creek, though she couldn't see the stream for the darkness relieved by only the sparkling starlight.

Erin's heart squeezed, and she felt her lips pinch together as she looked around at the crude but homey place. It was the kind of place that she and Jim's father, Daniel, had once wanted for themselves. But then Dan's father had died and passed the mercantile on to them, and they'd had no choice but to stay in town and try to give the business a go.

But they'd still hoped of one day having their own little ranch—a shotgun ranch—somewhere out in the piney foothills of the Big Horns, where the creeks ran cool and clear, and the nights smelled like wine.

Stanhope reined the gulla in before the main house. There was no porch, just a Z-frame door banded with iron. A hide-bottom chair sat to the right of the door, between it and a wooden washstand on which a rusty tin basin sat. A hand brush and a small, cracked mirror hung from nails over the stand. A rain barrel stood left of the stand, half-covered with a wooden lid.

A shadow moved in one of the windows. The curtain over the window opened slightly and a face appeared. After a few seconds, the curtain slid back in place, and the door opened with a wooden scrape. A tall, slightly bent man in an underwear shirt and suspenders came out, stooping beneath the door's low frame. He held a shotgun in his right hand.

Erin saw the curtain in the window part again. Another,

narrower face appeared in it, silhouetted against the lamp-light in the room behind the person looking out.

"Help you fellas?" asked the man with the shotgun.

Neither Stanhope nor any of the gang said anything for a time. Erin could hear the revolting, liquid sound of Stanhope moving tobacco around in his mouth before he leaned out to his right and spat into the dirt. Wiping his lips with the back of his left hand, he drawled, "This your place?"

"That's right. Mine and my boy's."

"You be Humphreys?"

"That's right. Who're you?"

"The man that's gonna kill you and your boy and bed down in your place for the night."

Humphreys stared up at Stanhope. Erin could see the lamplight from the windows flanking him glittering in his eyes. He looked uncertain, beetling his heavy brows, not sure if the ugly stranger before him was funning with him or not.

As tired and hopeless as she felt, Erin's heart leapt in her chest. "Oh, god," she moaned. "No. *No!*"

She raised a fist and hammered it against Stanhope's back. Too late. She heard the blast of his shotgun, saw the flash reflect off the cabin and the wide-open eyes of the man standing before the grulla. Erin rammed her fist again between Stanhope's shoulder blades to little effect. The killer laughed and crouched and the shotgun thundered one more time, the grulla skitter-hopping beneath him. The echo of the shot off the cabin was like a punch to Erin's face.

"Oh, god!" Erin cried when she heard the thump of a heavy body hitting the ground.

Just then the grulla turned sharply. She wasn't holding on to Stanhope or his saddle. She was flung sideways off the horse's right hip. As she piled up in the dirt before the cabin, she heard a boy cry, *"Pa! Pa!"*

In the corner of her vision, she saw a figure run out of the cabin. Then Stanhope and several of the other gang members opened up with their pistols. The guns flashed like lightning, the booms echoing loudly around the ranch yard. Erin flung her face down in the dirt and buried her head in her arms, sobbing.

"No," she cried so softly that she could barely hear it herself. "No, no . . . no . . ."

She must have passed out for a time, hearing voices only distantly. She woke to someone prodding her belly with a boot toe.

Opening her eyes, she saw that the horses were gone. Shadows moved in the cabin windows. Men talked and laughed loudly, drunkenly. Erin could smell meat cooking and tobacco smoke wafting out the cabin's front door.

She looked up to see Lester Stanhope, Clell's brother, standing over her, smoking a cigarette. He blew smoke out his slender nostrils, then glanced behind him and said to someone in front of the cabin, "Get her cleaned up."

"Why should I do it?" It was the faintly defiant voice of the whore, Trixie Tate.

"'Cause Clell says so." Lester turned away, taking another drag from his cigarette. "She's gonna have a job of work to do tonight."

He drifted into the cabin, chuckling.

The next morning, as they rode along the shoulder of a formation known as Anvil Ridge, on their way to try to break the trail of the Vultures who'd likely angled through the mountains two days before slightly north of the lawmen's position, Dusty Mason cast another wary glance over his right shoulder. He peered up the sparsely forested, tan slope that rose in the north toward the rocky, anvil-shaped crest of the mountain.

"What is it?" Spurr said, riding to his left. "That's the third time in about fifteen minutes you looked back. You think the Vultures cut around behind us, or you got the jitters over some jealous husband?"

Mason was on edge, all right. But there was no jealous husband. He wasn't that kind of jake, and Spurr knew it. The old federal lawman just tried to get Mason's goat whenever he had the opportunity, which was pretty much always.

Ignoring the older man, as was Mason's habit, he continued looking up the long, gradual slope that was the light brown of a mule deer's coat and sparsely stippled with firs and cedars. He felt as though there were a pair of eyes up there somewhere, staring down at him.

Occasionally, in the periphery of his vision, he thought he spied movement, but when he turned to look, as he was doing now, there was nothing. Maybe a pinecone falling from a fir bough. Maybe a cedar branch bobbing lightly with a breeze. But in the corner of his eye, he'd thought he'd seen a rider—a dark figure on a dark horse—moving amongst the trees. Moving along with Mason and the other lawmen. But furtive. Very furtive.

Finally, Mason brought his gaze back down and over to Spurr riding on the opposite side of the slope from him. "You don't feel like we're bein' shadowed?"

Spurr cast a cautious glance up the slope, deep grooves cutting into the leathery skin around his blue eyes. "Now that you mention it . . ."

"You see somethin'?"

"No. I haven't seen nothin'. But I got a little cool feelin' right between my shoulders, in the middle of my back. I been thinkin' it's just the sweat on this old shirt, but now when I dwell on it, it feels like a coin laid against my skin. And that feelin' usually means somethin'."

"Maybe Stanhope sent someone to double back and set up an ambush." Mason heard the doubt in his own words. It was a reasonable concern, but he just didn't think that the shadow he kept glimpsing—or thought he was glimpsing—had anything to do with Stanhope's gang.

Damn annoying, though.

Spurr ordered the other lawmen riding along behind him and Mason to keep their eyes peeled for a possible ambush, and the party continued around the shoulder of the hill, until they dropped down into a narrow canyon on the northwestern edge of it. They reined their mounts down at the bottom of a sandy wash in which slightly charred stones encircled a low mound of gray ashes and a black chunk of half-burned cedar.

Spurr turned to Mason. "Climb down and see how long them ashes been there."

Mason gave the older man an indignant look. "You're the tracker."

Spurr sighed. "I outrank you, Sheriff. And I'm old. Each time I swing down from ole Cochise's back might be my last. Now, git down there and poke your finger in them ashes."

"Ah, Christ, I'll do it." Calico Strang swung down from his white-dappled chestnut, cursing under his breath.

He bit off his right glove and, holding his horse's reins in his other hand, squatted over the fire ring and poked two fingers into the ashes. "Shit!" He pulled both appendages out quickly, snarling and rubbing the tips of both fingers across his checked trousers.

The others laughed. Spurr scowled down at the young Pinkerton. "Now, that was the most cork-headed thing I seen you do yet."

Ed Gentry, sitting his horse beside that of his fellow territorial marshal, Bill Stockton, said, "I think we oughta start callin' him Jim Bowie."

"*Mister* Jim Bowie," added Stockton, shaking his head and laughing.

Strang poked both fingers in his mouth and snarled at the others.

"All right, all right—joke's over," Mason grouched, soberly looking around. "Judging by them apples over yonder, and them tracks around the fire ring, it wasn't no gang that stopped here last night. It was just one man. One man, one horse."

Spurr said, "You act like you might know who's makin' you spooky."

"Hell, I don't know. I just know we gained a shadow somewhere along the trail. I'm thinkin' it must be one of the Vultures."

"What would be the point?" asked the second Pinkerton, Web Mitchell. "I mean, if he ain't bushwhacked us yet, what's he waitin' for?"

"And why would ole Clell only send one man back?" added Stockton, lifting his head to look a little anxiously around at the surrounding forested ridges.

"Who knows?" Spurr, too, was looking around and working his lower lip between his teeth. "One reason I and no other lawdog been able to run that pack to ground is they always seem to do the unexpected. Clell don't always do what you think he's gonna do. In fact, he hardly ever does." He hacked a wad of phlegm from his throat and spat it toward the fire ring. "I'll be damn glad to either kill that son of a bitch once and for all, or see him in leg irons."

Gentry removed his hat from his head and ran a red bandanna around the inside of the sweatband. "You know, fellas, if there is indeed someone shadowin' us, it don't have to be one of the Vultures. Could just be a line rider from one of the big ranches in these parts keepin' an eye on us, makin' sure we ain't throwin' long loops over their beeves with the intention of sellin' 'em to a crooked Injun agent over Dakota way."

Stockton nodded. "I'm gonna throw in with Ed on that one. He can't play stud for shit, and the whores in Casper say he hasn't gotten his pecker up since the end of the Civil War, but he occasionally comes up with a good idea."

"Why, thank you, Bill."

Web Mitchell chuckled at the two old-timers.

Spurr looked at Mason. "That's likely the best explanation."

"Yeah, pro'bly." Mason wasn't convinced.

Spurr canted his head to one side, and narrowed a shrewd eye. "You're thinkin' it's the hombre who kept your oysters out of the fire back in Willow City, ain't ya?"

"I reckon I am."

"What's that?" asked Web.

"Nothin'," said Spurr.

"Let's go." Mason booted his horse on across the wash. Behind him, Spurr said, "Hold on."

Mason halted his grulla and gave the older lawman an impatient look.

Spurr canted his head up the wash, which carved a narrow gap through the northern mountains. "If memory serves, Sweetwater is on the backside of this range."

"So it is," said Mason.

"If the Vultures rode through where you think they rode through, they would have rode through Sweetwater."

Mason thought about it. Spurr was right. The sheriff felt a little annoyed that the older lawman knew more about Mason's own territory than Mason himself did.

"So?"

"If they rode through there," said Gentry, catching Spurr's drift, his eyes gaining a serious cast, "they might have wreaked holy havoc. They tend to do that to towns."

"Or, hell," said Web Mitchell, smoothing his ostentatious handlebar mustache with two black-gloved fingers. "Maybe they liked it so much they decided to stay."

Spurr turned to Mason. "Let's you and me head up the wash and check in on Sweetwater. If nothin' else, we'll pick up Stanhope's trail there."

Mason felt frustration tugging on him like two opposing ropes around his neck. He looked up the wash, then toward the forested ridge rising on the other side of the canyon.

A game trail angled up the ridge through the conifers and aspens, skirting a small talus slide and curving around a lightning-topped pine. It beckoned him onward, farther west toward Utah where the Vultures were likely headed. Sidetracking to Sweetwater held little appeal for him. The Vultures had probably ridden straight on through, which meant Mason would only be wasting time, letting the outlaws who'd made a fool out of him get farther and farther away.

Farther and farther out of his jurisdiction.

Spurr was right, though. Damn the old lawdog. But that's one reason why Mason had wanted him around. To talk sense the mossyhorned federal had acquired through long experience, to keep Mason from becoming his own worst enemy in his haste to run the Vultures to ground and assuage his badly battered pride.

He turned to the others. "You fellas keep riding west while Spurr and I head on up to Sweetwater. Stanhope just might hole up somewhere around here to rest his horses for a day or two, so you might run into him. If you do, don't engage him till Spurr and I get there."

Mason winced against his frustration and booted the grulla on up the wash.

Spurr glanced at the fire ring. "Keep an eye out for our friend there, boys." He looked at Strang. "How're your fingers, Calico? Maybe you oughta put some lard on 'em."

"Fuck you, old man!"

"You're purty, but you ain't that purty," said Spurr, booting Cochise after Mason.

The others chuckled as they started up the forested ridge.

TWELVE

Spurr felt a rock drop in his belly as, two hours later, he and Mason followed a winding trail northward out of the mountains and spied a black wagon driven by a black-clad gent in a high hat moving toward him from the settlement of Sweetwater.

Folks on foot appearing dressed in their Sunday best followed the wagon, singing. Spurr could hear the mournful notes on the hot, still air. While he couldn't make out the words from this distance of a quarter mile, he recognized the melody of the old funeral song—"The Old Rugged Cross."

"Ah, shit," Spurr said under his breath.

Mason said nothing as he ground spurs against his grulla's flanks and headed down a shallow slope toward the funeral procession. The cemetery was on a low, bald hill on the left side of the trail, and just as the two horses leading the hearse began turning onto the two-track trace leading up to it, Spurr and Morgan caught up to the hearse and checked their sweaty horses down.

The driver wore a black clawhammer coat, white shirt, and black cravat. His round, steel-framed glasses glinted dustily as he regarded Spurr and Mason from beneath his black bowler.

"Well, it's about damn time, Sheriff!"

"Who you buryin', Crawford?"

"The banker, Earl Thornberg!" said another well-dressed man walking up from the rear of the wagon. He was short and fat, and a short, fat woman with curly white hair was trailing up behind him, holding a parasol that matched her gaudy black-and-pink outfit. "Just one of the folks the Vultures killed as they stormed through our once-fine town, Sheriff Mason—looting, robbing, killing, and kidnapping our citizens!" The fat man glowered, red-jowled, up at Mason. "Didn't you get my telegram? I sent it day before yesterday though I never got a response!"

"That's because I've been on the trail of the Vultures since they rode through Willow City," Mason said. Spurr noted the faintly sheepish tone of his voice and almost felt sorry for the sheriff, whose jurisdiction Sweetwater was in. Mason had no reason to feel as guilty as he did. The law always had an uphill battle on the frontier, especially in a place as remote as Sweetwater.

Especially when one of your own men turns on you like Mark Finn had. Spurr knew that Mason had a bullet with Finn's name on it. He knew, because that's what he'd do . . .

Another man walked up from the group behind the wagon, his face pinched with anger. He removed his beaver hat and pointed it like a finger at Mason. "Those men wiped out my gunshop of nearly every box of ammo I had on hand! Not only that, they broke out all my windows! I incurred several hundred dollars worth of damage!"

The man who was obviously the undertaker glowered down at the gunshop owner from the leather seat of his hearse. "Good lord, Dave—so you incurred a little damage!

What about that poor Wilde boy? He was gunned down right in front of his poor mother's eyes!"

Mason turned to Crawford sharply. "Wilde? Erin Wilde's boy?"

"Sure enough. Shot the boy down on the mercantile's loading dock. After they finished ransacking that store as well as several others, and stole around five thousand dollars from the bank—after shooting poor Thornberg here!—Stanhope himself grabbed Erin and rode off with her kickin' and screamin' over his saddle horn!"

"Good *Christ*!" Mason said, pausing a moment to take it all in, his horse leaping around beneath him as though sensing the sheriff's exasperation.

"We're waitin' to bury the boy," the undertaker said, "hopin' his ma returns home first."

"Mercer go after 'em?"

"Hell, no," said yet another man from the funeral procession. "Mercer's back here!"

Spurr turned to follow the man's hooked thumb toward another wagon, this one a buckboard. It was driven by a grizzled oldster in a threadbare suit. Mason heeled his grulla on back to the buckboard, and Spurr followed him.

He and the sheriff looked down at the open coffin riding in the buckboard's box. The coffin was open, and a suited gent lay inside, holding a spray of wildflowers in his knobby, sun-browned hands against his chest. A silver watch and a bowie knife with a carved bone handle rested in the coffin beside him. His brown eyes were half open and staring straight up at the sky. His salt-and-pepper hair, shiny and fragrant with pomade, was parted in the middle. He had a puckered, dark blue hole the size of a silver cartwheel in his forehead.

Spurr vaguely noted that his blue-checked suitcoat didn't match his brown broadcloth trousers that bore one patched knee. A middle-aged woman stood in the trail behind the wagon. She was dark, appearing to have some Mexican blood, and dressed all in black, with a black mantilla. She was leaning forward against the tailgate, both hands hooked over the top of the tailgate, sobbing as she stared at the man in the coffin. In one of her hands was a worn, leather-covered Bible. In the other she clutched a crucifix.

Mason opened his mouth to speak to the woman. Apparently seeing that there were no words that could comfort a woman so obviously bereaved, he turned to the townsfolk who'd formed a ragged semicircle around him and Spurr, regarding both lawmen expectantly, a little angrily.

Mason stared at the crowd, not saying anything. He looked chagrined; he didn't seem to know what to say. Spurr felt the burn of anger and stepped Cochise forward and a little in front of the sheriff.

The old lawman raised his voice as he said, "Did anyone back this man?" He canted his head to indicate the dead town marshal of Sweetwater.

The men and the women just scowled at him, their expressions growing faintly skeptical, as though they weren't quite sure what he'd said.

"I take it that's a 'no,' " Spurr said. "*Anyone* go after this group *at all*?"

A light hum rose from the crowd. Finally, a man several yards away raised his voice to yell, "Hell, no! Them's the Vultures, fer chrissakes! They shot ole Mercer down like he was a duck on a millpond! Besides, we ain't gettin' paid to go after 'em!"

"It's *you's* gettin' paid to risk your necks!" shouted another man from somewhere off Spurr's right shoulder. "If you was doin' your jobs, they wouldn't be runnin' around like a pack of wild wolves, anyhow!"

Spurr sighed.

Mason said, "Let it go, Spurr. Let's ride." He started walking his grulla forward.

Spurr ignored him as he hardened his jaws and cast his

angry gaze at the well-dressed crowd milling around him. The Mexican woman sobbed uncontrollably against the tail-gate of the wagon hauling her dead husband.

"That gang rode through here and killed a boy," Spurr said, feeling his old ticker skipping beats. "They kidnapped a woman whom they likely promptly raped and are still rapin' every chance they get . . ."

Several women in the crowd gasped.

One of the men said with an air of self-righteous indignation, "Now, look here, sir!"

"You look here, you little pipsqueak!"

The pipsqueak stepped back. His wife closed her hands over the ears of her pigtailed daughter.

Spurr pointed a gloved finger at the pipsqueak. "You and every man in this town who didn't do nothin' to back the play of your lawman is a yellow-livered coward. The law is only as strong as the citizens who stand behind it—especially when you got only one man wearin' a badge. The wolves outnumber us one hundred to one, and the only way we can keep a foot forward is if everyone does their part, and if that means risking your lives by formin' a posse, so be it!"

"We heard what happened to that posse over in Willow City!" the pipsqueak shouted. "Word spread like wildfire!"

Spurr looked at Mason, who had ridden slowly through the crowd and curveted his horse at the far edge of it, scowling impatiently over the hatted, bonneted heads toward Spurr.

"That's right," Spurr told the pipsqueak. "They paid the price for attempting to keep their loved ones safe, for standin' up against evil and maintainin' a foothold on their freedom. What you boys done—lettin' the Vultures run off with an innocent woman and not even makin' a decent *effort* to *track* 'em at the risk of your own sorry hides . . . hell, you all *deserve* what happened to the posse over to Willow City. Cowards, every damn one of you!"

He snapped the words like a whip, causing the men and even the women to collectively wince. The old lawman cursed and ground his moccasined heels against Cochise's ribs. The crowd parted in a sudden panic, making way for the enraged lawman, and Spurr trotted on up the trail and past Mason staring at him skeptically.

"Come on, Sheriff!" Spurr snarled. "What the hell we wastin' our time on these hoopleheads for?"

Mason decided to wait until they were on the other side of town and had picked up the two-day-old trail of nearly a dozen galloping shod horses before, riding abreast of the older lawman, he said, "You gotta remember you're from another time, Spurr."

"I been reminded of that every goddamn day of my life, Sheriff!"

The sun was almost down later that same day when, having ridden a good thirty miles west of Sweetwater, Spurr and Mason both reined their horses down sharply.

"What in hell was that?" Mason said.

As if in reply, the sound came again—a man's agonized scream. Spurr thought the scream was enough answer of its own, so he merely booted Cochise on down the grade they'd been descending between ever-darkening walls of evergreen forest. He couldn't run the horse too fast, because while the grade wasn't particularly steep, it was rocky, with here and there a blowdown they had to skirt and plenty of fallen branches.

The scream sounded once more, much nearer now. It was followed by several voices, and Spurr looked to his left where a stream threaded through the forest and crossed the trail he was on by way of a crude wooden bridge. Four horses stood along the edge of the stream, idly cropping grass, while four men were milling nearby. They appeared to have one man down and were working him over pretty good.

A bushwhack and robbery, Spurr thought.

He'd just reached for the butt of his Winchester when one of the men with a shelflike chin turned toward him, and he saw the round, brown-eyed face of Bill Stockton. Then he saw Ed Gentry standing over the man on the ground, tugging on one of the downed man's arms while Gentry braced himself with a boot on the man's chest.

The down man was one of the two Pinkertons—the older one, Web Mitchell. The younger detective, Calico Strang, stood a ways back from his partner and Gentry who, Spurr realized now, was trying to pop Mitchell's arm back in place. Judging by the shrill scream that loosed itself from Mitchell's wide-open mouth, and the faint wooden pop that accompanied it, Gentry finally got the shoulder bone yanked back in its socket.

"What happened?" Spurr asked as he swung down from his saddle with a grunt.

Bill Stockton was smoking a cigar butt, the aromatic blue smoke wafting around his gray head. His silver-streaked, dark brown hair hung to his shoulders. "The Pinkerton was attacked by a serpent. Downright biblical."

Gentry was breathing hard as he glanced at Spurr and Mason approaching the group. "Struck at him from atop a flat rock, and his horse spooked—threw him clear to last Sunday. That shoulder was damn near hangin' down the middle of his back."

"Woulda had an easier time wipin' your ass that way, eh, Mitchell?" Stockton said through a cloud of cigar smoke, prodding the white-faced Pinkerton's hip with his boot and laughing.

"He'll be fine now," Gentry said as he walked over to his horse and fished around in one of his saddlebag pouches.

He popped the cork, took a pull, then carried the bottle over to Mitchell. "Here ya go, Detective. Take you a swig of that. You'll be feelin' like you're shittin' in high cotton again in no time."

"Forget about shittin'," Spurr said as the detective took a hard pull off the bourbon bottle. "Can he ride?"

"We'd probably best camp here," said Gentry. "Give him a few hours to mend, then send him back to his home office."

The Pinkerton lowered the whiskey bottle and glared at the older men around him. His thick dark hair was mussed, a wing of it hanging over one gray-blue eye. "I'm just busted up a little, not dead," he said, taking another sip of the healing elixir. "And I'm not going back. The Pinkertons have a sizeable stake in running the Vultures to ground. I'll make a sling for this arm and be good as new."

"Might be better if you could ride another couple miles tonight," Spurr said.

Mason glanced at him. "You thinkin' about Waylon Humpreys's place on Cool Spring Creek?"

"Mitchell would be a whole lot more comfortable there than on the ground." The federal lawman turned to Mitchell. "And I know good ole Waylon'll pad out your belly right nicely for you. He got to be a good cook after that harpy of a woman left him and his boy."

"Maybe for all of us, huh, Spurr?" This from the ever-sneering Calico Strang.

"Yeah, for all of us," Spurr said, sneering back at the uppity young Pinkerton.

Mitchell extended his good arm to Gentry, who helped him to his feet. "I'll make it. I'm so tired of you fellas' cooking, I'd have to be a whole lot more beaten up than this *not* to make it."

While the others stood back to let Mitchell test out his land legs while holding his arm taut against his side and bent just a little, Spurr noticed Mason staring out toward the trail they'd ridden in on. Mason had a worried look.

Spurr said, "What is it?"

"This trail heads over into that canyon the Box Bar B's in, don't it? I mean, if you stay on this trail, it'll take you right to Waylon's front door, wouldn't it?"

Mason turned to Spurr. The sheriff's look was like a sucker punch. Spurr thought of Waylon Humphreys and his boy, Paul, as he ran his hand along his jaw and over his mouth, his old ticker hiccupping tightly.

Humphreys and his boy were likely alone at their place. Waylon usually only hired hands for the fall and spring roundups.

"That it does . . . that it does . . ."

He and Mason whipped around and hurried to their horses, Spurr yelling, "Come on, boys. Let's shake a leg, damnit!"

THIRTEEN

Spurr's group rode up and over a low pass and down into another, broader canyon sheathed in high, clay-colored ridges whose lower slopes were carpeted in firs and aspens. When they rode out of a pine forest, the old lawman and Mason reined up.

Stockton and Gentry rode out to either side of them, staring ahead across a broad mountain park that was a murky pool of dusk under a dark green sky. Beyond, the sun was drifting down through a narrow gap between indigo peaks and casting long crimson bayonets across the canyon behind it.

The only movement was a small herd of cattle, cow-calf pairs, grazing around Cool Spring Creek that ran along the base of the ridge to the right.

The only sound was the call of a mourning dove.

Spurr stared out from beneath his hat brim, dread tickling his belly. A hundred yards away lay the portal of Waylon Humphreys's Box Bar B Ranch headquarters. Beyond the portal, the buildings were brown smudges against the spruce-green forest. Spurr could make out the cabin. No lights shone in the windows.

Bill Stockton must have been reading his mind. "Getting late enough for a lamp or two."

A sound reached across the canyon from the direction of the cabin. Spurr pricked his ears, felt his blood warm. The sound came again—a loud grunt followed by a thud. At least, that's how it seemed. His old ears could just barely pick it up beneath the mournful cry of the lone dove and the steady whisper of the creek yonder.

It came again—a woman's agonized grunting groan along with a dull thud. The lawmen looked around at each other skeptically. Finally, Spurr slid his Winchester out of its scabbard, cocked it one-handed, off cocked the hammer, and swung down from his saddle.

"Mitchell, since you got an injured wing, you stay here with the horses while we walk in and check it out. Could be nothin'. Could be that the Vultures decided to hole up there in Waylon's cabin for a time. Maybe they like his cookin'."

"Doubt it," said Mason. "They're from this country. They know the Elkhorn Creek Cavalry Outpost is just south of here and that I likely would have wired ahead to have soldiers on the scout. They were in too big a killing frenzy to cut my telegraph wires."

"Yeah, shit," said Gentry, swinging down from his own saddle with a grunt, holding his carbine in one gloved hand and sliding a wad of chaw from one side of his mouth to the other. "They're likely headed off to their lair. I for one would sure like to know where that is."

Spurr kept his voice low. "Nevertheless, pards, let's step easy. Maybe Waylon and his boy are off herdin' cattle, but I don't like it that there's no light on in that cabin."

He and the others gave their reins to Mitchell, who had fashioned a sling with his belt buckle and tucked his right arm through it. He held the reins of the group's horses in his other hand and stood to one side of the trail, looking gaunt and pale as he frowned toward the ranch headquarters.

As the men started walking abreast across the trail toward the portal, the sound came again—a puzzling grunting sound and a dull thud. To Spurr it almost sounded like someone splitting wood and giving a grunt with every swing of the mallet, like maybe they were angry or maybe the implement was too heavy for them.

Spurr and Mason walked under the portal and into the ranch yard while Stockton, Gentry, and Calico Strang ducked through the fence on either side, old Gentry's bones audibly cracking when he straightened. He gave a curse under his breath, sighed, shook his head, and continued walking forward, the young Strang snickering.

"You'll be old one day," Stockton muttered at the young Pinkerton.

"Maybe, maybe not," muttered Gentry, his gravelly voice low-pitched with menace.

That the person grunting inside the cabin was female became obvious after Spurr and the others had moved to within fifty yards of the place. It was also obvious that she was in trouble. Vaguely, Spurr wondered if maybe she was in labor. Damn puzzling. Humphreys's wife had left him and the boy to head back East several years ago, having tired of the crude, lonely life out here—a common enough occurrence on the frontier—and Spurr hadn't heard of the rancher getting hitched again. Could he have found another one much younger than himself and slipped a bun into the oven?

Spurr stopped in the middle of the yard, staring at the windows that glinted dully in the last light, and waved to the others to hold their positions. He looked at Mason, who was standing about twelve feet to his right.

"Let's you an' me check it out," he said on the heels of another agonized grunt. They came in about ten- or fifteen-second intervals, not at all unlike the screams a woman gives when she's in the throes of delivery.

When the three others had taken cover behind a corral or off the corner of the main barn or behind a stock trough, Spurr and Mason moved quickly to the cabin. Spurr limped on his bowed legs; this was as far as he'd walked since he and Kenny Potter had taken down Philpot's Dogs in New Mexico three weeks ago, and the ground hadn't been kind to his feet in twenty years. He and Mason took up positions on either side of the half-open door.

The woman's screams—that's what they sounded like now, screams more than grunts—sounded again. She seemed to be kicking something with each agonized cry. Spurr glanced at Morgan, who stood with a shoulder pressed to the log cabin's front wall on the other side of the door.

And then Spurr, squeezing his rifle in his hands, yelled, "Law out here! Whoever's in there, you're gonna need to show yourselves pronto!"

He and Mason waited, staring at each other across the half-open door. The woman's screams died. Only silence issued from the bowels of the dark cabin.

"She must be alone," Mason said.

"Hold on!"

Spurr hadn't quite gotten that last out before Mason swung through the door and stepped to one side, crouching and loudly racking a shell into his Winchester's breech. Spurr cursed and turned into the cabin himself, stepping to the left so he wouldn't be outlined against the door. He thumbed his rifle's hammer back and stood staring into the dusky shadows.

Humphreys's wife, as discontented as she may have been, had fixed the place up homily before she'd finally pulled out a coulple of years ago, and Humphreys and the boy had kept it that way. At least, it had appeared a nice, tidy little hovel whenever Spurr had stopped through here over the past couple of years.

Now it appeared a twister had ripped through it. The kitchen was on the left, the living area on the right, but it was hard now to distinguish one section from another. The eating table was overturned, as were all the hide-bottom chairs and standing cabinets. Pots, pans, and skillets lay everywhere. Flour and sugar and other dry goods had been dumped out on the floor, their tin canisters tossed aside like trash. Several empty whisky bottles lay amidst the mess, as well.

The place smelled of tobacco smoke, whiskey, grease, and sweat. It smelled like a saloon.

The only thing that hadn't been turned asunder was the long, leather sofa in the living area, but someone had taken a knife to it, slicing the leather and pulling out the straw stuffing and tossing it every which way. The bull-horn rocker and two other armchairs and a grandfather clock lay in broken pieces upon the braided rope rug fronting the hearth at the back of the room.

When it was obvious that no one was in this main part of the cabin, Mason ran toward a half-open door in the far wall to his and Spurr's right. Spurr watched as Mason leapt the grandfather clock and crunched several of its broken boards before using his rifle butt to nudge open the door before him.

The hinges squawked with menace.

Then the sheriff froze. He just stood there in the doorway, his head turned slightly to his left. His rifle sagged, and his shoulders slumped.

"What is it?"

Spurr walked through the rubble of the living area. He stepped over the broken clock and several broken bird carvings that he knew Humphreys himself had whittled over the long mountain winters. Pitching his voice with annoyance, he shoved Mason aside as he stepped in around him. "I said, what the hell . . . ?"

He let his voice trail off when he saw the bed.

Rather, the figure on the bed. A woman. Nude.

She lay spread-eagle, her long hair a mess about her head.

She was naked and spread wide, like a gutted deer, her wrists tied to the two brass posts at the head of the bed. Her ankles were tied to the two brass posts at its foot.

She was a mess. They'd worked her over good. Her head was turned aside, facing away from Spurr and Mason. In the wan last rays of the sun pushing through the window on the far side of the room from the door, Spurr could see that her eyes were closed. Squeezed closed. Her naked belly rose and fell sharply as she breathed.

At first, he'd thought she was dead. But she was alive.

She was the first to speak. Her low-pitched, eerily calm voice almost made Spurr leap out of his boots.

"Please free me."

Her belly rose and fell.

"Please free me!" she screamed, keeping her head turned toward the window.

Mason just stood there. "Mrs. . . . Wilde . . . ?"

"Please free me!" she cried again.

Spurr set his rifle down against the wall, then pulled his bowie knife from the sheath in his right moccasin. Quickly, he cut the strips of white sheet binding her left ankle to the bottom bedpost. Then he hurried over and cut her other ankle free before moving up to the head of the bed, on the window side, and trying not to look down at her beaten and battered body, cut her right wrist free of its corresponding post. His heart fluttered and hammered against his ribs as he reached across her bare breasts to cut loose her other wrist.

The pent-up air in the room was sour with the reek of what the Vultures had done to her.

"How can I help you?" he asked her.

She rolled away from him, raising her knees to her belly, crossing her arms on her chest, and lowering her head.

"Please leave me," she whispered.

"Ma'am, if you're hurt bad . . ."

"Leave me," she said, stronger this time.

Spurr looked at Mason, who stared down dumbly, help-lessly at the woman. Spurr moved to the sheriff, canted his head toward the door, then followed Mason out of the room and closed the door behind him.

Both men stood in shock as they looked around the fast-darkening, ruined room. Spurr knew that Mason was as haunted as he himself was by the hollow look of agony in the woman's pale face

"Spurr, Mason!" Calico Strang called from the rear of the cabin.

There was a rear door to the left of the fireplace. Spurr and Mason made their way through the cluttered mess, threw the door open, and walked outside to where Gentry, Stockton, and Strang stood at the back of the yard, looking up at a cottonwood tree near the creek running along the base of the northern ridge. A privy and a woodpile stood left of the tree.

Two bodies hung from ropes from the same low branch.

The bodies of Waylon Humphreys and his son, Paul. Both bodies were bloody from bullet wounds to their chests and heads. Their faces were slack-jawed, blank, lids drooping lightly down over their eyes. They turned slowly in the same direction at the ends of their ropes—father and son perform-ing a bizarre death dance in the freshening evening breeze.

Strang turned to Spurr. His usual mocking expression was gone. "Cut 'em down?"

"They're not goin' anywhere," Spurr said. "They can wait. You fellas bring in wood and start a fire in the range, and fetch water—lots of it—from the creek. And we're gonna need to do a little house-cleanin'."

"What for?" asked Strang.

"Don't ask me what for," Spurr said, turning back into the cabin. "Just do as you're told, boy!"

FOURTEEN

Captain Davis Norbert twisted the quirley closed between his dirt-grimed thumbs and forefingers, then reached into a pocket of his dark blue cavalry tunic for a sulfur-tipped match and scratched the lucifer to life on his cartridge belt.

He touched the match to the cigarette. Puffing smoke and dropping the match into the finely churned dust at his feet, he glanced around the dilapidated cavalry outpost on the banks of Elkhorn Creek, in a snake-belly bowl surrounded by several Wyoming mountain ranges.

The sun was almost down, and the seven brush-roofed, adobe-brick buildings, including a bunkhouse for the enlisted men, an officer's quarters no larger than a chicken coop, and a barn and stable, were painted pink and saffron by the fading light. The forlorn little outpost, all but abandoned by the U.S. Army in favor of heavier patrols along the Bozeman Trail, hunkered beneath a broad arch of sky that had been turning all colors of the rainbow for the past hour but was now a sort of purple-green.

All but abandoned except when renegade Indians were

rawhiding off their reserves. Or when a contingent from
Fort Stambaugh was needed to quell a land or mining war,
or, in this case, to help lasso desperadoes cutting a wide
swath through this neck of still-wild Wyoming Territory.
Norbert and his twelve men—ten privates, a corporal, and
a seasoned career sergeant, Jake Pennyman—had arrived
here at the Elkhorn Creek outpost in the midafternoon. On
their way up from Fort Stambaugh, they'd scouted for sign
of the notorious and slippery outlaw gang who called themselves the Vultures, apparently on the run from nefarious
doings to the east.

Having had no luck in that regard, and according to
orders, Norbert and his men were now awaiting the arrival
of Sheriff Dusty Mason from Willow City whom they were
to assist by any means possible in running the killers to
ground. When Mason would arrive was anyone's guess. The
Vultures, if headed this way through a long corridor between
mountain ranges, might very well arrive here first. Most of
the gang had originated in Wyoming, so they likely knew
of the cavalry outpost, which, since its unofficial abandon-
ment four years ago, was used as shelter by cowpunchers
and scores of other passing pilgrims.

Scores of rats, as well, Norbert thought. Drawing deeply
on the quirley, he looked toward the long, low bunkhouse
in which most of the men not on guard duty or tending the
horses in the stable were now eating beans and hardtack or
playing poker and shooting occasionally at the vermin who
considered the bunkhouse home. Shots rang out occasionally, followed by a raucous stretch of cursing by none other
than Sergeant Pennyman himself.

Such an incident had just happened a few minutes ago,
and Norbert smiled at the memory. For all his earthy Scottish swagger, Pennyman was a cultured, somewhat pam-
pered city boy at heart and did not cotton to rough conditions.
Norbert, who had led the Forward Scouts of the Ninth

Missouri Rifles in the War Between the States, harbored no such prejudices. The outpost didn't bother him, despite he and his men having had to root a family of skunks out of the stable before putting their horses up for the night. He was just glad to have made it out of a certain Georgia prison alive . . . a prison in which he'd fought the rats for muddy drinking water so badly tainted that it had killed nine out of ten men who drank it.

No, a rat or two, or skunks in his stable, would never bother him again as long as he had food, fresh water, and freedom. He would leave his own musty quarters to the heat and the rats, and sleep out here on the ground. Norbert found fresh air and starlight soothing.

"Riders, Captain!"

An adobe-brick wall partly surrounded the place, on the side facing Elkhorn Creek, from where trouble in the form of Indians had been most likely to come. Originally, the wall had been meant to surround the outpost, but the post had been abandoned before the wall had been finished.

The stockade was only about six feet high, but it offered a modicum of cover for soldiers shooting from behind it. There was a fifteen-foot-high guard tower on each end of the fort, and on the end near where the stockade's wooden doors used to be, before someone had used them for firewood, stood one of the towers.

Private Homer Early was manning the tower while another guard patrolled the creek on foot and another held the scout on the fort's northern end, which faced flat, open country rolling up toward the far eastern foothills of the Wind River mountains. Early was pointing beyond the creek now, his head turned toward Norbert, his slender body silhouetted against the sky, which had now turned purple and lime.

"How many?" Norbert called.

"Can't tell fer sure. Looks like three horses. Comin' at a trot."

"Call Scarborough in," Norbert ordered. Turning toward the bunkhouse, he yelled, "Pennyman!"

When the sergeant's bulky body appeared in silhouette against the open doorway lit by yellow lamplight, Norbert said, "Riders headed this way. Just three, but bring your men."

Pennyman saluted with the same hand in which he held a smoldering, half-smoked cigar. Norbert walked into his quarters that stood a ways off from the bunkhouse and barn with its connecting corral, near a springhouse. He stopped just inside the doorway and heard a sharp breath leap out of his throat.

He'd dropped his hand to the Colt .44 holstered on his right hip, but stayed his hand when he saw the yellow eyes of the coyote standing atop his small, square eating table staring back at him. The coyote's back legs were on Norbert's chair, its front legs on the table, on either side of the plate on which the captain had left a few scraps of food before he'd wandered out to the parade ground for air.

The coyote gave a low, guttural mewl, then leapt up onto the table and then out the open window on the table's far side. Its fur glowed tawny gold in a vagrant ray of light before it dropped down beneath the window. It hit the ground outside with a soft grunt and ran toward a clump of brush. It stopped suddenly. Norbert watched it, frowning. The beast growled and sort of mewled, hackles raised, as it stared into the brush. Suddenly, it switched course and ran off around the stables, as though it had been afraid of something in the shrubs.

Norbert blew a relieved breath, chuckling to himself sheepishly at the start the beast had given him. He'd fought so many Indians in the past out here that he supposed he was still looking for a wild-assed Sioux or Arapaho behind every rock and sage shrub.

He grabbed his tan kepi off the table and his Sharps carbine from where he'd leaned it against the wall near his cot and the tack he'd piled on the earthen floor. He opened the

Sharps's breech, making sure it showed brass, then quickly adjusted his kepi on his head and headed outside to see what the fuss was about.

Probably just drifting punchers, but in this country, you never knew . . .

FIFTEEN

As Norbert strode toward the stockade wall, Pennyman and six or seven enlisted men were streaming out of the bunkhouse, some tucking their shirts into their trousers, others making sure their carbines were loaded.

They were a good-looking lot as far as today's frontier cavalry went—no cottontails amongst them. Norbert had handpicked the contingent himself. Most soldiers posted as remotely as Fort Stambaugh would desert first chance they got, but this crew took their jobs relatively seriously—mostly, Norbert guessed, because they'd been on the dodge from one thing or another in their civilian lives and had enlisted into the cavalry because they'd heard it was a good place to hide.

"You men stay inside the wall," the captain told the soldiers, then turned to Pennyman, whom he was on a first-name basis with, often carousing with the sergeant during furloughs in Laramie or Rawlins.

"Jake, join me outside the wall," Norbert said, smoothing down his salt-and-pepper, dragoon-style mustache with his fingers. "Probably no one of any significance out there, but since the Vultures are supposed to be on the prod in these parts, no point in getting caught with our pants down."

"Like to have me a shot at one o' them," said Pennyman, smoothing down his long, thick tangle of hair and then setting his leather-billed forage hat on his big-eared, rocklike skull.

The two men walked toward the opening in the wall.

"Just approaching the creek now, Cap," said the private standing atop the guard tower, holding his Sharps carbine up high across his chest, ready.

"Thank you, Private," said Norbert as he and Pennyman walked out through the gap in the wall.

Private Scarborough, short and squat but good with horses and not one to scare in a Sioux attack, stood just ahead, at the lip of the creek that was mostly brush-lined sandbars this late in the year. Norbert heard the thuds of the oncoming riders before he picked them out of the dark stretch of sage-stippled desert beyond the creek.

Two men leading a riderless horse. One of the men held what to be appeared a straw-haired woman in front of him, the woman's head flopping against his chest. Norbert squinted, vaguely incredulous. The woman's body was a pale smudge in the growing darkness.

Could she be nude?

As the three riders approached the creek, Norbert raised his pistol and triggered a round into the air, the maw sparking in the purple shadows.

"Hold on, there!" he shouted, making his presence known. "I'm Captain Davis Norbert. Who goes there?"

The riders reined their horses to skidding halts atop the shallow creek's opposite bank. "Holy shit—you spooked the devil's own hell out of us!" The voice of the rider riding single was loud in the dusky silence.

"You occupyin' the outpost, Captain?" asked the rider who was carrying what did indeed appear to be a naked woman.

"What's it look like? You didn't answer my question."

"I'm Lawton. This is Burns. Line riders for the Tilted W. We got an injured girl here. Found her along the trail a ways back. She's messed up good. You got a medico with you, Captain?"

"Of sorts," Norbert said, nodding, his blood quickening when he saw the girl's obvious dire condition. "Bring her on over!"

Norbert holstered his Colt as the rider with the woman booted his buckskin down the draw's opposite bank. He galloped across, then up the side near Norbert, Sergeant Pennyman, and Private Scarborough. The second rider followed, both horses blowing and kicking up dirt and gravel.

The lone rider was tall and thin but vaguely Comanche-featured and not an attractive hombre by anyone's standards. He was dressed nearly entirely in black but with a red vest under his black wool coat. But there were few good-looking men this far out on the devil's backside, and you didn't need to be a dude to be good at punching cows. The man holding the girl was sandy-whiskered and built like a bull, with close-set eyes and no neck to speak of and a broad-brimmed tan hat with a torn brim.

He looked down at Norbert and Pennyman moving up to him, and his eyes flashed anxiously beneath his hat brim. "Found her out yonder near her torn dress and this hoss standing over her."

"Jayzus H.," muttered Pennyman in his faint Scottish brogue. "Looks like she's been shot."

Norbert's eyes had taken their natural man's look at the blonde's voluptuous body before straying to the bloody hole in her right side. The blood flashed wetly in the fading light. It trickled down her side, across her hip, and down her naked right thigh. She lay back against the bull's broad chest, eyes squeezed shut, groaning and sort of whimpering as she shook her head from side to side. Her heavy, sloping breasts rose and fell sharply as she breathed. Her eyes opened slightly, and she pinned Norbert with a look of fierce agony and—something else—fear? Vaguely, the captain thought the look was almost like one of warning, but then the girl squeezed her eyes closed once more as pain visibly rippled through her, and the captain let the thought go.

Norbert looked at the bull, Lawton. "You don't know her?"

"Not from Adam's off ox. Just know she's gonna die we keep jabberin'."

Norbert turned toward the opening in the stockade wall in which a half-dozen soldiers stood, all holding rifles and staring toward the captain and the naked blonde. "Donner over there?"

"Here, Captain," said the medico, Donner, as the string-bean corporal stepped out away from the group, handing his rifle to one of the others.

Donner walked over to Lawton's horse. He paused a moment, flushing a little behind his round-rimmed spectacles, as he looked at the girl's lush body.

"Go ahead, Donner—take a look at her," Norbert said. "You think there's somethin' you can do?"

"We'll need to get her into the bunkhouse so's I can examine her," said Donner, his voice quaking nervously.

He wasn't really a medico, just a farm kid who'd helped out his hometown doctor a few times and was fairly adept at setting broken bones and tending the usual bruises, lice-infestations, snakebites, heat stroke, and minor wounds that were part and parcel to military life on the frontier. His skills were mostly only used on details like this, away from the main pill roller at Fort Stambaugh.

Norbert looked up at Lawton. "Ride her on up to the bunkhouse. Make way, men!"

"Yes, sir," said the bull-like man, whipping his rein ends across the flanks of his mount.

He and the other rider lunged through the gate as the small cavvy of soldiers made way for them, staring in awe at the naked woman in Lawton's arms. As though they'd never seen a nude girl before. Maybe some of them hadn't, silently mused the captain as he and Pennyman jogged after the horses. Donner overtook them both, nudging his glasses up his nose as he ran like a kid late for school, pumping his arms and legs, eager to recuse the naked damsel in dire distress.

When the riders hauled up in front of the bunkhouse, whose open windows were lit from within, Donner was hot on their horses' heels. Breathless, he reached up to take the blonde out of Lawton's hands. Then the kid carried her through the low door and into the bunkhouse, both Lawton and Burns dropping their reins and anxiously following.

Norbert and Pennyman, both breathless, walked in behind them. Norbert removed his hat out of habit in the presence of ladies—even unconscious ones—and watched as Pennyman hurried over to help the other two men clear the long eating table of tin plates and forks and other paraphernalia left from the men's supper, swiping it all onto the floor with a raucous clatter.

Then Burns helped the young medico lay the girl onto the table, where Donner nudged his glasses up his nose once more, then nervously wiped his hands on his pale blue trousers before crouching over the wound in the moaning girl's side.

Once again, Norbert, standing back by the door, his hat in his hands, noted how comely she was. Big-breasted, with rounded hips and a waist not overly thin nor round. A nice, soft belly—one man, especially a lonely soldier, could really bury his face in while he kneaded her big . . .

The captain shook his head with chagrin as he realized the direction his thoughts had taken. Christ, what was wrong with him? Too long this far out in Wyoming, he reckoned. Few whores in Laramie or Rawlins looked anything like the golden-haired, round-faced young creature moaning and groaning on the table before him.

Who in hell was she, anyway? Norbert had never seen her before though he figured he'd seen most everyone who lived in these parts—and that wasn't very many folks at all. There were way more cattle than people. Maybe she was some rancher's daughter run down by brigands, roughed up and shot and left to die so she couldn't identify her abusers.

Donner lifted his head from the girl's bloody side. The young man's eyes were dark behind his spectacle lenses winking in the dull light from the three flickering lanterns. "Doesn't look good, Cap. Appears she was shot at close range. I think the ball went all the way through, but she's most likely scrambled up pretty ba . . ."

The medico let his voice trail off. His eyes went to the door flanking Norbert. Norbert turned to see all the rest of the soldiers crowding close to the open doorway, nudging against each other like penned cattle, trying their best to see over and around each other at the naked girl on the table.

Norbert raised his hands to shoo the men away, but his eyes caught on something behind them.

Not something.

Some*one*.

Men moving around, their shadows long and thick in the twilight as they walked spread out in a line from the direction of the barn and corral. By ones and twos, the young soldiers turned around to follow the captain's puzzled gaze with their own, until they saw the men walking toward them.

"What is it, Cap?" Pennyman said behind Norbert.

The captain felt a thousand reptiles of dread crawling up his legs and back. He glanced at the sergeant beside him and saw Lawton and Burns standing around Donner and the naked girl on the table. They were looking at Norbert.

They were both smiling greasily.

As Norbert heard the chinging spurs of the men walking toward the bunkhouse, he shared a horrified glance with Pennyman. And knew then that Pennyman knew what had suddenly dawned on him, as well.

That Lawton, Burns, and the girl were merely a distraction—a mighty effective one, too—so that the other Vultures could steal into the outpost from the open country to the north.

At the same time, Norbert and Pennyman reached for their sidearms.

Too late.

Burns and Lawton had already drawn theirs. They shot the captain and Pennyman twice each before swinging their pistols toward Donner, who screamed as he backed toward the small sheet-iron stove behind him. Three bullets plunked through his chest and sent him howling over the stove to pile up at the base of the wall, where a rat watched him hungrily from a ragged hole in the disintegrating bricks.

The other soldiers had stood frozen in shock at the mind-numbing vision of the feral gang of unshaven gun wolves strolling toward them, the pistols in their fists glinting redly in the light from the bunkhouse. Just as the privates and one corporal started yelling and slapping leather, the Vultures opened fire.

Their pistols flashed, flames lapping toward the jerking soldiers. The young men were blown into the open doorway or back against the bunkhouse's front wall. A few were merely wounded during the first barrage and tried to make a run in several opposite directions only to be cut down, howling, before any had made it more than a few hobbling strides.

Aside from a couple of soldiers groaning as they died, silence descended. Gunsmoke wafted on the still, cool air of the Wyoming night.

The Vultures stopped to peer down at their handiwork. Hector Debo stepped in front of one near-dead soldier who was trying to crawl away and rammed his spur down on the soldier's left hand, grinding the rowel deep into the knuckle. The soldier stopped crawling and, lifting his head and arching his back, loosed one last scream until Lester shot him

through the eye. Debo laughed as the man's brains spurted
out the back of his head, toward the hole the bullet had made
in the dirt beneath him after it had missiled through his
skull.

Chuckling, Clell Stanhope stepped over a couple of dead
soldiers clogging the doorway and entered the bunkhouse.
Doc Plowright, aka Lawton, and Magpie Quint, aka Burns,
stood grinning with satisfaction as they plucked empty shells
from their pistols to refill the empty cylinders from their
cartridge belts.

Stanhope looked down at the soldier with the captain's
bars on the shoulders of his dark blue tunic. The man sat
against the wall near the door, head canted to one shoulder,
eyes open. A thick mustache mantled his mouth. Dark mut-
tonchops framed his cheeks. Blood dribbled from a bullet
hole one inch in front of his left ear, and continued making
a red line down his unshaven neck. There was another hole
in his high, dome-like forehead, which was white down to
the edge of his hat line. The wound oozed blood down his
thick nose and into his mustache.

The bigger man with sergeant's chevrons on his sleeves
lay twisted facedown on the bunkhouse floor. His legs
jerked. He farted loudly, and Stanhope, Magpie Quint, and
Doc Plowright laughed.

Then Stanhope turned to the naked blonde on the table.

"Ah, dear Trixie," he said, raising his sawed-off shotgun
and ratcheting one of its two hammers back. The girl's eyes
opened halfway.

They were pain-racked, terrified. "No," she begged, tears
streaming down her pale cheeks. "Please, don't kill me."

"You finally did earn your keep, after all," Stanhope said,
aiming the savage popper at the girl's head. "For that, I
thank ye."

SIXTEEN

Spurr set one bucket of steaming water and one bucket of cold water down in front of the closed bedroom door.

Hesitating, he wiped his hands on his buckskin breeches, then lightly rapped the knuckles of his right hand against the halved-log door.

He turned an ear to the door, listened for a moment, then cleared his throat. "Uh . . . uh, ma'am . . . I set some water down here outside the door. Some hot, some cold."

Spurr paused, stared in consternation at the door, trying to think of something else to say. On the other side of the door rose no sound whatever. Finally, the old lawman ran a hand down his patch-bearded jaw, turned away, and walked back across the living area that he and the other men had straightened as best as they could.

Mason was the last one at the eating table in the kitchen section of the house. The others had eaten and were now sitting outside in chairs they'd hauled out from the cabin. They weren't saying anything though above the crackling of the fire in the kitchen range Spurr could hear the occasional gurgling of a bottle being tipped back, the wooden squawk of the chairs as the men shifted around.

None of the others had said much of anything since they'd found the woman. They'd gone about their chores of straightening the cabin to make it liveable for themselves for one night, and out of respect for Mrs. Wilde. They'd buried Waylon Humphreys and his son, Paul. Then Spurr had cut some steaks off the side of beef he'd found in the root cellar outside and fried them up along with some potatoes.

This, despite the fact no one was really hungry. Finding the dead rancher and his boy, and the woman, had hit them all hard. It had cast a dark pall over the dark mountain night.

Mostly, they'd all just wanted to drink. But they knew they had to eat.

Spurr looked from Mason to the raw chunk of steak he'd left in a pan on the plank cupboard near the dry sink. He'd fetched it for Mrs. Wilde, in case she wanted to eat something. But they hadn't heard a peep out of her since Spurr and Mason had left her in the room they'd found her in.

Spurr sat down in the chair he'd vacated when he'd fetched the water for Mrs. Wilde and leaned forward on his arms. He stared down at his quirley smoldering on his plate on which only his steak bone and a smear of grease remained. A bottle stood on the table between him and Mason—one of the bottles of brandy they'd found in Humphreys's cellar, which had been overlooked by the Vultures. Mason grabbed the bottle, plucked the cork from its lip, and dumped a goodly portion into his coffee cup.

There was no coffee in the cup. Spurr had noticed that the sheriff had only drunk about half a cup of coffee before switching solely to brandy, which wasn't like him. Spurr had never known the man to be much of a drinker. Tonight, however, he had that cockeyed, slightly wild look of a man who wanted to get good and drunk. Spurr thought that maybe Mason wasn't such a soulless devil, after all.

Mason slid the bottle toward Spurr, inviting the old law-man to overindulge with him, then lifted his cup in both his hands. His dark, moody eyes were already a little red-rimmed. They seemed to stare off behind Spurr at nothing.

"Gotta run 'em down fast, Spurr. They're crazy—the lot of 'em. Devils straight out of a hell, with the devil's own blessing. They know they're tougher and meaner than any son of a blue-eyed bitch within a thousand square miles, and they can do whatever they damn well please. That means they'll rape and murder at every ranch or settlement they come to until we bring 'em to bay."

"Humphreys has some extra horses out in his paddock. We'll each take us a spare saddle horse when we light out of here tomorrow. Switchin' horses regular'll buy us extra time."

"Funny Stanhope didn't take 'em."

"Hell, he's in no hurry," Spurr said with a scoff, splashing brandy into his own empty coffee cup. "He's havin' fun. He don't care if the law catches up to him. He's no more afraid of us than a yard full of schoolchildren. He knows the kind of holy terror he puts in the hearts of most folks." The law-man sipped the brandy, plucked his quirley off his plate, and took a long puff, sucking the rich smoke deep into his with-ered lungs. "He'd probably like it if we did catch up to him. So he can drive his point home."

"What point's that?"

"That no one can stop him from raping and killing to his heart's content," Spurr said, blowing a wobbly smoke ring over Mason's right shoulder. "From wreaking just as much havoc as he feels like wreaking."

"Yeah, well he's got that wrong!"

"Yes, he does."

"Looks likes he's headin' along the old Oregon Trail." Mason dug a half-smoked black cigar out of his shirt pocket. "You reckon he'll follow it all the way to Oregon?"

"No." Spurr shook his head as he stared into his brandy.

"You sound mighty sure."

"After all these years, when I'm trackin' a man I find I get a handle on his notions. Stanhope's a big fish in a little pond here in Wyoming. He'll stay here. Maybe even for the winter or at least *until* the winter. Then, who knows? Maybe he'll split his gang up and whatever loot they have, and they'll head south by separate routes."

Mason touched a lit match to his cigar and squinted through the billowing smoke at Spurr. "What do you mean—here?"

"Like you said, he's generally headed along the old Oregon Trail. I'm guessin' he'll continue on to South Pass City where he'll load up on supplies, then swing north into the Wind Rivers."

"You think that's where his hideout is?"

"I do."

Mason smiled with a wry curve of his mouth. "Again, you're just so damn certain. Don't you ever think you might be wrong?"

"I was wrong once."

"No shit? About what?"

"Thinkin' I was wrong." Spurr curled his own wry smile as he lifted his brandy cup to his lips.

Mason snorted. "Why the Wind Rivers?"

"'Cause they're the biggest range around. Ten men could get lost in 'em easy-like. There's a chance they might swing south into Colorado, but I got a big-bosomed witch whisperin' in my ear they'll swing into the Wind Rivers."

Mason nodded. He and Spurr sat and drank and thought for a time, listening to the dwindling fire snap occasionally in Humphreys's range.

Mason looked at Spurr again. "We're gonna need help with 'em."

"Most likely help would be wise."

"We should hook up with the soldiers at Elkhorn Creek

just after midday tomorrow. I requested a man I know, a good soldier named Captain Norbert. He's a crack tracker and fighter—cut his teeth during the Little Misunderstanding and then up on the Bozeman against Red Cloud."

Spurr winkled a brow. "What side did you fight on, Dusty?"

Mason studied the old lawman for a moment and acquired a guarded look. "What about you?"

"None of your damn business," Spurr said.

Mason gave a wry chuff, then puffed his cigar for a time before sliding his eyes toward the closed bedroom door. "What about Mrs. Wilde?"

"We'd best send her back to Sweetwater with Mitchell. Soon as she's ready to ride."

"Helluva thing to go back to, after all she's been through herself . . . her boy's funeral."

"How well do you know her?"

Mason shrugged. "She's a looksome woman. A widow. And she lives in my jurisdiction."

"I see," Spurr said, nodding knowingly.

Obviously uncomfortable by the personal turn the conversation had suddenly taken, Mason splashed more brandy into Spurr's cup, then rose from his chair, hefting the bottle against his chest. "I do believe I'll get some air."

When Mason had tramped on outside with the others, Spurr dug his makings sack out of his shirt pocket and glanced toward the closed door. He frowned. The water buckets he'd set in front of the door were gone. She must have quietly opened the door and hauled both buckets into her room while Spurr and Mason were jawing.

Spurr felt a little guilty. He should have noticed and offered to haul them into the room for her. But likely, she wanted to be alone after what the Vultures had done to her.

Spurr dropped his makings sack on the table, rose, and went over to where he'd left the raw chunk of meat near the dry sink. He glanced once more at the woman's closed door, brushed his fist against his nose in speculation, then grabbed the big pan he'd fried the other steaks in. He levered up one of the stove lids, shoved a couple of chunks of pine through it, then set the pan on the lid. He smeared some butter around in it. When the butter was bubbling along with the grease from the previous steaks, he forked the raw steak into the pan.

He didn't know how the woman liked her steak, so he cooked it the way he liked it—charred on both sides, half raw in the middle. He plopped it onto a clean plate, smeared a little butter around on it, then poured a fresh cup of coffee. He grabbed the salt and pepper and a fork and a knife and carried it all over to the closed door.

Again, he hemmed and hawed outside the door. He could hear no sounds on the other side of it. Finally, he cleared his throat. "Ma'am . . . I've got a steak out here for you . . ."

He waited.

Nothing. The silence was a slap. He winced. Christ, she probably just wanted to be left alone. You think's she *hungry*?

"I'll just sit it right down here on the floor, Mrs. Wilde."

He waited another few moments, then set the plate and tin cup of coffee on the floor with the fork and knife. He set the salt and pepper canisters down, as well. Then he returned to the kitchen, picked up his makings pouch, and turned to the cabin's front door that stood half open to relieve the heat from the cooking range. He stopped at the door, glanced once more toward the woman's room and the steak resting on the plate in front of it.

Finally, he went out.

The lawmen and the Pinkertons bunked on the cabin floor, each man taking a turn keeping watch outside. They rose before dawn and ate a hurried breakfast of ham and eggs— both of which they also found in the well-stocked cellar. They washed the food down with hot coffee.

Spurr dropped his fork onto his empty plate, finished his coffee, and glanced at the closed bedroom door. The woman had made no appearance, but when he'd entered the cabin last night to spread his bedroll on the floor, he'd seen that the food he'd left for her was gone. Good to know she wasn't giving up, he thought.

He grabbed his hat and slid his chair back from the table. "Time to pull our picket pins, boys."

The others yawned or groaned or threw back the last of their coffee. When Web Mitchell, his arm still in a sling, slid back his own chair, Spurr said, "Not you, Mitchell. We're sending the woman back with you."

Mitchell frowned. "Huh?"

"You heard me. You're no good with an injured wing. Besides, when Mrs. Wilde's ready to ride, she's gonna need an escort back to Sweetwater."

"That ain't gonna be necessary," Mitchell said.

Spurr and the others stared at him.

"Hell, I thought you knew," the Pinkerton said. "I was keepin' watch on the hill behind the barn, and she came out and saddled a horse and rode out. You boys musta still been sawin' logs."

They all continued to stare at him.

Finally, Spurr said, "Which way'd she go?"

"West," Mitchell said.

Calico Strang said, "Hell, Sweetwater's east."

SEVENTEEN

Jimmy was calling for his mother.

Erin Wilde closed her eyes and shook her head as she galloped the steeldust she'd taken from the stable of the dead rancher down a mountain shoulder through widely scattered jack pines and onto a broad flat. Her boy kept calling for her. She knew it couldn't be possible that she could hear him, because Stanhope was too far ahead of her.

Jimmy was too far away.

Just the same, she could hear her boy's pleas in her head.

"Ma! I'm scared, Ma! Don't let the badmen take me!"

"I'm coming, Jimmy," she heard herself scream beneath the blasting of the wind in her face and the loud thuds of the steeldust's hooves. "I'm coming! I'm coming! Oh, god, I'm coming for you, Jimmy!"

She closed her eyes and gritted her teeth against the misery the horse's lunging stride caused her. The pain that the Vultures had inflicted on her, one after another the night before, was now like bayonets driven deep into her battered womb. But the physical pain was nothing compared to the mental anguish of knowing that Jimmy was in the hands of Clell Stanhope.

She had to get her boy back. She couldn't lose him now, too. Not after losing Daniel. *Oh, god, how could she live knowing that both Daniel and Jimmy were dead? Leaving her here in this awful world alone?!*

After she'd retrieved her son, she would do everything she could to make sure that Stanhope could never cause such horror to herself or to Jimmy or to anyone else again.

She patted the holster on her hip. She'd found it in a trunk in the rancher's cabin, in the room in which the Vultures had so mercilessly and seemingly endlessly violated her. The pistol was a Remington .44. She knew the make because her brother and father had taught her all about guns when she'd been growing up around Gillette, before she'd met Daniel, who had never been fond of firearms of any kind. In fact, Daniel had never owned a gun, hadn't even wanted to keep one in the house. Having been raised in an eastern city before coming west with his parents to sell dry goods in Colorado mining camps, he'd been afraid of them. Erin had not held that against him. His delicate sensibilities, so rare on the frontier, had been what had charmed her most about him.

In a land of brutish men, he'd been a rare yet masculine flower.

It had been a while since Erin had fired a pistol, but she felt certain that she could fire one again quite effectively. Anyway, she'd find out soon enough. Because she would not stop until she'd run down the Vultures and rescued her son and blown a hole through the dead center of Clell Stanhope's vile head.

She had no idea how she would accomplish that task. The complexities and practicalities of it were a strange, mysterious fog behind her eyes. All that was clear to her was that she would get Jimmy back and she would satisfy this raw, burning need within her to kill Stanhope. Slowly, if possible.

Somehow, she'd do so without getting herself or her boy killed. She was certain of this. Only a very remote part of her was at all worried. Mostly, in spite of her physical agony, she felt very powerful indeed. In fact, she felt almost indestructible.

She booted the horse into a lope, keeping her back straight, reins held high against her chest and loosely in her hands. She'd grown up riding horses and was a natural rider. While her body ached from the abuse she'd taken, she knew how to ride to keep the jarring to a minimum.

Occasionally she paused to make sure that she was still on the Vultures' trail, which was not hard, because they had made no effort to disguise the clear prints of nearly a dozen shod horses they'd left in the sand and gravel of this high-desert country. Ahead, the broad flat she'd been following narrowed into a canyon with high, steep sandstone walls. A stream curved along the wall on her right, and it was lined with aspens whose leaves flashed gold in the sunlight.

As she continued on into the canyon, she began to hear the stream's rush, and she found herself reining the steeldust away from the Vultures' trail and over toward the water. Despite the sponge bath she'd taken the night before, with the water the old lawman had provided, she felt as though a million tiny snakes of filth were crawling over her, even coiling and uncoiling inside her.

The cool, clean water—snowmelt water from high in the mountains—beckoned. Chickenflesh of anticipation rose on the back of her neck. She imagined the filth washing off of her like a thick layer of coal dust.

Jim needed her. But she could not ignore the clean chill of the stream, the chance to rid herself of the stench and the slime that Stanhope and the other Vultures had left on her.

At the edge of the woods, she checked the steeldust down and swung gingerly down from the saddle. The horse tried to edge away from her and continue through the trees toward the stream, but she held fast to the reins.

"Hold on, fella," she said, with one hand brushing her chestnut hair back away from her face and looking carefully around. Making sure she was alone here in this clean, fresh-smelling canyon with only the whisper of the aspen leaves and the murmur of the cold water nearby.

When she saw nothing more threatening than a mule deer doe grazing near where two spotted fawns lay at the opposite edge of the canyon, Erin led the horse into the woods and slipped its bit from its teeth, so the mount could freely draw water from the stream.

She dropped the reins, let the horse continue on by itself toward the water. She strode slowly toward the water, continuing to look around cautiously before removing the serape she'd found in the ranch house. Her dress had been too badly torn to wear; besides, she'd wanted clothes more rugged for the chore she had ahead of her. So she'd taken a pair of balbriggans down from a peg in the ranch house, and she'd donned them under a pair of loose, ragged denims that she'd also found in the ranch house, and the serape that smelled like camp smoke and man sweat but would have to do. The nights were cold this high above sea level.

At the back of a wardrobe, she'd found a pair of beaded moccasins. They were sound except that the soles needed new thread. They must have belonged to a woman or a boy, because they were only a little large for Erin but would in time conform to the shape of her feet. Most importantly, they were comfortable.

And they were quiet, which would come in most handy when she finally ran the Vultures down.

She stopped just inside the woods about fifteen feet from the stream and tossed the serape onto the ground. She stooped to remove the moccasins, then slid the pistol from behind the wide leather belt holding the baggy denims on her lean hips. She set the pistol down on the serape, then shucked out of the denims and the balbriggans and, crossing her arms on her breasts, looked around once more.

There were only the trees, a few peeping chickadees, the stream, and the tan ridge on the other side of it. It rose nearly straight up a good thousand feet from a gravel shore and a thin line of aspens. A few birds—robins and mountain jays—watched her from the trees.

Before her, the river slid, cool and inviting over the rocks. To the right and only a few feet out from the bank was a gently turning, dark pool.

She headed toward it, feeling the brittle grass and gravel under the soles of her feet, which, when she'd been a girl, had been hard and calloused from running barefoot but which now were so tender that she could feel the poke of every grain of sand and every blade of grass. She stepped off the grass and into the water. It was cold. Colder even than she'd expected. The way it numbed her feet and then her ankles and calves was wonderful.

She continued into the water, feeling better, cleaner already. Angling out to the right where the black hole beckoned her near a gouge in the bank, where a tree must have been at one time, she dropped down into it. A smile spread her lips wider and wider as the water moved up past her belly and over her breasts. When it had inched up to her neck, she closed her eyes.

She felt the slime slithering off of her. The grime and the stench washed away in the water sliding around her and continuing downstream as it sent up little tea-colored stitches where it bubbled over rocks.

After a time, she moved up to shallower water, nearer where she'd entered the stream, and lay down on the sandy, gravelly bed. She closed her eyes, letting the sound of the water and the birds and the blowing leaves fill her head, cleansing her brain the same way the water had scoured her body.

The steeldust whinnied.

Erin opened her eyes and lifted her head, turning toward where the steeldust stood on the bank, reins dangling. The horse was looking across the stream and to the woman's left, twitching each ear in turn.

She followed the horse's gaze and gasped, sitting up and crossing her arms over her breasts. A man in a white shirt, suspenders, and broad-brimmed black hat sat a horse near the edge of the stream's far side. He must have just ridden out of a draw. Another rode slowly up from behind him, from behind a bulge in the canyon wall. The second man was short, and he wore a red plaid shirt and dark trousers stuffed into mule-eared boots.

Both were bearded. They were trailing pack mules loaded down with burlap supply sacks and picks and shovels and other mining implements. Prospectors. The man in the white shirt and black hat was staring toward Erin. He glanced at the smaller gent just now riding up beside him, facing the stream, and jerked his chin in her direction.

Erin scrambled up out of the water, retrieved the serape, and dropped it over her head. The red-and-white-striped garment fell to mid-thigh. As she stooped to retrieve her oversized balbriggans, she saw the first man drop the lead rope of his pack mule and boot his horse into the stream and angle it toward her. He did not come quickly but held his horse at a walk. He canted his head to one side, his eyes slitted beneath the broad brim of his hat. He had a cold, lusty look on his face.

An expression that Erin knew well.

Her heart leapt, and her blood turned to ice.

The snakes of slime were slithering over her again.

She dropped the balbriggans and started running toward the steeldust. She stopped, looked toward the man riding toward her. The other, shorter man was following him. The smaller man had a red beard and a big grin on his thin face.

Erin felt the ice thaw in her veins. Her blood warmed. She turned to where she'd dropped the gun in the grass, walked over to it, and picked it up. Her heartbeat slowed.

Calm inched over her. Certainty. Confidence that she would never again be abused the way the Vultures had abused her. At least not without her pain coming at a very high price to her attackers.

If she didn't discourage these two men, they'd likely dog her as she trailed after the Vultures and reduce her chances of rescuing her boy from the killers' savage clutches. Purposefully, feeling the strange calm steal over her just as the cold water had only a few minutes ago, Erin walked to the edge of the stream. The breeze nudged her wet hair. It tickled her shoulders and back.

The rider was within twenty yards of her now, a little more than halfway across the stream, the other man a horse length behind him. Erin took the pistol in both her hands, raised it, and clicked the hammer back with both her thumbs and a slight curl of her upper lip.

She felt her hands shake and willed the shaking to cease.

The man's eyes dropped to the gun pointed at him. He stopped his horse, as did the smaller man riding behind him. His mouth slackened inside his dark brown beard. His eyes grew hard. "Put that gun down," he said above the stream's even rush.

"Just ride away, mister."

The man's cheeks drew up into little red balls under his eyes, which crossed a little with anger. He jabbed a gloved finger at Erin.

"You put that gun down, goddamnit! I won't have no woman aimin' a gun at me!"

Erin was vaguely surprised by the almost serene tone of her voice. "Just ride away, mister."

She felt her lips curl a cordial smile.

"Goddamnit!"

The first man glanced at the second man. They shared a quick, conniving look.

Then the first man rammed his heels into his horse's

flanks, and the mount lunged toward Erin, who squeezed the Remington's trigger. The man grunted and jerked slightly back in his saddle, drawing his horse's reins taut, using the ribbons to keep himself seated.

When his horse had stopped, he looked down at the blood oozing from the hole in his grubby white shirt, just left of his heart. It bubbled frothily. His head bobbed as though he were having trouble lifting it, and he said with a weird chuckle, "Good lord—this little bitch done shot me, Bryce."

The smaller man shuttled his wide eyes between Erin and his partner, blinking, letting his jaw hang lower and lower, as though he wasn't quite sure what had happened. He rode up beside his partner and turned to look at the front of the man's shirt. He gasped, then jerked his exasperated, blue eyes at Erin, who had recocked the Remington and stood at the edge of the shoreline, bare feet spread shoulder-width apart. She drew air slowly, evenly into her lungs, and blew it out the same way.

The congenial smile was still on her lips.

"Just ride away, mister."

That seemed to enrage him. He pulled the pistol he wore wedged behind his broad brown belt and gigged his horse forward.

As he raised the big Colt, Erin squeezed the Remington's trigger a second time. The horse kept lunging toward her as the red-bearded man screamed and triggered his pistol off to the side and flew back over the mount's left hip. He hit the stream with a splash, his head striking a rock with a hollow bark.

His pinto gave a startled whinny as it galloped past Erin and up the bank and through the trees. The red-bearded man lolled facedown in the shallow water, blood spreading out around his torso and his cracked skull.

Erin looked at the first man, whose horse had turned and was now carrying him across the stream. Slowly, the man slumped lower and lower until his head hit his horse's neck.

He rolled down his right stirrup and hit the water with a splash. The horse nickered and ran off across the river while the current grabbed its dead rider and carried him like so much flotsam downstream.

"You should have just ridden away."

Erin lowered the pistol and turned to retrieve her clothes.

EIGHTEEN

A rifle cracked once, twice, three times.

Spurr checked Cochise down and swung the horse around to gaze behind him. Mason, riding to Spurr's right, did the same, both men sliding their Winchesters from their saddle boots. Gentry and Stockton were riding a couple of horse lengths back, and now they swung their own mounts around, Ed Gentry yelling, "Goddamnit—what's that?"

They were each trailing a spare horse taken from Humphreys's Box Bar B.

"What's it sound like?" asked Stockton.

Only Web Mitchell and his own extra mount were behind the two territorial marshals. Calico Strang was nowhere to be seen.

Again, the rifle spoke, the report flatting out around the ridges of the canyon that Spurr's group was riding through along the Sweetwater River. Spurr dropped his spare mount's lead rope and rammed his heels against Cochise's flanks and, levering a shell one-handed, galloped the big roan back down the trail. He set the rifle's butt on his right thigh. The shooter fired twice more, and as Spurr rounded a bend in the trail, the other men in his group following close behind, he sawed back on his reins.

Calico Strang was hunkered down behind a boulder just right of the trail, firing up the southern ridge. Spurr couldn't see anything up the slope but rocks and pinyon pines, a few cedar. Strang's bullets merely puffed dust up around the rim, near where a large thumb of limestone jutted toward the canyon.

Spurr turned to Strang. "Hold your fire! Hold your fire, there, you goddamn dunderheaded tinhorn!"

Crouching behind his covering boulder, his carbine resting atop the boulder itself, Strang turned toward Spurr. "I'm tired o' that damned devil! It's time he either comes down here and introduces himself or gets his ass drilled! He's just tryin' to get under our skins!"

He pressed his cheek to the rifle's stock once more and pulled the trigger. The hammer pinged on an empty chamber. Spurr swung down from Cochise's back. He strode over to where Strang rose from behind his boulder, regarding the old lawman with open disdain.

Strang held his carbine across his chest defensively. "What are we supposed to do—wait for him to bushwhack us?"

Spurr bunched his lips and rapped the butt of his rifle across the young Pinkerton's right cheek. Strang hadn't seen it coming; he hadn't expected such a quick move by the old federal. He gave an indignant scream as the hard blow threw him back and around. He lost his footing and hit the ground with a raucous ching of spurs, splayed out on his belly. Twisting back around, he glared up at Spurr, both his dung-brown eyes wide, his long red hair pasted across his pale cheeks.

"You old bastard," he spat out, sliding his hand to the Colt resting in its black, oiled holster strapped to Strang's skinny thigh clad in checked wool.

Spurr aimed the Winchester from his right hip and triggered it twice, blowing up dust and gravel to the right and left of the young Pinkerton. Sand blew across the younker's store-bought three-piece suit and his face. He gave another indignant cry and sort of lurched backward on his heels and elbows, shielding his face with his hands.

"You crazy old coot! What're you tryin' to do?"

"Teach you a lesson, you cork-headed coon! If that fella up there was fixin' to ambush us, he would have done so by now. He ain't what we oughta be worried about. If you do anymore unsactioned shootin', I'm gonna follow suit and drill you a third eye, then cut your damn head off, box it up, and send it via the U.S. Mail to Allan Pinkerton himself!"

Mason had ridden up behind Spurr, and he glared at the young Pinkerton. "If the Vultures are anywhere within ten miles, they'd have heard your shots, you damn fool!"

"Hell, they're a day ahead of us, at least!"

"We don't know that!" Mason said, his eyes bright with exasperation. "For all we know, they're holed up another half mile up trail, waitin' to see who's foggin' em."

Spurr sighed heavily as he swung around and grabbed Cochise's reins. He looked at Mason. "How far are we from the Elkhorn Creek outpost?"

"'Bout two miles."

"You fellas push on ahead and pick up the soldiers. I'm gonna drift up this ridge and see if I can get a look at the fella ghostin' us."

"What for?" asked Mason. "You yourself said if he had any bad intentions, we'd likely have knowed about 'em by now."

"'Cause he might not have had 'em before, but he might now!" Spurr threw another bright-angry glance at Strang. "Besides, I'm curious!"

Red-faced, tired of riding with too damn many men when he was used to riding solo and not having to explain himself—or suffer fools like Calico Strang—Spurr swung into the leather. He reined the roan around, pinched his hat brim to Stockton and Gentry. "You boys pick up my spare hoss, will you?"

When Gentry said they would, the old lawman galloped on up the trail. He came to a feeder ravine opening on the left and paused to look it over. The brushy cut rose at an easy angle toward the top of the southern ridge, along which the mysterious stranger who had saved Mason's life back in Willow City had been keeping a close scout on Spurr's posse. Or, at least, they thought it was the man who'd saved Mason's hide.

It was time to find out. And it was time to learn what in hell the man wanted—if that was possible now that Strang had tried to beef him.

Spurr booted Cochise up the trail that ran along the side of the ravine—a game trail, possibly a cattle trail. He hadn't ridden far before he spied the bones of a long-dead cow that had either expired from old age or coyotes, or had gotten hung up in the heavy buckbrush and wild currant shrubs, which the stupid beasts were wont to do now and then.

As he rode, he kept an eye on the ridge above him, to which the ravine climbed to within about thirty feet, before it became a jumble of rock down which, judging by the abundant green around it, a spring likely seeped. He continued on up past the rocks and halted Cochise at the crest of the ridge, under a lone jack pine.

A rider had passed recently in front of the pine. The tracks continued on down the other side of the ridge. Distant movement grabbed Spurr's attention, and he lifted his gaze to see a rider riding up a far ridge at an angle from left to right. All Spurr could see from this distance of a quarter mile was a black horse and a man with a black hat.

He reached back for his spyglass, raised it, telescoped it. When the single sphere of magnification had cleared, he caught a fleeting, jerky glimpse of the horse and rider—the rider with long, Indian-black hair wearing buckskin breeches and a calico shirt with what appeared claws or teeth of some kind hanging around his dark neck—cresting the ridge.

Then all Spurr could see for about four seconds was the man's broad back and the stallion's black tail swishing from side to side before they disappeared down the other side of the ridge.

Spurr stared at the opposite ridge for a time, wondering who in hell the man was and what he wanted. Possibly, he was one of the Vultures, but it was only an outside chance.

Cochise gave a weary blow. Spurr looked at the horse. The roan's neck was sweat-lathered. The late summer sun poured down like liquid gold, hot as a skillet. And the blackflies were buzzing.

Remembering the thick grass and moss he'd seen in the rocks at the mouth of the ravine only a dozen yards away, he reined Cochise back down the way they'd come, then followed a deer and elk trail into the ravine's bottom. Instantly, he felt the coolness here of the rocks and the water and the shade that the low, steep banks offered.

A good place to rest his horse as well as his old, tired bones. He shouldn't take the time—he had a job to do—but by god he'd take a breather. There were younger men on the trail ahead of him.

He swung down from the saddle, dropped the reins, and loosened Cochise's latigo, to give the horse a rest from the tight belly strap. Doffing his hat, he went over to where water slithered over the mossy stones spotted with mineral deposits. He set the hat under a slight ledge in the broken rock wall; a couple of slender streams trickled into it with ticking sounds. He sat back and rolled a cigarette. When he'd finished building the quirley, the hat was about a third full, so he set it down in front of Cochise, who lowered his snout to draw the fresh, cool water.

Spurr set the quirley aside, leaned down near the rocks, and cupped his hands to a couple of good-sized trickles, then raised the water to his lips, drinking thirstily of the cold, pure brew. There wasn't enough of a flow here to fill his canteen—he'd fill it later on at Elkhorn Creek—but there was enough to refresh himself.

He sat back in the shade near the run out from the spring, crossed his ankles, smoked half his quirley, then drew his hat down over his eyes and allowed himself to doze. Good being away from the others. That Calico Strang needed a bullet in his ear. The others, including the other Pinkerton, Web, were good men, but there was no man so good that Spurr would enjoy riding with him for long.

He and Mason had partnered up in Colorado and New Mexico, when they'd gone after the firebrand Cuno Massey. But it had just been him and Mason then, and the sheriff had turned out to be a passable partner, being as how he didn't talk much and didn't seem to mind that Spurr did.

No, Mason was a good man. Spurr might even recommend him to take Spurr's place when the old lawdog finally retired, if he ever did. Maybe he'd just die in the saddle.

Half dozing, he watched the pretty, mature, brown-eyed face of Abilene float up out of the murk to smile at him from just behind his eyelids. Regret was a little white varmint nipping at his oysters.

Damn, maybe he should have married her. God knew he'd had the chance. They could have gone to Mexico together and had a few good years before the iron crab in his chest got the better of him.

Now she'd married some mucky-muck in a tailored suit who owned a ranch nearly as large as some eastern states, and Spurr had let the opportunity slip through his hands. A damn fool was what he was. When you got to be Spurr's age, shots at new beginnings were few and far between.

And he really had loved her. At least, he thought he had. Still did. Hard to tell. Could he merely be jealous of the rancher?

"Well, shit," the old lawdog said, poking his hat brim back up on his age-spotted forehead. "That'll be enough of that! If you ain't gonna sleep but just sit here and make yourself glum, you'd best haul your fuckin' ass."

He leaned over, filled his cupped hands with the spring water, and washed his face and the back of his neck, then heaved himself to his feet. His ticker gave a hiccup, chugging almost audibly. He lost his breath, and black javelins swam in his eyes.

He stumbled back against the brick-like wall, fumbled a pill from the pouch in his pocket, swallowed it, and held himself steady with his hands on the wall behind him, wincing, enduring the throbbing pain in his chest while he waited for the spell to pass.

Gradually, the steel trap eased its grip on his heart. Then he just stood there, the image of Abilene fading in his head, looking around at the rocks and the sky. Hearing the wind, birds. He suddenly felt very old, looking back over all those years, all those faces and track downs, all the lonely nights in distant places, drinking whiskey and feeding brush to a fire.

Yes, he was old. Back when he was a kid, he remembered an uncle returning from the Rocky Mountains after spending nine years fur trapping, and the man had been considered an old-timer though he'd not yet turned forty. Spurr was sixty. That was as old as dirt even for these modern times. What the hell was he still doing here?

Turning down pretty women's requests that he take them to Mexico . . . ?

He chuckled at that. He kept the mental quip in his head as he mounted up and rode back down the ravine to the main trail, a smile lifting the corners of chapped lips inside the patchy, ginger-gray beard. He looked back up the ridge for sign of the Indian or half-breed, possibly a Mex, who'd been trailing him and the others, then booted Cochise into a lope.

A mile or so ahead, near where the trail curved to the north toward the outpost on Elkhorn Creek, the Vultures' trail curved south. More recent tracks followed the trail toward the outpost. That would be Mason's men.

Spurr pondered the situation, then decided he'd scout the Vultures' trail for a mile or two. It would likely take an hour for the cavalry boys to get mounted up and on the trail with Mason, anyway. Spurr would ride back to meet them when he was sure of the direction the killers were headed.

He followed the Vultures' trail until it curved back toward the Sweetwater River. But after the day-old trail reached the river, it swung back north, in the direction of the Wind Rivers looming huge on the northern horizon, Gannett Peak touched with the white of last winter's snows.

From here, had Stanhope headed directly into the mountains—without outfitting himself with supplies from South Pass City?

There was a distant cracking sound, like firecrackers being ignited from a mile or two away. The dry, thin air carried it crisply.

Spurr looked across a broad sweep of tan-yellow valley to the north, rising gradually toward the apron slopes and elk parks of the mountains. He could see the brush lining the creek along which the Elkhorn Creek Cavalry Outpost lay, out of sight beyond a low, cedar-stippled, hogback ridge.

The crackling continued.

And all at once Spurr knew what it was.

"Oh, Jesus," he said, stumbling forward, a helpless expression on his withered face. "Oh, no—*dear lord*!"

NINETEEN

Twenty minutes before, Mason had ridden up over a low, grassy rise to spy Elkhorn Creek curling below, at the lowest point in the broad valley that rose gradually in the north to the foothills of the Wind River mountains. In the south it sloped off toward the Sweetwater River into which Elkhorn Creek flowed.

Just north of the creek, up a slight hill, lay the Elkhorn Creek Cavalry Outpost. As Mason kept his grulla and his spare mount moving down the other side of the rise toward the stream, he scanned the post that appeared little more than a ruin remaining from a long-defunct, ancient civilization—and a small ruin, at that.

The buildings appeared little more than brown dimples on the tan plain tufted with silvery green sage shrubs. A wall stretched across the front, paralelling the creek, and ran for a few dozen yards along the post's western side. A waste of time and manpower, for in its unfinished state it offered little protection. There was even a ten-foot gap in the wall where the gates had once been.

Despite the fort's dilapidated appearance, Mason was relieved to see horses milling in the corral off the barn that flanked the long, L-shaped, enlisted men's quarters, which, in turn, sat to the west of the small officer's hut. The soldiers must have brought extra mounts out from Fort Stambaugh, because there were a good twenty, twenty-five horses kicking up dust in the corral or standing statue-still in a wedge of shade angling out from the barn.

There was a line of dark blue tunics sitting low along the south wall of the enlisted men's bunkhouse—soldiers lazing there, waiting on Mason. The sheriff could see the tan or blue kepis on their heads, the yellow neckerchiefs billowing around their necks. There was another bluecoat standing outside the gap in the crude stockade, yet another walking in a desultory fashion along the top of the creek's far bank.

Mason frowned slightly as he ran his gaze across the outpost's remuda once more, only vaguely conscious of a twinge of apprehension flicking around between his shoulders, as he booted his grulla on down the hill, jerking his spare mount along by its lead rope. The others followed, spaced widely out behind him, Gentry leading Spurr's spare horse as well as his own, Calico Strang looking like a whipped schoolboy after Spurr had laid his rifle butt across the arrogant young Pinkerton's cheek.

A purple bruise had risen around a quarter-inch cut on the kid's cheek, and Strang kept brushing at it with his hand and spitting to one side, muttering angrily under his breath. His partner, Web Mitchell, his right arm in a sling, ignored his younger partner, as did the others.

Mason bottomed out in the creek bed, then let his horses stop to draw water from between the sandbars. The soldier who'd been walking guard along the far bank had stopped to stare toward the newcomers, holding a Spencer carbine on his right shoulder. He canted his head to one side—a big man with long black hair gathered in a ponytail, and an impatient scowl.

In a thick Texas accent, he said, "You Sheriff Mason, is ya?"

"That's right," Mason said, jerking his horse's head up. The mount had had enough water until it had cooled down. "Captain Norbert over yonder?"

The big man in the corporal's uniform, the tunic of which had a large stain over the belly, nodded. "Waitin' on you, sir. Said we'd be foggin' them Vultures with ya'll."

"That's right. Judging by their tracks, they must have ridden right past here not a day ago—just a mile to the south."

The corporal kept his head canted to the right and hiked a shoulder noncommittally. Then he grinned. "I sure would like to be part o' the bunch that runs them wolves to bay. Get my name in the history books."

"I reckon you'll get your chance," said Stockton as he jerked his buckskin's head up from the trickle of water twisting between sandbars.

"Let's go, fellas," Mason said as he booted the grulla on across the creek and up the opposite bank. "We'll rest our horses for an hour. By that time, Spurr will likely show, and then we'll head out again, get a few more miles behind us before sundown."

Strang muttered again under his breath, and Mason curled a wry smile. Spurr had a way with folks.

The soldier standing near the opening in the stockade wall was smoking a cigarette, his rifle leaning against the wall behind him. As Mason and the other men approached, the man put his head down slightly, and the shade from his kepi brim slid down over his eyes. He, too, had a stain on his uniform—on the thigh of his right, pale blue pantsleg. In the middle of the stain was a hole.

Mason was so eager to get his horses rested and to take off after the Vultures that he paid little heed to the shabby uniform. After all, this was the frontier army, and supplies as well as fresh uniforms were often few and far between.

But when he'd ridden through the gap and into the parade ground and continued on toward the small collection of rough-hewn buildings sixty yards beyond, worms of foreboding began crawling not just between his shoulders but up and down his spine.

He looked again toward the corral off the barn, and it was Ed Gentry who voiced the sheriff's half-formed concern: "When'd the cavalry start ridin' pintos and Appaloosies?"

Stockton, riding to Mason's left, chuckled. "The ranchers must have run out of bays down around Fort Stambaugh."

Mason reined up. The others walked their horses a little farther ahead and then, regarding the sheriff curiously, stopped their own mounts around him. Mason stared toward the bunkhouse.

The soldiers gathered there had all gained their feet and were now walking toward Mason and the others. A tall, broad-shouldered hombre walked in the middle of the group. He wore a uniform with captain's bars on the shoulders and a broad-brimmed blue kepi.

Mason couldn't see the man's eyes because the captain was walking with his chin down, just like the guard outside the stockade had done. Something in the way the man moved looked familiar.

Just as Mason's heart began to quicken, he saw the birds circling in the sky behind the bunkhouse.

Buzzards.

He jerked his gaze back to the big captain striding toward him, fifty yards away and closing with the others, their spurs chinging. They all had stains on their uniforms.

Dark stains. Bloodstains.

And then the two vultures tattooed on Clell Stanhope's cheeks spread their wings as the man lifted his chin and smiled.

"Mason," he said, "if I woulda killed you back in Willow City, like I intended, you'd have all the pain behind you now!"

"Well, I'll be goddamned," said Gentry, drawing the words out tensely as he dropped the ropes of his two spare horses.

"Holy shit!" said Calico Strang, his chestnut sensing his fear and leaping around beneath him.

Keeping his eyes on the hard-eyed, unshaven gun wolves forming a semicircle before him, Mason said, "Everybody take it easy." But his calm voice belied the thundering of his pulse in his temples. Fear and shame burned through him.

He'd seen all the signs of an ambush—the non-bay horses, the stained uniforms—and still he'd ridden right into it. Worse, he'd led other men into it.

He glared at Stanhope, ran his gaze across the others all decked out in the uniforms they must have taken off the bullet-torn soldiers whom they themselves had killed. The whole gang was here—Ed Crow, Clell Stanhope, Red Ryan, Santos Estrada, Quiet Boon Coffey, with Magpie Quint and Doc Plowright, who'd been scouting the creek bank and the outside of the stockade wall, respectively, now moving up behind the lawmen.

The latter two Vultures separated, circling Mason and the others, smiling as they held their rifles across their chests.

The lawmen's horses had all turned skittish now, sensing their riders' anxiety as well as the killers' antipathy.

Clell Stanhope started to laugh. Then his brother followed suit. The other killers looked at him, and his humor became infectious. They all started laughing, the guffaws rising eerily around the parade ground and rising above the nickers and whinnies and hoof thuds of the frightened horses. As he laughed, Clell Stanhope pointed at Mason, mocking the sheriff's obvious fear and chagrin.

Mason glanced quickly at the other lawmen and the two Pinkertons. They were all swinging their heads around at the laughing cutthroats. None of Mason's men had his hand on his gun, knowing that as soon as they reached for their weapons, the set-to would begin. And while the Vultures had not yet drawn their own pistols or leveled their rifles, they had the lawmen outnumbered nine to five.

Not horrible odds. Mason had seen worse. But the fact that he and the others were mounted on nervous horses reduced their chances even further.

Mason heard someone laughing beside him, and turned to see that Gentry was laughing now, too. Then Bill Stockton slapped his whipcord-clad thigh and threw his gray-bearded head back, sending his own resonant guffaws careening toward the clear, blue sky.

The laughter was indeed infectious. Mason himself grew heady on the danger. He felt a chuckle roll up from his own chest as he looked around at the others and heard and saw them laughing—even Web and Calico Strang albeit with slightly less vigor than the others—and began laughing himself.

Hell was about to pop, and there was nothing anyone could do about it.

Mason locked eyes with Clell Stanhope. Stanhope's hand dropped to the pistol wedged behind his black cartridge belt, and Mason slapped leather, as well. Just as Mason triggered his Colt, the grulla pitched hard to the right, and the sheriff saw with a sinking sensation his slug puff dust far behind Stanhope and the others.

Mason felt a crushing pain in his side as the horse turned once more. All around him, guns popped and men shouted or screamed. The sheriff saw Calico Strang's horse rear wildly and caught a brief glimpse of the young Pinkerton tumbling off the back of his mount as Strang fired his own pistol in the air.

When Mason's horse had turned a complete circle, he felt another punch-like blow—this one to his shoulder. He cocked his pistol, extended it toward Clell Stanhope, who was down on one knee, laughing and shooting into Mason's pitching crowd.

But the sheriff's horse continued bucking and squealing horrifically, and Mason's shot nearly blew the hat off Magpie Quint's head. Quint returned the shot, glaring indignantly, and the Vulture's shot found its mark in Mason's chest.

The sheriff heard himself groan as the bullet punched him back in his saddle. Turning his head slightly, he saw Bill Stockton on the ground, his bloody, hatless body being pummeled by his own horse's prancing hooves. Mason grunted loudly, gritting his teeth, as he lifted himself to a sitting position once more and triggered another round at the Vultures though his crow-hopping horse made it impossible for him to see if his lead struck any of the laughing, shooting killers.

He did see Gentry standing nearly straight up in his stirrups, firing a pistol in each hand while howling like a poisoned coyote, gobbets of blood and chunks of flesh being blown out of his body by the Vultures' fierce fusillade. Then Mason's horse took off at a gallop through the Vultures, and all the sheriff could do was grab his saddle horn, dropping his pistol in the process, and hold on.

TWENTY

Hunkered low in his saddle, Spurr ground his moccasin-clad heels into Cochise's flanks and whipped his rein ends against the horse's right hip, urging more speed. The wind basted his hat brim against his forehead. The ground slid by in a green-tan blur though he kept his eyes straight ahead, toward the low ridge on the other side of which sat the Elkhorn Creek outpost.

The shooting had died several minutes ago.

It was a good five-mile ride to the outpost from where Spurr had first heard the shooting, and he wouldn't have been able to keep up the hell-for-leather pace without killing his horse. He was too experienced a frontiersman not to stop the horse when he felt Cochise's stride begin to falter.

He was just too far from the outpost to be of much help to Mason's crew. Cursing continuously and casting his ter- rified gaze toward the north, he rested the horse, then walked him before running him again. Gradually, the outpost shifted into view on a distant slope. A string of riders was riding away from it to the north, angling westward.

The Vultures.

Dread grew like a grapefruit-sized tumor in the old law-man's belly. His heart hammered, hiccupped, and hammered again. As the fort grew before him, the line of riders drifted out of sight behind a distant ridge.

Spurr drew rein suddenly. A horse stood about a hundred yards away from him as well as from the outpost beyond it. Spurr urged Cochise ahead more slowly. Gradually, the horse grew in his vision until it became obvious that the horse was not alone. A rider straddled it, the man slumped forward against the grulla's neck.

Mason's horse.

Spurr pulled up to the sheriff's mount, which nickered and shied away, curveting. Mason's head hung down along the side of the horse's neck. The sheriff's pin-striped shirt was pink in places, crimson with fresh, oozing blood in others. The horse continued to turn, rolling its eyes around wildly, thoroughly terrorized but also exhausted, and before it could trot away, Spurr grabbed its reins. He swung down from his saddle and walked over and looked up at Mason.

"Dusty . . . ?"

Spurr grimaced as he placed a hand on the sheriff's left shoulder. He was shot up bad. He might have been dead. He wasn't moving. Spurr jerked the man's shoulder slightly and was surprised when Mason stiffened and lifted his head a little.

The man grunted, tried straightening his back, but cursed softly and rested his chest back down against the grulla's neck. His hat was gone, and his thin, sweat-matted hair was mussed.

"Easy, Dusty," Spurr said. "I'll get you down."

Mason turned to him. Even the man's face was splattered with blood—likely from the many wounds in his chest and belly. Blood slithered down from both nostrils, matting his mustache. He ground his jaws. His eyes were dark and flat with pain.

"Spurr . . . ?" His voice was a wheeze that barely made it through his lips.

Spurr squeezed the man's bloody arm, his own knees threatening to buckle. "I'm here, Dusty." He blinked hard as tears oozed out of his eyes to roll down his cheeks.

"Spurr," Mason said again, only slightly louder this time. His eyes bored into Spurr's for a full ten seconds, his jaws quivering as he ground them together. And then he said between quick, shallow breaths, "Kill 'em . . . ," before his eyes fluttered and he rolled off the saddle toward Spurr.

Before Spurr could catch him, Mason hit the ground and expired with a sigh at the old lawman's feet.

Spurr was tired and so was his horse. He wanted nothing more than to hightail it after the Vultures, but if he didn't blow himself out within a few miles, he'd blow out Cochise. And then he'd have failed miserably in his endeavor, leaving the Vultures free to continue looting, raping, and killing.

With much back-and-bellying, he managed to lift Mason up onto the grulla, belly down across his saddle, arms and legs dangling. Breathless and cursing his nearly useless body, hoping he could squeeze enough juice out of it for one more job—the biggest job of his entire career—he hauled himself back into the leather and led the grulla onto the outpost.

As he'd suspected, the Vultures had killed his entire group, shot them down like coyotes in a pen. Mason's group hadn't had a chance. They'd been surprised, outnumbered, and burdened by their horses, two of which lay amongst the twisted dead and puddled blood. The rest had fled.

The soldiers probably hadn't had much more of a chance than Mason had. Stanhope had the cunning of a crazy man—a crazy killer who lived to draw blood—and sane men had little chance against him. Spurr saw the buzzards circling beyond a rise to the north and knew that that was most likely where the soldiers were.

   Staring down at the two old territorial marshals, Spurr's
knees turned to water. He dropped to one knee and doffed
his hat, ran a gnarled hand through his thin, long, brown
hair streaked with gray. Anguish gripped him as he gazed
down at Gentry, who lay with his head propped on the back
of one of Stockton's boots. The Wyoming lawman's jaws
hung wide, and flies buzzed around him, flicking in and out
of his mouth. Spurr waved his hat futilely over both men,
trying to disperse the insects.

   Finally, he gave up, dropped his hat, lowered his head,
and massaged his temples. He felt old and defeated but managed to heave the heavy feeling aside by working up a furi-
ous fire within him. Lifting his head once more, he looked
in the direction the Vultures had ridden off less than a half
hour ago.

   They'd gain another half day to a day on him, but their
sign should be easy to follow. When he'd rested himself and
his horse and picked out a spare horse from the outpost's
corral, he'd get back after them.

   Alone?

   *Hell, why not alone? Ain't that how I've always worked
it before?*

   *I'll manage. At least, I'll kill one or two, slow 'em down
a mite before I can summon more lawmen onto their trail.*

   He considered riding south to Fort Stambaugh for help
and decided against the idea. That would set him back at
least a week. He could telegraph both his own boss, Chief
Marshal Henry Brackett, and Fort Stambaugh from South
Pass City, if there was still a working telegraph in the old
mining town.

   Spurr straightened, donned his hat, and led Cochise over
to the holding corral. He unsaddled the horse, set his tack
over the corral's top rail, then led the horse inside amongst
the wary, inquisitive others—all bays belonging to the soldiers and which the Vultures obviously hadn't wanted to

fool with—and grained and watered him under the lean-to shelter angling off the barn.

He chose one of the bays to help him with his burial detail. When he'd saddled the mount, he used it to drag his dead partners out to the creek that wound along the south end of the fort. He'd found a spade in the barn, and, removing his sweat-soaked shirt, began digging a hole in the sandy creek bottom, where the loose sand made for fairly easy work. He'd dig only one grave and roll the bodies inside. They deserved better, even young Strang, but they'd understand that it was all he had time for.

Shadows grew long there in the creek bottom, the water trickling along the bed's far side. A box elder growing up from a nearby island offered shade, but it was still hot, and the blackflies were biting. Spurr didn't push himself too hard, taking a couple of smoke breaks, pausing frequently to drink water and to nip from a brandy bottle he'd brought from Humphreys's ranch. His hair, beard, and sinewy, powder-white torso were slick with sweat.

He'd almost cleared a grave four feet deep and four feet wide when he stopped digging suddenly, dropped the shovel, and reached for the rifle he'd leaned against a boulder. Racking a round into the chamber, he brought the rifle to bear on the man sitting on the creek's far bank, on the other side of the box elder.

"You just hold it right there, you sneaky devil!"

"I been holdin' it right here," the half-breed said. "For the past ten minutes." He had his knees up near his bear claw necklace, his arms wrapped around them. He opened his hands as though to show that they were empty.

Spurr stared at him. He was the man who'd been shadowing him and the others. A half-breed, all right. Wearing buckskin breeches and a red-and-black calico shirt over his broad, hard chest and rounded shoulders. He could have been a full-blood, with that large, flat-featured face and hawk nose, but the jade-green eyes set off vividly by the cherry color of his sun-leathered skin said he had at least a quarter white in him. He was in his early or mid-thirties.

His stygian hair tumbled straight down from his low-crowned, flat-brimmed black hat to hang loose about his shoulders. On his feet were traditional, well-worn stock-men's boots. A horn-gripped pistol jutted from a holster thronged low, pistolero-style, on his right thigh.

A half-breed, all right. Something about the mix of white and red blood made for especially tough nuts. Spurr thought it might have been because most, straddling two worlds, belonged to no one but themselves. That, in turn, made them cold-blooded, devilish. The end of a small knife handle jut-ted just above his right shoulder, under his shirt, likely from a sheath strapped behind his neck.

The green eyes bored into Spurr, though a faint, casual smile had etched itself on the man's wide, handsome mouth. Spurr couldn't tell if it was a sneer or a real smile.

"One o' them that pride yourself on bein' quiet, huh?" Spurr lowered the rifle from his shoulder but kept it cocked. "So you can sneak up on white men and feel all proud about it, like an actual full-blood."

"I don't know too many full-bloods who can move as quiet as I can." The half-breed hiked a shoulder. "I reckon they don't need to."

"Who in blazes are you and why you been followin' us?"

"I been followin' Mason since Willow City."

"You the one saved his hide?"

The half-breed's eyes moved to Mason lying with the others about ten feet from Spurr's hole. "Wasn't much point, I reckon. Only got him a few extra days." He looked at Spurr. "I was tryin' to tell you about the ambush when that one there, the younker, started throwin' down on me."

Spurr looked at Calico Strang lying between Gentry and Web Mitchell. Like the others, the kid lay on his back, hands crossed on his bloody belly. His half-open eyes stared at the sky, the tip of his tongue nestled in a corner of his mouth. Spurr had the urge to go over and kick the young Pinkerton, who as much as anyone was responsible for the ambush.

But hell, he had the starch taken out of him now. For good. And there was no bringing the others back.

Spurr depressed his Winchester's hammer. "You one o' them shape-shiftin' Injuns or somethin'?"

The half-breed blinked at him dully.

"Thought maybe you could change yourself into a bird— somethin' like that. Since you seem to be keepin' such a good scout over all of us."

"One man alone can move quicker with less chance of bein' seen than a posse."

"Why you so damn secretive—keepin' to yourself on them ridges?"

"I sort of answered that, didn't I?"

Spurr narrowed an eye at the half-breed. "What's your piece of this? You a bounty hunter?"

The Indian shook his head. "Nope." He looked off. "I been a cowpuncher for the past four months for the Triple X brand outside of Willow City. I was sent to town for supplies when them Vultures busted their ramrod out of Mason's jail. Heard the shootin', saw the killin'."

"I don't get you, mister. You save Mason's bacon but don't show yourself till now, near a hundred and fifty miles outside of Willow City. I'll ask ye again—what's your stake in this?"

"I don't have a stake in it. I reckon I wanted to see some justice for the innocent men those Vultures killed. For the women they took. But I'm only one man."

"You coulda thrown in with us."

"And end up like them?" The half-breed cast his gaze once more at the dead men. Then he turned his sharp, cunning, suspicious gaze back to Spurr. "Besides, how do I know you're any more upstanding than them Vultures?" He smiled. "'Cause you wear a badge?"

He placed his big hands on his knees and straightened. He must have stood at least six foot three—an imposing figure of a green-eyed Injun. He wheeled and started walking away.

"Hey," Spurr yelled after him, "what the hell's your name, friend?"

The big Indian stopped and turned back toward Spurr. He stared hard at the old lawman for a time, shrewdly taking his measure. "Yakima Henry," he said and walked away.

"Yakima Henry," Spurr muttered, chewing on the name, then shaking his head. He set the rifle aside and grabbed the spade. "Never heard of you, mister."

TWENTY-ONE

---✳---

Spurr was beat when he'd finished burying his dead comrades. But his horse was rested, so, trailing the bay who'd helped with the burial, he pushed on. As he left the outpost, he saw the buzzards circling above the backside of a near rise.

"Rest easy, soldiers," he said, pinching his hat brim to the dead men.

He booted Cochise into a lope, following the Vultures' fresh trail up and down the hogbacks stretching like wrinkles in a paper fan from the higher, more rugged foothills of the Wind Rivers looming as though behind smoked glass in the northwest, their tips touched with white.

It was hard to get a fix on where they were headed, as, true to habit, they stuck to no trail. Like a pack of chicken-thieving, calf-killing coyotes accustomed to being hunted, they switched direction slightly but often.

Most likely, they were headed for South Pass City. It was the only town of any size around. Filled with rawhiders and ringtails of every brand, it was also the only town they could ride into without sticking out like pink tigers in a rodeo parade and load up with enough supplies to get them through a couple of months' hole-up amongst the high, snowy peaks.

Also, there was generally no law in South Pass City, as lawmen tended to simply disappear or contract lead poisoning not long after being sworn in. While there was a town marshal position in the rough-and-tumble jumble of unwashed humanity there along the old Oregon Trail, it was rarely filled by anyone but some twelve-year-old orphan or some whore having fun. That was how Spurr remembered it from a few years ago, anyway.

So the Vultures wouldn't have to waste any lead there, either, unless they wanted to, of course. Which they probably would.

Spurr holed up for the night in a wooded hollow between two hogbacks. After he'd tended Cochise and piled his tack near a run-out spring, he grabbed his rifle and headed out to look for supper. Most likely, the Vultures were well out of earshot.

He brought down a rabbit with one try, dressed it out, and spitted it over a fire he built of pine and fir branches. He sat against his saddle smoking and drinking coffee laced with brandy, watching the flames dance around the big jack and a pot of beans, unable to rid his mind of the images of his dead brethren.

Maybe that was why he had little wish to retire. What would he do—sit out on some flophouse porch, rocking and letting the demons dance around in his head until he became a simpering fool whizzing down his leg and flinching at the clangs of a blacksmith's hammer?

He'd known a lot of good men, most of them now dead. He was just sorry that Ed Gentry, Bill Stockton, and Dusty Mason were amongst them. Hell, he hadn't known Web Mitchell all that well, but even he and Calico Strang had had a right to grow old. Maybe Strang would have even made a man.

A soft thud rose from the darkness beyond Spurr's fire. Or a cracking sound.

Staring into the darkness, Spurr grabbed his rifle, rose with a grunt, wincing at his popping knees, and stepped off to the left of the fire. The noise had probably only been a curious deer, maybe a coyote—hell, maybe only a pinecone tumbling from a jack pine growing out of the far bank.

Still, he slowly, quietly levered a shell into his Winchester's breech, keeping his ears pricked, his eyes boring into the darkness beyond where the firelight stretched.

The sound came again. Spurr scowled. No, not a deer. And not a coyote. The thud or crack wasn't of the right pitch for either.

Spurr's eyes narrowed shrewdly. A faint smile took shape inside his gray-salted beard. "Maybe you ain't so quiet at night, eh, Henry?"

The sound came again, a little farther off.

The fire cracked. Juices from the rabbit popped and sizzled. Otherwise, silence down here in the dark, secluded hollow.

Concern poked around beneath Spurr's collar. Maybe it wasn't the half-breed out there. Had someone else heard the shot Spurr had used to take down the jack and been attracted by it?

Possibly the Vultures. Or, more likely, some other wolf on the prowl. God knew there were more badmen than only Stanhope's bunch rawhiding through Wyoming. Maybe earlier they'd seen an old man with a couple of horses that would fetch a nice price in South Pass City or Rawlins. Enough, leastways, for a tumble with a percentage gal, good whiskey, and a few games of stud.

That finger of apprehension continued to tickle the back of the old lawman's neck as he drifted farther left, away from the fire, then stole silently forward on his soft moccasins, heading toward the hollow's far bank. Whoever lurked out there was likely hunkered down behind a tree or a boulder, trying to draw a bead on the old-timer so they could steal his food and his horses.

Spurr ground his back teeth.

Another thud—closer this time.

Spurr whipped his head toward the left where he saw some of last year's fallen aspen leaves ruffle—like the surface of a calm lake disturbed by a skipping rock. A footfall sounded behind him and right, and he turned around, drawing his index finger back on the Winchester's trigger, to see someone dash toward his fire. He—no, *she!*—crouched over the flames, grabbed his rabbit off the spit, and bolted back in the direction from which she'd come.

The woman gave a painful groan, likely finding the rabbit a tad hot for tender hands, as she sprinted back into the darkness on the far side of Spurr's camp. He caught a glimpse of long, wavy, dark brown hair bouncing across narrow shoulders sheathed in a brown knit poncho, heard the legs of her baggy denim trousers scrape together as she ran.

Spurr bolted forward. "Stop!" He raised the rifle to his shoulder but held fire. What was he going to do—shoot a woman in the back for stealing his supper?

Knowing in the back of his mind that she could have been the bait in a deadly trap, he took off running in his shambling way. He ran along the edge of the firelight, then cut away from it and into the aspens, his way lit by starlight. Trees and rocks danced around him, black as ink.

He couldn't see or hear the camp-robbing woman, but the hollow's banks formed a bottleneck just ahead. There was nowhere for the woman to go but through it and into an open area that led to a creek. As he passed through the bottleneck, keeping the Winchester aimed from his right hip, he looked around.

Ahead, a thud sounded. The woman cried out. Spurr saw a dark shadow flailing around on the ground just in front of the creek on the surface of which starlight glistened like blue scales. A silhouetted horse stood on the far side of the

creek, turned toward Spurr and the woman now, lifting its
head and nickering fearfully. Spurr could see that its reins
were tied to the upthrust branch of a deadfall log.

"Hold it right there, you thieving little trollop!"

She was trying to clamber to her feet when Spurr grabbed
her arm and jerked her toward him, causing her long hair
to fly around her head.

"Please!" she cried. "I was hungry!"

Spurr stared at her. The starlight danced in her brown
eyes. He could see the pretty, heart-shaped face, the cuts
and bruises on her lips and one cheek, dark against the sun-
burnished skin. She had a one-inch, swollen gash above her
right brow.

"You," he said, recalling her name. "Mrs. . . . Wilde . . . ?"

After all that had happened since his leaving Humphreys's ranch, he'd forgotten about her, including the fact
that she'd lit out early that last morning, ahead of Spurr and
the others, headed west . . .

"I'm sorry," she said. "I was hungry. Please, let me go."

Spurr realized he still had a firm hold of her arm and
opened his hand. Her arm dropped, and she sank back away
from him. Her eyes stared back at him; they owned a wild,
animal-like fear. She had one hand wrapped around the
grips of a pistol wedged behind the belt securing her baggy
men's denims that she wore with the bottoms rolled.

"Just let me go," she whispered, scuttling slowly back
away from him on her butt.

"You have no cause to fear me, ma'am. Don't you remember who I am?"

He could see that she did, but she still continued to move
her hands and the heels of her moccasins across the gravel,
inching toward the creek and the horse flanking it.

As he stared at her, not sure how to quell her obvious fear
of him, she stopped suddenly, sank down on her rump. The
starlight flashed less sharply in her eyes. "I dropped your
rabbit. It was hot."

She turned onto her hands and knees, heaved herself to her feet, and started walking through the shallow stream.

"Ah, that ain't nothin'," he said, rising to a standing position and pitching his voice a little softer. "I bet we could find it, clean it off. There's enough for two. And a pot of beans."

She stopped midway through the stream. The water washed over her moccasins, making little white wavelets just above them. She turned toward him, her expression oblique there in the darkness with the nickering horse behind her pulling at his reins.

Spurr spread his arms, shrugging. "It's up to you."

He turned and started walking back toward his camp, casting a half-furtive glance over his shoulder. She remained standing there in the shallow creek, a nightbird calling from somewhere on the velvet-black escarpment beside her horse. Spurr continued walking forward, moving through the bottleneck in the rock wall. As he neared the glow of his fire, he found the rabbit lying in the brush, picked it up, and brushed it off.

He glanced behind once more, spying no movement. Then he continued on back to his camp, washed the rabbit off with his canteen, then returned it to its spit over the flames. He added a small branch to the dwindling fire, set the bean pot on a rock away from the flames, and poured himself a fresh cup of coffee.

He'd taken only one sip when he heard the slow clomp of hooves behind him. The woman's horse snorted. One of Spurr's mounts, tethered off to his right about thirty feet, loosed a whinny, and the woman's horse responded in kind as she led it into the camp.

She stopped there at the edge of the light, looking uncertainly, almost suspiciously around. "I'm alone," he said, setting his cup aside and climbing to his feet.

"I figured you were."

"Oh?"

"I saw what happened at the outpost."

She'd reported the information with an almost shocking lack of emotion, as if the carnage hadn't surprised her at all.

When she offered nothing more, Spurr took her steeldust's reins from her. "I'll tend your horse. You sit down there by the fire and dry your feet. There's coffee and an extra cup. A bottle, too, if you've a mind."

She hadn't looked at him since she'd entered the camp, but now she did, just brushing his face slowly with her eyes that now, in the firelight, looked vaguely haunted. Likely, she was exhausted from the long ride out from Humphreys's place, and probably still in shock from what the Vultures had done to her. Spurr couldn't fathom how she'd come so far, astraddle a horse, after all she'd been through.

He glanced once more at the pistol snugged down behind her belt, then stepped behind her and led her steeldust toward the trees where he'd tied his own. When he'd unsaddled the gelding with Cochise and the cavalry horse, he checked him over carefully as he rubbed him down briskly with a scrap of burlap.

After a few minutes, he returned to the fire, carrying the woman's saddle and bedroll. That was all she had. No saddlebags stuffed with trail supplies. No wonder she was hungry.

She sat across the fire from where his own saddle and bedroll lay. She'd taken off her mocassins and set them about a foot away from the fire. Barefoot, she sat with her legs bent in front of her, leaning forward, hands wrapped around her feet. She almost seemed to be in a daze, the vacant way she stared into the flames, tugging on her toes.

Spurr regarded her skeptically, not sure what to make of her, as he set her gear down beside her. She did not look up at him but only stared into the flames. Her pistol sat beside her on the ground.

He said, "You didn't get a cup of coffee."

"Just the food'll do me."

"It's probably done. Help yourself."

Without ado, she grabbed the two tin plates off the rock Spurr had set them on, and grabbed the stick skewering the rabbit. She laid the rabbit across both plates and, wincing and sighing as the charred meat burned her hands, pulled the jack apart, depositing half on each plate.

She set one plate down, then folded her legs Indian-style, set the other plate in her lap, and hunkered over it. She tore off a leg quarter, then picked small bits of smoking meat away from the bone, blowing on them before tipping her head back and dropping them into her mouth, chewing hungrily.

Sensing Spurr staring down at her, she looked up at him, frowning almost indignantly, then reached over, grabbed the other plate, and thrust it toward him.

Spurr took the plate. As she resumed eating, Spurr regarded her again curiously as he walked back around the fire and sat down against his saddle. She ate hunkered almost childlike over her plate, not looking at him and making no attempt to converse.

Touched. No doubt about it. Poor woman.

What in hell would he do with her?

TWENTY-TWO

"You're still going after them—alone?" Mrs. Wilde asked Spurr later as she finished eating and set her plate aside, brushing her greasy hands across her sun-faded, dusty denims.

"I reckon I am at that," Spurr said with a sigh.

"Are you a good tracker?"

"Few better. Maybe Kit Carson, but he's dead."

"Then I'm going with you." She stared across the fire at him. Her face could have been made of granite, for all the emotion it displayed. No emotion, only hard resolve.

Spurr studied her as he ran his last bit of rabbit around in the last of the beans on his plate with his fork. "So that's what all this is about—you being out here."

She gave an expression as though he'd been crazy to question it. "Oh, I have to get my boy back. He's probably terrified half to death. He's all I have, you see. I'm all he has."

Spurr stared across the glowing coals at her. "But I thought . . ."

He let his voice trail away, instinctively knowing that he should leave the thought unfinished. Maybe he was wrong in his assumptions; maybe the Vultures really did have her son. But . . . no, he was sure that the undertaker in Sweet-water had said they'd killed him and he was waiting to bury the child if and when his mother returned.

Spurr looked at her again, saw her sitting there near the fire, examining one of her moccasins. As preoccupied as a child. All at once, a great bubble of sorrow rose up from his belly, and he tried to swallow it down while tears came to his eyes. The sorrow lodged in his throat like a hard pine knot, and he quickly raised his cup to cover it.

He cleared his throat, sipped his coffee twice, tears streaming down his cheeks, and swirled the cup to busy himself.

The poor woman.

Her son murdered in front of her eyes, and the only way she could keep from unraveling entirely was to allow herself to believe the Vultures had him, and that she would get him back.

"You do the tracking," she said suddenly, jolting him out of the incomprehensibly sad thoughts swirling through his head, against his will visiting the woman's own suppressed suffering, "and I'll do the cooking."

She smiled, squeezing the toe of her left moccasin, trying to return some pliance to the old doeskin. "And I do apolo-gize for stealing your rabbit, Marshal . . ."

"Spurr," he said thickly.

"Marshal Spurr. That was shameful. I was just fright-ened. Amazing what fear can drive a person to do. Before tonight I'd never stolen so much as a sewing thimble!"

"You don't need to fear me, Mrs. Wilde."

"Please, do call me Erin." Her eyes snapped wider. "My closest friends do. And I have a feeling, knowing now that I can trust you, and that you're a thoroughly decent

man—having offered me food even after I stole from you—
that we're going to be friends."

Spurr swiped a tear that had made its way through his
beard to dangle off the end of his chin. "Don't you think,
Mrs. Wilde . . . that perhaps I should ride on alone after your
boy? I mean, you've never done anything like this before,
I'd wager."

"Nonsense. Jim is going to need me there to comfort him
when he's rescued, and to take him on back to Sweetwater
with me. I'm sure he's terrified, but I've prayed to the lord
our savior to keep him strong and to let Jim know that I'm
here. Right behind him. And when I . . . er, *we* . . . get a
chance, we're going to swipe him away from those brigands,
and he and I will return to Sweetwater, and I'll fix my boy
his favorite meal—fried chicken, creamed garden carrots,
and milk gravy for his 'tatoes."

The pine knot grew larger and harder in Spurr's throat,
but he managed to say, "I reckon he'll be more than ready
for that, ma'am."

"Erin."

"I mean, Erin." Spurr added a splash of whiskey to his
coffee, trying desperately to assuage the sorrow that was
making him as sick as sour milk, his heart quivering, and
frowned across the fire at her. "You saw what happened to
the other lawmen, did you?"

"Yes, I'd stopped my horse along the creek," she said
plainly, pulling a sock onto her right, bare foot, grunting
softly with the effort. "I heard the shooting and looked up
to see the soldiers tumbling off their horses."

Her eyes turned bright, and she smiled painfully as she
drew the sock up to her calf, then grabbed the other one off
the rock she'd draped it across. "I hope Jimmy didn't see
that. I think he was in one of the buildings, or maybe Miss
Tate was caring for him somewhere a ways from the fort."
She sniffed and gazed across the fire at Spurr. "Surely

Stanhope's men aren't so callous as to allow a child to be
privy to their depradations. They simply couldn't be—could
they, Marshal Spurr?"

He'd forgotten about the whore whom the Vultures had
kidnapped in Willow City. The poor girl must still be in the
Vultures' talons, if she was still alive.

"Most likely, you're right, Erin."

He wondered why she thought the Vultures would have
the boy, anyway. What worth could little Jim be to them?
Of course, Spurr had no inclination to voice his question.
The woman he was sharing his camp with had had her wits
dulled by an overload of sorrow. He almost envied her.

And he hoped for her sake that she never got them back.

The next day, in the early afternoon, Magpie Quint stared
through the field glasses he'd stolen from the soldiers he and
the others had gunned down at the Elkhorn Creek outpost
and said, "Well, I'll be hanged!"

Clell Stanhope was on his knees beside a narrow but
hard-running creek tumbling out of the stretch of low,
wooded mountains they'd been riding through, holding his
head under the water tumbling down from a beaver dam.
He turned to Quint now, opening his eyes as the water continued to wash over him, soaking his beard and pasting his
hair against his head. "Didn't your ma say somethin' like
that?" the outlaw leader mocked. "Just after she done
squeezed you out?"

The others, drinking or washing along the stream,
chuckled.

"Just after she squeezed him out and tried to shove him
down her privy—'cause he was so damn ugly!" Lester Stanhope added, tossing his wet head and laughing too loudly,
lower jaw hanging nearly to his skinny chest.

The others stopped laughing and cast him dubious
looks. The dull-witted brother of their leader was an embar-

rassment to them all. They put up with the scrawnier, younger of the two Stanhopes for obvious reasons, though Clell himself often had to resist the temptation to drill a .44 ball through his younger sibling's head.

And he would have, too, if he hadn't promised their dear mother on her deathbed to look after the turnip, as god knew he wasn't able to fend for himself. He could rape and kill just fine. It was the little things like securing food and lodging that he struggled with, just as their dear old pa had, as well.

Clell himself took after his mother—a Tennessee mountain woman tough as a hickory knot and meaner than a shoat with its tail dipped in tar.

Quint, perched on the steep side of a ridge about thirty feet up from the stream and its narrow canyon, glared down at Stanhope and the others. "All right, never mind," he said with feigned indifference.

"Never mind what?" Stanhope said, pulling his head out of the falls.

Quint let the glasses dangle from the cord around his neck and began making his way down the steep ridge, his black coat blowing out around his long, black-clad legs. Not looking at the others, he adjusted his black, broad-brimmed hat as he stepped around the boulder, heading for the horses gathered between him and the other gang members. His faded red vest fairly glowed in the crisp light.

"Ah, come on, Magpie!" Clell said, wringing his hair out as he faced the man he considered his first lieutenant despite the man's thin skin and generally pissy nature.

"No, that's all right. You fellas would rather laugh and jeer and taunt like a bunch of six-year-olds than take anything serious."

The other men looked around at each other, chuckling sheepishly.

"Magpie, for chrissakes!" Clell said, setting his hat on his wet head. "Don't be that way. What'd you see?"

Magpie leapt from a low ledge to the bottom of the canyon, then walked over and deposited his field glasses in his saddlebags. The others watched him, waiting. Magpie didn't look at them but appeared to be concentrating only on buckling his saddlebag flap.

Hector Debo slicked his short black hair down with his hand and set his sugarloaf sombrero on his head as he stepped out away from the river. "Come on, amigo—we apologize, huh? We were just havin' a little fun."

"Yeah, we was just havin' a little fun," added Lester Stanhope. "I was just kiddin' about you bein' ugly. Hell, you ain't no uglier than Hector here."

He laughed at that. But he was the only one. Debo gave him a half-tolerant look, then turned back to Magpie. He and Quint had been partners several years before they'd thrown in with Stanhope's group during a raid up in Montana, so they were closer to each other than to the rest of the group.

"You fellas are too much, you're just too much," said Magpie. "I'm right tired of all your funnin'. Might just ride on alone—to hell with you." He walked over and took his time untying his reins from a stunted cedar.

"Oh, for chrissakes!" Stanhope stomped on over to Magpie's black-and-white pinto, unbuckled the saddlebag flap, and pulled out Magpie's field glasses.

"Be careful with them, Clell," Magpie said, his reins in his hand, his indignant look in place. "I took them myself— they're mine. And I don't want 'em gettin' broken."

"Ah, shut up, ya damn Nancy boy," Stanhope said, pulling the glasses out of their case, dropping the case to the ground, and heading up the ridge. "Can't take a damn bit of funnin'. Well, this group likes to have a good time, and if your skin's too damn thin, I suggest you pull foot." He stopped halfway up to where Magpie had been and turned an angry look back to the sore-headed Quint, who was sulkily leading his horse up along the trail skirting the creek.

"But don't expect to be ridin' off with any of that bank loot, by god. You quit this group, you quit your cut, too!"

"Yeah, that's right, brother Clell," Lester said. "You quit the group, you ain't gettin' your cut, Magpie!"

"Shut up, Lester!" Clell said with a weary air as he continued climbing the ridge. The elder Stanhope wasn't worried about the big, black-and-red-clad killer leaving the group. Because of his thin skin, he often threatened to leave the group when his feelings were hurt, but they'd likely catch up to him farther up the trail, and all would be well with Magpie and the gang in no time.

A couple of the other riders—Red Ryan and Doc Plowright—climbed the ridge after Clell.

"Well, I'll be hanged," Clell said after he'd stared through Magpie's binoculars. "Is that who I think it is?"

"Who do you think it is, Boss?" asked the tall, red-bearded Ryan, running a finger across the gold spike in his right ear.

In the two semicircles of magnified vision, Clell watched two horseback riders trot their mounts along the edge of the creek about a quarter mile east of the Vultures' position. A man and a woman. At least, the second rider, riding behind the man, appeared a woman though she wore men's shabby trail clothes and a man's brown hat. But she was willowy, and she had two nice-sized lumps in her flannel shirt. And long brown hair bounced across her shoulders.

Stanhope had no idea who the woman was, but, as he adjusted the focus wheel on the army-issue field glasses, he brought up the grizzled, patch-bearded features of the man riding a big roan ahead of her, until the name Deputy U.S. Marshal Spurr Morgan fixed itself in the outlaw leader's brain.

He smiled and said almost fondly, "Ole Spurr."

"Say again, Boss," said Red Ryan, standing next to Stanhope.

"You remember ole Spurr Morgan, don't ya?"

"You mean we got that old mossyhorn doggin' us *again*? Must be the third or fourth time."

"Third," said Clell, grinning as he handed the glasses to the big, burly redhead. "We must be one helluva thorn in that old lawdog's side. Heard tell he was once—some say he still is—the best lawbringer in Henry Brackett's remuda."

"Ah, hell," said Doc Plowright, scratching at a food stain on the wool vest he wore over a grimy red undershirt, a set of human teeth dangling from the twine hanging around his stout neck. "He's older than the Rockies themselves!"

"Gotta remember," said Ryan, staring through the field glasses, his brown teeth showing inside his beard, "he almost always rides solo—too ornery for a partner, they say—and he's the only lawman that ever even came close to catchin' up to us." He poked his tongue through the gap between his two front teeth. "Wonder who the woman is. Can't make her out from here."

"Prob'ly some whore," said Plowright. "He's an old whoremongerer, Spurr is. Said he married up with a squaw once, long time ago, before the war."

Clell said, "You know, fellas—maybe it's time someone taught Spurr this is a young man's country. Old mossyhorns like him just don't have what it takes to survive out here. They're like old bull buffs; only thing is, unlike the buffalo, they don't have sense enough to just wander away and die."

Red Ryan smiled delightedly at the leader of the Vultures. "So, chew that up a little finer for us, Boss."

"Red, how would you and Doc like to ride back and fetch that old lawman for me?" Clell slid his bowie knife from his belt sheath, flicked his thumb across the razor-sharp blade. "Might be time to show the lawbringin' bastard how much of an old fool he really is—thinkin' he can bring down the Vultures alone. Insultin' us like that. Maybe relievin' him of both his whore and his topknot, and sendin' his scalp back to ole Henry Brackett along with the whore's head, would finally convince him it's time for ole Spurr to go, and that the Vultures ain't no bunch to be trifled with such as that!"

Red Ryan and Doc Plowright chuckled and shook their heads, always fascinated by their indominatable leader's refreshing ideas.

"But don't you kill him—understand?" Clell said, jerking the bowie's hooked point up beneath Plowright's chin. Gritting his teeth angrily, he added, "No, don't you dare kill him. I don't want him dead. I want him brought to me alive, so I can carve him up myself—understand?"

Both men said they did.

Then they ran down the ridge, swung up onto their horses, and galloped back in the direction from which they'd come.

TWENTY-THREE

Red Ryan gigged his big claybank up the narrow canyon's sloping north ridge. Doc Plowright followed close behind, both men glancing down canyon toward where they'd seen through a screen of willows the two riders crossing over from the stream's south side to the north.

Spurr and the woman riding with him.

Since they were following the Vultures, they'd likely pass along the bottom of the north ridge in about five, maybe ten minutes, judging by how far away they'd been when Ryan had last seen them, and by how fast they were riding. They were only walking their horses. Spurr had had his head canted toward the ground, keeping an eye on the Vultures' hoofprints.

Ryan's broad, sunburned cheeks above the bleached red beard rose in a self-assured smile. He could just see him and Plowright taking down the old badge toter, riding him tied to his saddle up to Stanhope and the others, who'd elected to ride on as it was getting late in the day and they wanted to reach the abandoned ranch shack before sundown—just one of many hideouts they used when they were running roughshod over this stretch of Wyoming. A well-hidden place in a canyon just west of here, about twenty miles from the next town along the trail, South Pass City.

Near the top of the ridge, a limestone finger of rock jutted from a wagon-sized escarpment that was aproned with scree. The scree appeared fairly firm, with a game path angling through it, and the two Vultures followed the faint, narrow trail up and around behind the finger. Both men dismounted, led their horses back into the cover of several boulders, tied the horses to scrub cedars, and slid their Winchesters from their saddle boots.

Ryan stepped out from the boulders to the blocky chunk of sandstone, edged a look around the right side of it toward the canyon floor. The stream ran down the middle of the canyon, sheathed in sage and willows. It didn't run as fast here as it had farther upstream, where Ryan and Plowright had left the other Vultures. And it was a little wider and shallower, stippled with rocks around which it licked up white froth.

Ryan gently levered a shell into his Winchester. Plowright flanked him, holding his own rifle high across his chest in his thick, beringed hands.

Ryan glanced toward another large chunk of rock jutting from the slope about thirty yards ahead and also aproned with scree. He glanced at Plowright. "Doc, head on over yonder. If I miss the old dog from here, you'll get another shot at him from over there."

"I thought we wasn't supposed to kill him."

"I don't intend to kill him," Ryan said. "Just wing him, get him off his horse. Hurry, now, goddamnit, before he shows!"

"I don't take orders from you, Red. I don't believe your name is either Clell or Stanhope, but seein' how I see you got a point on this one, and I'm a big enough man to say so, I'll do your bidding." Plowright offered a bitter smile. "This time. But you'll be buyin' me a beer and a whore in South Pass City."

"The hell I will," said Ryan, his own eyes shining with acrimony. "I don't owe a goddamn thing to no Missouri fool with shit between his ears. Now, git, Doc, before you make me mad." He edged his rifle barrel slightly toward Plowright's chest.

Doc looked at the rifle, licked his lips, and flared his nostrils. "This ain't over, Red."

"For now it is."

Plowright tugged on the brim of his filthy hat, from which thick, tangled brown hair tumbled over his torn coat collar, and walked away, crouching down to keep out of view from the canyon. Ryan gave a caustic chuff. Nothing quite like bedeviling that heel-squattin' Missouri trash. Ryan himself hailed from Kansas, though he'd hightailed it when he was only twelve. If he'd been going to pull on teats the rest of his life, it sure wouldn't be cows' teats! He pressed a shoulder against the sandstone, peered out around the side of it and into the canyon.

He could hear the creek chiming over the rocks, the rising and falling sigh of the breeze, and a distant crow cawing. That was all. The only movement was the breeze-brushed willows and the occasional lifting of dust along the trail, well churned by prospectors' wagons.

He looked straight across the slope. Plowright was just now moving out from behind a hump of rock and dropping to one knee behind the boulder that Ryan had directed him to. Plowright glanced at Ryan, made a lewd gesture, then turned his head to stare down into the canyon.

Ryan grinned, then jerked his head back suddenly behind the large chunk of sandstone when he heard the clomping of horse hooves. Snapping his rifle to his shoulder, he dropped to a knee and aimed down into the canyon.

The thuds of the shod hooves grew louder. A horse appeared, trotting along the trail. Ryan gritted his teeth and tightened his finger on the Winchester's trigger, then slackened it. The horse had no rider. Its reins were tied to its saddle horn, the stirrups bouncing freely.

Just as Ryan's heart kicked up nervously, "Hold it," sounded from close behind him. A gravelly, raspy voice pitched low.

Ryan froze though his heart went wild, beating erratically.

The man behind him kept his voice down as he said, "You call out, Red, and I'll blow your head off."

Ryan looked across the slope toward where Plowright knelt, aiming his own rifle down into the canyon but staring toward Ryan. He was too far away for Ryan to see the expression on Doc's face, but he knew the man was wondering about the riderless horse—the horse whose rider was now somewhere behind Ryan himself, likely not more than ten or fifteen feet away.

"Shrug, Red."

"Huh?"

"You heard me," said the man behind Ryan. "Shrug to your friend over there. Do it now, or I'll blast you into little bits—won't be enough left to send home in a croaker sack."

Ryan stretched his arms out and hiked his shoulders. He hoped Plowright would see the tense look on his face, but his partner merely turned to stare down into the canyon, then straightened and moved around to the other side of the boulder. Ryan could hear his boots clacking on the slide rock.

"Move back toward me, Red," said the man behind him.

Ryan sighed, considered making a try with his rifle.

"This your day to die, Red?" asked the man behind him, as though it were a serious question.

Ryan stepped back behind the boulder, then turned around to see Spurr Morgan on one knee atop a flat-topped boulder, about five feet behind and above Ryan's own cover and out of sight from Plowright. Ryan's and Doc's horses milled in the shade of the rocks beyond Morgan, switching their tails and twitching their ears.

Spurr stared down the barrel of his old-model Winchester, narrowing his aiming eye so that Ryan could see the blue of the orb just over the rifle's fore and rear sights. The lawman's bearded face was as weathered as an old, abandoned barn, but the eyes looked alert, calmly menacing. A stubby mole grew out of one of his grizzled brows.

Ryan felt the heavy weight of a fool descend on him like a blacksmith's anvil. He'd let the geezer get the drop on him by using the oldest trick in the West. How had the old lawbringer seen him and Plowright climb the ridge from that far away?

"Seen your dust, Red," Spurr explained, reading the would-be bushwhacker's mind. He chuckled. "These peepers still got some seein' left in 'em. Now, why don't you go ahead and ease the hammer down on that rifle and lean it against the base of my rock here."

Ryan sighed again, more raggedly this time, as he saw the cold stare the old man was giving him down the barrel of his cocked Winchester. If Red Ryan couldn't figure a way out of this, he was done. The thought was as raw as the chafing from a new pair of denims on a long, hot ride through rough terrain. Maybe Doc could do something, once he figured how the old lawman was playing them. If he ever did, that was.

Ryan set the rifle aside.

"Now them pistols."

Ryan held his hands shoulder high, fingers curled toward the palms. "Why should I, Spurr? You got the drop on me, but I might could snap off a shot before I give up the ghost."

"You might could," Spurr agreed, not blinking as he stared down his rifle barrel. "But prob'ly not. You'll just die, Red. Back to the dirt from whence you come."

"Hell, I'm dead, anyway."

"Who are you—god?"

"Ah, Christ!"

Ryan winced as he turned his head to stare back in the direction of Plowright. But he couldn't see his partner from this angle behind the large chunk of sandstone. Spurr had him. The thought of dying right now, right here, was a hard, cold rock in his belly. Before he knew what he was doing, he was sliding his three pistols from their sheaths and tossing them into the brush growing up around the base of Spurr's boulder.

"You old mossyhorn," Ryan said with supreme frustration. "Ain't you ever heard of retirin'?"

"Retire? Hell, Red, retirin's just a sad, slow way to die." Spurr rose to a crouch, glanced toward Plowright, then, keeping his rifle aimed on Ryan, sat down and dropped his legs over the edge of the boulder. He took his rifle in one hand and pushed himself off the rock, dropping straight down to the ground in front of Ryan, bending his knees and cursing with the impact.

Ryan jerked forward, intending to take advantage of the lawman being off balance for a second.

"Uh-uh," Spurr said, jerking his rifle back up and clasping his left hand around the walnut forestock. "Eyes still got some seein' left, the old legs still got some jump in 'em. Step back if you don't want an extra belly button."

"What about Doc?"

"That's Plowright over there? Well, hell, I reckon I'm gonna have to go over and say howdy-do shortly." Spurr recognized all the Vultures from their wanted dodgers, much in circulation over the past five or six years. "Wouldn't be polite not to." He kept back just out of quick-lunging range of Ryan, his Winchester aimed straight out from his right side at the big redhead's rounded belly. "Where's the rest of your gang headed?"

Ryan smiled without mirth, shaking his head. "Can't tell you that, Spurr."

"Where's your hideout, Red?"

"Now, I sure as hell can't tell you *that*."

"Why not?"

"If you don't kill me, Stanhope will. *Slower.*"

"To hell with ya, then." Spurr lurched forward and before Ryan could do more than widen his eyes in shock, smashed his rifle barrel across the big killer's left temple, bending his hat brim down over his forehead.

Ryan's chin dropped and his knees buckled. He fell hard at Spurr's feet, out like a blown lamp.

A rifle barked three times in quick succession. The reverberations batted back and forth between the canyon ridges. Spurr lurched forward, stepped over Ryan, and peered down the steep, talus-slick slope to see Doc Plowright crouched about halfway down the ridge, aiming a rifle into the canyon and back along the trail a ways, in the direction from which Spurr had sent Cochise.

Keeping his cheek pressed against his rifle's stock, Plowright shouted, "Come on out of there, Spurr, or the woman dies!"

TWENTY-FOUR

Spurr cursed and looked down the slope. On the canyon floor, Erin Wilde's steeldust was spinning in a flurry of rising dust. The woman was on the ground on the far side of the trail. As the horse swung around once more, mane flying, it pointed itself up trail, whinnied shrilly, and galloped off in the direction in which Spurr had sent Cochise.

When he'd climbed the ridge through a sloping trough, he'd left the woman in the canyon, hidden behind a bend in the northern wall. She must have gotten restless and ridden out into the canyon to see what had become of Spurr.

Well, now she knew, damnit.

Spurr bit his lower lip as she pushed up onto her elbows and peered up the slope through the still-wafting dust at Doc Plowright bearing down on her with his Winchester. Plowright triggered two more quick shots. The woman twisted around and lowered her head, shielding herself with an upraised arm, as two more bullets blew up dust and gravel within a foot of her.

"I got her dead to rights, Spurr!" Plowright shouted,

casting a quick glance up the slope at the lawman flanking him, as Doc savagely levered a fresh cartridge while ejecting the spent one. It clinked and rattled briefly on the scree.

He pressed his cheek up against the stock once more, steadying the rifle on the woman, who was now looking up over her arm.

Spurr chuffed in disgust. "Goddamnit."

His old heart chugged as he slid his glance between Plowright and Erin Wilde. She stayed down on the trail, knowing that if she tried to run the gunman would kill her. Spurr measured his chances at drilling Plowright before Doc could kill the woman. The brigand seemed to read his mind, as he cast a cool glance toward the lawman and showed one eyetooth between his thin lips mantled by a brushy brown mustache.

"You kill her, I'll kill you, Doc!" Spurr set his sights on the side of the rifleman's head, just above his ear.

He wanted to take the shot. But there was a good chance that Plowright would trip his own trigger and drill a round through Erin. He didn't know what else to do, however, so he tightened his trigger finger. The faint ching of a spur sounded behind him. His blood chilled, remembering Red Ryan.

A rifle cracked. For a quarter second, he thought he'd fired his own Winchester but then he felt the bullet burn along the side of his head, just over his right ear. The jar spun him around on his heel, and he whipped his rifle around to see the hatless Ryan staggering toward him, his rifle aimed out from his hip, blood smeared across his left temple.

He ground his teeth and lowered his cocking lever but before he could rack a shell, Spurr triggered his Winchester, knocking Ryan back against the boulder from which Spurr had first gotten the drop on him. Ryan screamed as he rammed the cocking lever up against the underside of his rifle and, screaming again, triggered the rifle down low, blowing the toe off his left boot to reveal a bloody nub poking up out of his white sock.

That bullet blew up shale a foot in front of Spurr.

Down on his butt, Spurr raked out another frustrated curse, brushing his hand against the side of his head, and ignoring the blood on his glove, twisted around to gaze down slope. Plowright was running down the slope toward the canyon, howling like a crazed coyote. Erin lay where she'd fallen, propped on her elbows and looking dazed behind the screen of her mussed hair.

Spurr raised his rifle and fired while lying on his hip. Both shots were long, striking the canyon trail beyond Plowright. One came close enough to cause the outlaw to lose his footing on the scree; one of his boots slipped out from beneath him, and he hit the ground hard on his ass.

Spurr fired again too quickly. His bullet blew the hat off Plowright's head. The outlaw left his rifle on the ground, palmed one of his pistols, and snapped a quick shot toward Spurr, the bullet twanging off scree to Spurr's left.

Then Plowright heaved himself to his feet and set off running down canyon toward Erin. Spurr climbed to a knee and, ignoring the burn of the bullet across the side of his head, aimed toward the running cutthroat. He removed his finger from the Winchester's trigger and raised the barrel. Plowright was in line now with Erin, and Spurr was liable to hit the woman with a ricochet.

He knelt there, staring in dread.

On the canyon floor, propped on her elbows, Erin watched the crazed desperado running toward her, howling. Near the foot of the slope, his boots slipped out from under him again, but he quickly regained his feet, dropped onto the trail running along the base of the ridge, and ran toward where Erin had been deposited by her horse.

He was the man whom she'd heard called Doc. He was

the one responsible for the cut over her left brow. He'd smacked her while he'd lain between her legs for no more reason than he'd wanted to inflict as much pain as possible.

Fifteen feet away, Plowright stopped suddenly, boots skidding in the dust, throwing his arms out for balance. He stared in shock down at Erin, recognizing her. He held his pistol negligently in his right hand.

"Well," Plowright said, chuckling softly under his breath. "I'll be damned."

"You got that right, mister."

Erin wrapped her right hand around the pistol wedged behind her belt, and slipped the gun out from behind her waistband. Plowright regained his shocked look and snapped his pistol toward her. Erin took her own revolver in both hands and steadied it. Plowright fired, his slug screeching past her ear and thumping loudly into the ground beside her. Erin centered her pistol's sights on the man's chest, but she must have nudged the gun high at the last quarter second.

At the same time that the pistol roared, nearly leaping out of her aching hands, Plowright twisted around, lower jaw hanging, blood blossoming from his left cheek as blood and white bits of teeth blew out the other cheek and onto the trail.

"Gnaahhh!" the desperado cried. It was like a gargle, and it caused more blood to spew out onto the trail.

Erin bit her lower lip as she raked her revolver's hammer back with both thumbs and steadied the gun on the outlaw. She fired just as Plowright gave a garbled curse and jerked toward Erin, and her bullet blew off his right earlobe before spanging off a rock a few feet up the canyon slope.

Plowright's shot sailed far wide as he screamed again, twisted around, and dropped to one knee before lunging back to his feet and staggering off up the trail. He started howling again but not with victory; he was howling now like a dog with its ass peppered with buckshot.

Erin gained her feet, ignoring the ache in her twisted left

ankle, and stumbled forward, gritting her teeth, remembering the hard, taunting, sadistic look in the man's eyes as he'd pounded against her. She thought of Jim—poor Jimmy, probably used as a slave by these cutthroats to gather wood and tend their horses.

The image of her poor son amongst these killers jerked an exasperated scream out of her throat, and she stopped suddenly about ten feet behind the stumbling Plowright and raised the revolver. She thumbed the hammer back. Doc must have heard the ratcheting click of Erin's pistol because he stopped and turned half around, eyes widening when he saw the gun.

"No!"

His cry was punctuated by the revolver's belch. The slug punched through his collarbone, sending him staggering back and dropping his chin to watch the blood oozing from his shoulder. He fell on his butt and lay flat on his back, shaking his bloody head and grinding his heels in the trail. He was no longer yelling, just whimpering and staring at the sky as though for help that wasn't likely to come.

Meanwhile, Spurr had worked his way down the ridge. He walked over to where Erin stood a few feet from Plowright, holding the gun straight down in both hands, sobbing.

"Good," Spurr said, placing a hand on her shoulder while gazing grimly down at Plowright. "You done real good, Erin."

She looked at him, sniffed, then turned full toward him and frowned. She placed her hand hand against the side of his head. "Spurr . . . you're . . ."

He took her hand in his, lowered it. "Cut myself worse shavin'." He gave her a reassuring smile and then, spying movement in the willows along the creek, shoved her aside and raised his rifle, loudly racking a shell into the chamber.

"Come on out of there!"

His heart twisted and lurched. If the other Vultures were

part of Plowright and Red Ryan's ambush, he and Erin had likely come to the end of their trail.

The willow branches bobbed and swayed around a broad, round face sheathed in a white beard streaked with gunmetal gray. Two eyes blinked beneath a leather hat brim.

"Why, I'll be hanged!" the lurker said as he pushed up out of the brush, sort of stumbling toward Spurr and Erin, the mule ears of his high-topped boots buffeting. He was clad all in buckskins, with dyed porcupine quills adorning his big-front buckskin tunic. If he was one of the Vultures, he was one Spurr didn't recognize—and one even older than Spurr himself. The graybeard said, "Should have known if there was gunwork around, ole Spurr Morgan wouldn't be far behind!"

Spurr studied the oldster moving toward him, felt his jaws loosen. Slowly, absently depressing his rifle's hammer and lowering the piece, he said, "Chris? That you, you old scalawag?" Relief washed over him like a cool, refreshing breeze.

"Sure as mad around a hornet's nest!" Chris Nordegaard came hobbling up out of the brush, lowering his old Sharps carbine and poking the brim of his ragged leather hat back up off his broad, liver-spotted forehead. Before the war, he and Spurr had once worked for a stage line up along the Platte River, and they'd gotten together after the war to hunt game two summers for the Central Pacific Railroad. They'd run into each other a few times since, but it had been a good six, seven years since they'd seen each other last.

Nordegaard stopped in front of Spurr, sniffed and snorted, and slid his gaze from Spurr to Erin and back again. "How you been, you ole lawdog? Still sportin' that badge, I see. Still shootin' up the territory." Chuckling, he glanced down at Plowright, who was still struggling as though against invisible hands pinning him flat on his back. "What'd this one do?"

"He's done enough," Spurr said. "What in the hell you doin' out here, Chris? Last I seen you, you was homesteadin' down around Camp Collins."

"Wildfire burned me out. My wife, Two Stabs, knew of a quiet spot left here in the shadow of the Wind Rivers, so we come out here to raise a few sheep and get old in peace. *Been* peaceful, too, till I heard you shootin' up the place. Shoulda known it was you causin' all that racket. Could hear that thunder all the way to my cabin yonder." He glanced at a narrow ravine mouth gouged into the ridge on the opposite side of the stream.

Both men fell silent as Erin walked around Plowright, glancing down at him stonily, then walked off toward where her and Spurr's horses grazed off the side of the trail, about fifty yards away.

Chris glanced sidelong and wolfishly at Spurr. "She, uh . . . yours, you old buzzard?"

Spurr stared after the woman, who, with each step she took up the trail, favored her right ankle more and more, until she groaned and dropped to the opposite knee, wrapping both hands around the ankle in question.

Spurr walked over to her, as did his old trail partner, Nordegaard, and crouched beside her, wrapping an arm around her shoulders. "Best rest that ankle, Erin. We'll find you some shade over by the creek, wrap a bandage around it."

She looked up with chagrin at the old lawman. "I'm sorry I didn't hold my position like you said. I guess I just lost patience. I have to get to Jimmy, Spurr. I don't have time to rest this ankle. Will you fetch me my horse?"

"Like ole Spurr says," said Nordegaard, crouching on the other side of the the woman, "you'd best rest that ankle. Might be broken."

"It's not broke." Erin sucked a sharp, painful breath and squeezed the ankle once more, sobbing. "I have to keep moving. My son needs me! Please, Spurr—fetch my horse."

Spurr stared at her. He was on the verge of telling her that her son was not with the Vultures, but he wasn't sure what the news would do to her. If she'd even believe it.

"Come on, now, Erin. We've ridden far enough for one day. You can't ride with that ankle. We'll rest it a night, then . . ."

"No!"

"Now, Erin, them other Vultures might be close, and we can't linger out here flappin' our jaws. I'm afraid I'm going to have to insist we hightail it back to Chris's cabin." He glanced at his old friend, and when Chris didn't object, he continued: "We'll get us a blow and pick up their trail bright and early tomorrow."

"Damn!" the woman cried angrily. "They're close, Spurr. They must be real close!"

"If it's the Vultures you two are after," Nordegaard said, warily looking around, "they're *too* close if they're anywhere west of Denver."

Spurr glanced at his old partner. "You got a horse over yonder?"

"I got a wagon *and* a horse over yonder."

"Good. Can you help Mrs. Wilde to it, and take her on back to your digs?" Spurr didn't want to involve his old partner in his trouble with the Vultures, but the woman needed food and shelter, and she needed her ankle tended. In the back of Spurr's mind he was hoping she wouldn't be able to continue fogging the cutthroats' trail. She'd be safer with Chris, and Spurr could continue trailing the Vultures without having to worry about her.

"Sure, sure. My Two Stabs—don't worry about the name; she's over all that—will know just what to do about that ankle. Come on, honey. Just wrap your arms around ole Chris, and I'll carry you over to my wagon. It ain't much, but I got some buffler hides to make the ridin' softer."

Spurr grabbed his friend's beefy arm clad in a badly

smoke-stained buckskin sleeve. "Chris," he said, giving the man a grave look. "Might be trouble."

"With you, when's there ever ain't been trouble?" Chris scoffed as he picked up a sobbing Erin in his arms. "We'll head on back to my cabin. If you can still track, you old catamount, you'll find us."

TWENTY-FIVE

Spurr looked down at Doc Plowright, who lay groaning and mewling and turning his head from side to side in agony. Blood dribbled from his ear, the lobe of which had been shot away, and from his upper right chest and both cheeks. The dirt and gravel beneath him was as red as a red-velvet settee in a plush whorehouse parlor.

The killer stared dimly up at Spurr, who said, "I can't do nothin' for you, Doc. Even if I wanted to, which I don't."

Plowright stopped moving his head to glare up at the old lawman. He spat a large gob of blood through his lips, then said as though around a mouthful of rocks, "Red dead?"

"Red's deader'n hell."

"You ever thought of retirin', you old mosshorn?" Doc said, wincing as pain spasmed through him.

"You know, Red asked me the same thing—just before I killed him."

A faint smile curled the desperado's bloody lips.

"No use you an' him facin' the fires of hell alone," Spurr

said. "Where're the others headed? Where's your hideout, Doc? The Wind Rivers, I'm guessin'."

Another little, dark smile curled Plowright's upper lip. "You go to hell, you old bastard."

All at once, his eyes turned opaque, a long sigh gurgled up from his throat, and his body fell slack.

"You first, Doc." Spurr looked up the trail. No sign of the other Vultures. They must have been so sure that Red Ryan and Plowright could take Spurr and the woman down that they'd ridden on ahead.

How far?

Spurr and Erin had caught up to them unexpectedly. Lucky they hadn't ridden right up on them. The gang must have taken their time after leaving Elkhorn Creek, maybe celebrated the killing of the soldiers as well as Mason and the other lawmen in one of the ravines they'd holed up in. Earlier that morning, Spurr had found several whiskey bottles along one such encampment.

Good to know that now they were only a few hours away.

Or was it? He thought of Erin and old Chris and the wife he'd mentioned. Best if Spurr didn't linger here but rode on early the next morning. There was a good chance that when Red Ryan and Doc Plowright didn't show up at their next camp, Stanhope would send more of his group back to look for them.

Spurr thought about that as he dabbed at the bullet burn above his ear with his neckerchief, staring down at Plowright. He gave a little chuff of satisfaction, then walked up the trail and fetched Cochise from the patch of grama grass he was grazing on.

Then he grabbed the reins of Erin's steeldust. His extra bay was grazing along the stream down near where Spurr had told Erin to stay until he'd called for her. He'd pick up the army remount later. For now, he had a chore to finish out the afternoon with . . .

A half hour later, he'd led Plowright's and Ryan's horses down the ridge, Red Ryan draped over his saddle and secured to the stirrups with ropes. Spurr swung down from Cochise's back, took a hard pull from his brandy bottle, then back-and-bellied Plowright over the cutthroat's own saddle. When the exhausting chore was finished, the old lawman ate a nitroglycerin tablet washed down with whiskey, then slapped both horses' asses.

He dug in his pocket for his makings sack and rolled a smoke as he watched the mounts gallop on up the trail through the heart of the narrow canyon, along the pictur-esque little stream bubbling through wolf willows. The dead men's heads and arms flopped stiffly down the horses' sides. They drifted around a bend and disappeared.

"There you go, Clell, you son of a bitch," Spurr said, firing the quirley and sucking the acrid smoke deep into his tired lungs. He trickled the smoke out his leathery nostrils. "Now you don't have to worry about 'em."

"She sleeps," said Two Stabs, Nordegaard's current wife in a long line of wives, most of them Indian women. This one was a Ute with cool brown eyes, a birthmark under her right eye, and a thin mouth that curved downward. Spurr figured she was about ten years younger than Chris, who was five years older than Spurr. "She will sleep the night with the tea I gave her."

"How's her ankle?" Spurr asked the woman from the couple's kitchen table. Chris sat across from him, smoking an Irish clay pipe.

"Swollen," said Two Stabs, taking the basin of water to the cabin's open front door and tossing the water into the cool mountain night. "But the bone is not broken, I think." She turned from the door and gave Spurr a direct look, odd for an Indian woman, as he'd usually found them shyly indi-rect. She'd probably learned Chris's directness. "She fought the sleep, and she will try to walk on the ankle before it is ready. She keeps saying the name of a boy—Jimmy." Two Stabs arched a brow. "Her son?"

"Yeah." Spurr sipped his coffee and poked a fork around on the tin plate littered with the leavings of the antelope steak and potatoes that the Ute woman had prepared and that had more than adequately filled the old lawman's belly.

Chris puffed his pipe and spoke around the stem. "Vultures got him?"

"No." Spurr shook his head. The coffee spiced with his own bourbon suddenly made his gut sour. "She thinks they got him, but the boy's dead."

"The hell!"

"Somehow she got it in her head the boy's alive and ridin' with the Vultures and she has to save him." Spurr shook his head slowly and looked around at the spare, humble cabin outfitted with a hodgepodge of hand-hewn furniture and animal hides on the floor and stretched on the walls. There was the smell of wood smoke and the coal oil lantern flickering from a ceiling support post and hanging opposite a massive rack of elk horns. "I haven't had the heart to tell her the boy's dead. Seems to be all that's keepin' her alive— the prospect of gettin' little Jim back."

Two Stabs had refilled the basin from a bucket of water and sat with a weary sigh in the hide-bottom chair next to Spurr. "Does she have a man?"

"Dead, too." Spurr lifted his quirley to his lips but jerked his hand back down when Two Stabs pressed a wet cloth to the side of his head. "What're you doin' there?"

"I am cleaning your cut. Don't be stubborn. It needs cleaning. You already have a barrelful of dirt in it, mixed with the blood."

Embarrassed by the woman's ministrations, Spurr glanced at Chris, who smiled around his pipe. "If anyone needs tendin' in this ole tipi, Two Stabs's gonna tend 'im and there ain't nothin' you can do about it but sit there and take it. Mind her name—she mighta got it long ago but she got it for a reason."

"Ouch!" Spurr hissed when the woman dabbed too hard at the burn.

Two Stabs arched her black brows, regarding him dubiously. "What—you are going to start to cry now? That would be a display for a man who wears a badge."

Spurr submitted once more to the woman's tending as he scowled across the table at Chris. "Where in hell'd you find this one?"

"Hell, I didn't find her. She found me—knocked me over me head, hog-tied me, and here I sit!"

Chris slapped the table and laughed nearly silently, jerking his shoulders. Spurr snorted while the woman clucked and shook her head as she continued cleaning the shallow wound. When she finished, she retrieved a tin of homemade salve that smelled like coal oil and skunk piss—it probably was!—and rubbed it brusquely into the cut while Spurr scowled and ground his teeth while old Chris continued to laugh.

When the woman tamped the lid back on the tin and rose from her chair, Chris winked at her. "Don't expect me to be sharin' my woman with you tonight, Spurr. I know it's traditional amongst Two Stabs's people, but it ain't tradition in this house!"

He slapped the table and started to howl, but Two Stabs sushed him with: "Hush, you old fool! The woman sleeps!"

With a castigating chuff, but also wearing an embarrassed flush on her still-handsome face, she headed up the stairs that rose from the far right side of the cabin to a dark loft with a full-log rail. Spurr watched her as she climbed the stairs, holding the hem of her colorful skirt above her ankles, moving slowly, tender with age, the wooden steps creaking softly beneath her. Her long black hair, threaded by only a few strands of gray, fell straight down her back.

At the top of the stairs she became a shadow melding with the loft's darkness until she lit a red lamp.

Watching her, Spurr felt sadness creep into him though he wasn't sure why. Maybe he wouldn't mind having a woman like Two Stabs—a woman he could watch retire at night, after he'd sipped coffee around the table with her, chatting about the day's events and whatnot. Maybe that's something he'd given up and regretted now, just as he regretted not lassoing Abilene when he'd had the opportunity.

"Reckon I'll sleep out yonder," he said, rising with a grunt from his chair, pushing himself up with both hands on the table. Thrusting the regret back down deep inside him. "I'll be able to keep watch out there, in case we have any unwanted visitors tonight."

"You'd best sleep, lawdog."

"I will sleep, like I always do." Spurr grinned at his old friend, who looked a stranger now with his thick gray beard and only a few strands of coarse gray hair swept back from an age-spotted widow's peak. "With one eye open!"

But he didn't sleep. Not right away. He sat back in one of the two rocking chairs on the cabin's front stoop, his blanket roll pulled up to his chin, stockingfeet crossed on the porch rail before him, and stared at a distant storm flashing over the Wind River Range looming blackly in the north. He felt the refreshing chill in the air, smelled the rain.

Long after the cabin's lights had been extinguished, he heard someone moving around in there. The front door clicked. Chris Nordegaard stepped out wrapped in a robe, his white beard fairly glowing against the darkness, leaving the rest of him a murky silhouette.

Instantly, Spurr smelled licorice. Chris had something in his hand. He walked over and held it out to Spurr.

"What's that?"

"Medicine pouch. Two Stabs ground some roots and herbs for you."

Uncertainly, Spurr took the hide sack in his hands, the rawhide cord sewn into the pouch's neck dangling down against his blanket.

"She says it's for your heart," Chris said quietly, standing over Spurr, holding his hands together in front of the round paunch pushing out his bathrobe.

Spurr looked up at the man, incredulous. The lawman hadn't mentioned his ticker. A wave of emotion swept over him, making his tongue thick. He looked at the pouch, then lifted the rawhide thong over his head.

"I'll thank her in the morning," he said hoarsely.

Chris walked to the cabin door and stopped, glanced back at the old lawman. "We all gotta die, Spurr."

Spurr jerked a surprised look at him. Irritation slithered up out of the loneliness and regret, and the tenderness he was feeling toward Two Stabs, for going to so much work for him. "What the hell's that supposed to mean, hoss?"

"Ain't that why you keep workin'—trailin' gangs like the Vultures? 'Cause you're afraid to hang up the irons? Well, you get you a woman, Spurr. Makes the process a whole lot easier."

Spurr saw his old friend give him a wink and a half grin before Chris opened the door and went inside, softly latching the door again behind him.

Spurr blinked tears from his eyes, his chest heavy and raw. He thought of Abilene for a time, and he felt like a fool when he heard himself sobbing, but he finally managed to sleep. He woke surprised—how much later he didn't know— to hear the door of the barn slide open on the other side of the yard.

So much for sleeping with one eye open!

Could it already be time for Chris's morning chores?

Hooves clomped, echoing woodenly inside the barn. Then the silhouette of a horse and rider passed out the open door before swerving sharply to Spurr's left. The horse bounded off into the night.

Spurr was still half asleep, fisting sleep from his eyes, wondering where in hell Chris was headed so early in such a hurry.

The fact that the rider wasn't Chris dawned on him at the same time the door opened and Chris's voice said, "That Mrs. Wilde done slipped out the back, Spurr!"

"Again?" the half-asleep lawman said, pushing to his feet. "Ah, hell!"

TWENTY-SIX

Erin dropped low over her horse's neck and gave the mount its head. The wind blew her hair, caressed her face. The night air was cool. The stars swept a purple-blue swath across the heavens, so the horse had little trouble picking its way back along the trail that she and Mr. Nordegaard had taken in his wagon the previous afternoon.

She couldn't remember how far they'd come from the main canyon—she'd been too preoccupied with getting to Jim, as she was now. When the horse stumbled as they traced a particularly dark part of the trail, however, she checked it down to a trot. If the horse went down, her chance of retrieving Jim would be lost. She couldn't walk far on her twisted ankle.

She had to be patient.

Patience wasn't easy, but she tried to concentrate on her surroundings as she put the horse across the stream that threaded the main canyon and onto the trail. It was here that she'd shot Plowright, though she couldn't see the killer's body. Maybe Spurr had buried him.

She let all thoughts of Plowright and the other men she'd killed pass through her mind like water over a beaver dam. As she booted the horse along the trail, she closed her hand over the handle of the Remington revolver wedged behind her belt. The solid weight of the gun was reassuring. After she'd dressed in Nordegaard's back bedroom, having slept a couple of relatively refreshing hours, she'd made sure to reload the revolver from the shells she'd stuffed into the pockets of her denims.

Now it was loaded and ready to go. Ready to assist her in rescuing her son.

She wasn't sure where she was going. She let the horse pick its own way. The Vultures had to be close around here. She and Spurr must have nearly ridden right up on them earlier in the afternoon. That wouldn't have bothered her even if it had gotten her killed. It would have been worth it for just one more look at Jim.

Nonsense, she thought now, turning her head to rub her cheek brusquely across her shoulder. If she died, Jim would die. She had to remain rational. And careful. If the Vultures caught her again, neither she nor Jim would have any chance at all.

She scoured the ground for tracks, and she saw a few but only irregularly and only where the starlight shone brightest on open ground. Swinging her head from right to left, she probed the dark, rolling land for lights—lights of a cabin or the lights of a cookfire.

Ahead lay a hogback ridge with a notch in the top. The trail that she was following—if it was a trail and if the horse wasn't just following its nose—rose toward the notch. Upon reaching it, the horse breathing hard from the climb, she saw that she was on a low pass, with a field of boulders strewn along both sides of the trail, deadfall lying amongst the rocks like giant jackstraws that glowed eerily in the starlight.

Beyond the boulders, menacing black forest stretched toward high ridges.

Rocks rattled to her left. Erin drew back hard on the horse's reins. "Whoa, boy," she whispered. "Whoa!"

A shadow moved on a ledge about ten feet above the trail on her left. A man! Erin closed her hand over the revolver's grips, slid the gun from her pants. A keening screech erupted. It filled her head, blurred her vision, rattled her eardrums painfully. Her heart leapt into her throat.

When the sound was abruptly clipped, she saw the silhouette of the bobcat against the stars as it took long, fluid strides up the side of the ridge to a cabin-sized boulder. It was outlined briefly against the sky, curling its long tail, before it dropped down the boulder's opposite side and disappeared into the pines carpeting the long, steep slope rising toward a granite spire that shone pearl blue in the starlight.

Normally, running into a wildcat while riding alone in the middle of nowhere would have scared the hell out of Erin Wilde. Now, however, her heart slowed with relief that she hadn't been caught in a trap set by the Vultures.

She booted the horse on down the ridge. At the bottom, she stopped the horse again suddenly, sniffing the air. There was the slight tang of wood smoke. The slight breeze was out of the north. She stared across a long, flat stretch of pale desert stippled with cedars and sage.

There were no lights but the arching stars. But since the breeze was from that direction, the smoke had to be coming from that direction, as well.

Tension tightened her shoulders. But eagerness made her breathing shallow. It took the pain from her twisted ankle. She turned the horse off the trail's right side. She followed the scent of the wood smoke for half a mile, finding that the flatland wasn't as flat as it had appeared.

Ahead lay a ravine bristling darkly with trees. It angled out of some chalky bluffs on the right. Probably a creek at the ravine's bottom. Maybe a cabin. The occasional whiffs of wood smoke were growing stronger.

Erin followed a deer path down the side of the ravine and into the trees that started about halfway to the murkily forbidding bottom—twisted conifers and aspens. It was cooler down here. The air was humid, and she could smell the pungency of a slow-moving stream. As she'd expected, the creek twisted along the ravine's bottom, glistening darkly through black, weblike branches.

There didn't appear to be a cabin down here. Nor a camp. Maybe up the other side? She could tell from the smoke that the fire wasn't far away.

Dismounting, Erin tied the horse to an aspen sapling along the stream's muddy shore. The twisted ankle barked when she put weight on it, but she'd have to ignore it. She couldn't ride the horse up out of the ravine without risking giving herself away.

Hobbling, chewing her cheek, keeping one hand on the handles of her pistol still wedged behind her belt, she crossed the stream and gingerly climbed the opposite bank. She continued to try to ignore the ankle, but she could feel it growing warmer, swelling. A nerve like an angry snake kept striking.

She cursed it, cursed herself for the impatience that had led to the injured limb, and dropped to both knees three feet from the crest of the bank. As she edged a look over the top, she gasped and reflexively jerked her head back down.

She'd seen lights against the outline of a broad, low structure of some kind.

Her heart beat almost painfully in her throat, in her ears. Licking her lips, sliding the pistol out of her pants, and holding it firmly in her right hand, she lifted her head above the lip of the bank.

Indeed, a cabin sat about a hundred feet away, on a broad, flat area amongst the chalky buttes. It was built of stones and logs, with a slightly pitched brush roof. Starlight reflected off bits of other structures behind it, including a corral in which horses milled, the starlight shining like dull sequins on the backs of a few. Only one was moving restlessly, trotting in circles, pale dust rising.

Erin could see four of the cabin's windows from her vantage—two in the front, two in the right-side wall. The shutters were thrown wide against the cabin. The two windows in front were brightly lit. The nearest one in the sidewall was dimmer, the fourth one, near the shack's rear, was dark.

Erin's mother's instinct told her that Jimmy was in that dark room. Probably locked inside. But she might be able to get to him through the window.

Patiently, she held her position for fifteen minutes, looking around carefully for any sign of patrolling Vultures. The only movement she saw besides the restless horse, however, were the shadows of men behind the cabin windows. Their voices emanated, chillingly familiar, on the cool, silent night.

Wincing at pain stabbing up from her ankle, Erin gained her feet and stole up out of the draw. She limped across the yard, holding her pistol down low in her right hand, where the starlight was less apt to find it. Someone inside the cabin laughed raucously, and there was a thudding sound, as though someone had slapped a table, followed by the chinking of gathered coins.

"If I find you been cheatin', little brother, I'm gonna cut both your ears and your pecker off!" Clell Stanhope's distinctive, mocking voice stopped Erin in her tracks. A chill swept her, lifting gooseflesh across the backs of her arms.

Fear gripped her. It was like an invisible hand shoving her back toward the ravine and her horse. Why not wait there for Spurr?

Because he likely wasn't crazy enough to try what she intended—to slip into the cabin and pluck her son away from the Vultures at the risk of her own life. No, a rational person would not do what she must do. Only a mother would attempt what she was attempting.

Pushing forward against the unseen hand splayed across her chest, she limped ahead. Boots thumped loudly inside the cabin. The front door scraped open. Her heart pounding, Erin froze and dropped to both knees in the yard about fifty feet in front of the cabin, staring in horror at the shadow moving on the stone stoop that was propped on short, stone pylons.

Erin crouched low, pressing the pistol against her right knee. Her heart hammered like a piston as she watched the shadow stop at the front edge of the stoop, just over the two stone steps. A pin-sized light glowed beneath his hat. Smoke wafted in the darkness as he stood there at the edge of the stoop.

Erin gritted her teeth.

Had he seen her?

The man grunted. There was a soft rustling of cloth, another grunt. Then she saw a thin arc of reflected starlight, heard the wooden dribbling of the man's urine against the ground.

Erin stared at the man, her eyes wide, silently willing him not to see her against the dark velvet of the ravine behind her. He peed for an excruciatingly long time, the stream giving out gradually, sporadically as the man grunted and pivoted his hips and bent his knees.

Finally, with one last grunt, he tucked himself back into his pants, turned, blew smoke into the darkness around his head, and clomped back inside the cabin from which the other men's voices and the chinking of coins continued to issue.

Drawing a deep breath, Erin rose and continued to limp more quickly across the yard toward the side of the cabin. At the front corner, off the end of the stoop, she stopped. Two long, dark objects lay before her. She crouched down until she could see the face of Doc Plowright. Beside him lay Red Ryan. Neither man wore a hat. The fetor of blood was so strong that Erin slapped her free hand to her throat, suppressing a gag.

She dragged her injured ankle around the dead men—how had they gotten here?—and continued limping down the side of the cabin. She stopped suddenly, turned sharply right, hearing a soft gasp escape her throat.

Crouching down along the side of the cabin, she stared into the ambient light and shadows around the corral and what appeared a small stable. She'd heard something. None of the horses was moving now. Nothing moved around the stable or, as far as she could tell, around the buttes jutting pale as flour behind and around it.

She could have sworn she'd heard something—a man's low whisper.

She remained crouched there for five minutes, trying to listen above the slow, hard thudding of her heart in her ears. Finally, convinced that what she'd heard had only been in her mind, she rose slightly and stole down the side of the cabin to the second window.

Its shutters were closed. She could have sworn they'd been open a few minutes ago. It was too dark back here to have seen clearly.

Erin lifted her head, tried to peer between the boards in the window's left shutter. She thought she saw a slight movement through the crack. Eager anctnicipation made her groan, and she said in a loud whisper through the crack, "Jim? Is that you, Jim? Oh, Jim—it's your mother!"

Both shutters burst outward, slamming against her head and throwing her backward. Two large hands jutted from the opening, and grabbed her shirt. She stared, awestruck, at two tattooed vultures pushing toward her beneath two dark, glistening eyes. Stanhope's lips spread to show white teeth inside his beard as he guffawed loudly.

"I reckon you didn't get your fill of us—eh, little ma?"

Erin screamed. She tried to bring her pistol up but realized that she'd dropped it when Stanhope had grabbed her. She tried to fight free of his iron grip, feeling her shirt slip down off her shoulder, and saw in the periphery of her vision three men strolling toward her from various points in the yard, all holding rifles down low by their sides.

Stanhope had posted pickets, after all. They must have seen her and were waiting for their rabbit to walk back into their lair.

The Vultures' leader's sawed-off shotgun hung from his stout neck, dancing against his chest.

She gave another agonized scream, kicking and fighting wildly, as a loudly laughing Clell Stanhope pulled her through the window and into the cabin.

TWENTY-SEVEN

A harrowing scream cut the night.

A woman's scream. By its pitch and duration, it seemed to express all the sadness and horror in the earth and the cosmos. It echoed shrilly for a long time, leeching into the old lawman's brittle bones.

"Whoa!" Spurr jerked back on Cochise's reins. He'd left the spare horse with Nordegaard.

He looked around, trying to pick the original scream out of its echoes. Blood pumped in him. Fear. Sorrow that the scream conveyed was a heavy weight against the back of his neck, a cloying smell.

It had come from the north. Spurr reined Cochise off the trail he'd followed from the Nordegaard cabin, having to take his time so as not to lose it in the darkness. He booted Cochise into a dangerous gallop across a sage- and cedar-stippled flat, swerving around the shrubs and occasional boulders. At times he could see beneath him by starlight the tracks of shod hooves.

The hooves of Erin's horse.

He reined up at the edge of a deep, inky-black ravine. Looking around, he saw where Erin had dropped down from the tableland and into the cut. Anxiety clawed at the old lawman. Urgency. She could be dying while he debated his course of action.

He made a conscious effort to calm himself, slow his thinking. If he rode down there at a breakneck pace, he could not only kill Cochise but risk riding into the Vultures' trap and getting himself killed without being able to do a thing for Erin.

He slid his rifle from its boot and heaved himself out of the leather. He dropped the reins, patted Cochise's sweat-lathered neck. "Stay here, boy."

Slowly, he followed a game trail down the steep slope, taking mincing steps so he wouldn't slip on occasional patches of gravel. At times, he could barely see his feet. With his free hand, he reached out and grabbed small tree trunks and branches to break his momentum. All the while, he looked around, expecting to see the flicker of a campfire but there was nothing except darkness nearly as dense as that of a well bottom.

On the breeze was the faint smell of wood smoke.

Erin's scream echoed in his head. He knew it was her. He recognized her voice. Something told him it hadn't been a scream of terror. It had been an expression of unbearable agony.

Like the agony of a mother learning that she'd deceived herself. That her boy hadn't been alive as her mind had fooled itself into believing, that little Jim was dead.

Equal to Spurr's anxiety was his sorrow. A close second was rage. He wanted to go in blasting at the Vultures, to kill as many as he could and in the process snatch Erin out of their clutches as she'd wanted to take back her boy. But if he went about it in such a corkheaded way, he'd only get himself and probably Erin killed. If she wasn't already dead.

At the bottom of the steep, twisting trail, he stopped to

rest his legs. His knees and thighs ached. He drew a deep breath and did not like the whine of his tired lungs. They sounded like an unoiled winch.

"Gonna have to go easy on the tobbaco, I reckon," he whispered to himself, knowing he wouldn't.

Drawing another breath that squeaked like some little animal in his shirt, he walked forward but stopped after only two steps. He dropped to a knee. He'd heard the quiet ring of a spur off to his left.

Raising his Winchester slowly, he resisted the temptation to rack a shell into the chamber. The scrape could be heard for a quarter mile along this silent ravine. He'd let his opponent or opponents make the first move.

He didn't have to wait long. A gun boomed and flashed about twenty feet away, on the other side of a darkly glistening stream. The slug spanged loudly off a rock over Spurr's right shoulder. The rifle's report reverberated between the slopes, dying slowly as though sucked straight up to the stars.

Spurr pumped a round and fired at the red spot only now fading from his retinas. In the flash of his own fire he saw a pair of legs and spurred boots flying behind a rock. The man had known Spurr would fire at the man's own blast, but he'd thrown himself to cover only a half a second before Spurr's slug would have drilled him.

As it was, the slug hammered a tree but even before the echo of the shot had died, he fired three more shots toward where the killer had gone to ground. He couldn't see enough to know if he'd hit anything, so on the heels of his third blast, he threw himself hard to the left with the desperate abandon of a much younger man.

He paid for it, too—the racking pain hammering through his left shoulder and hip. Something prickly ground into that knee. Knowing he couldn't lie here and cry over his aches, he heaved himself to his feet and bolted straight up the ravine, running hard, holding his rifle in one hand and pumping his arms and legs.

Behind him, the killer's gun sparked in the night once, twice, three, then four more times. The slugs slapped the water to Spurr's right, thumped into the brush, cracking branches. One slug screamed off a rock, and a shard ground itself into Spurr's right cheek.

He brushed the shard away and dropped behind a tree growing at a dark angle from the left ravine bank.

"He's down here!" shouted the gunman now sixty or seventy yards away from Spurr, though the lawman couldn't see him in the darkness. The man laughed crazily. "Hey, Spurr, that you? Why, you old devil—we got the telegram you sent!"

Spurr raked air in and out of his lungs. Sweat dribbled down his cheeks. His heart chugged tiredly, racking his ribs.

"Hell, we got *both* of them telegrams you sent strapped over their saddles!" shouted a voice up the slope on the far side of the stream. This man, too, laughed. "You might still got some hunt left in you, old dog, but you're all alone out here or I miss my guess!"

The big talker was likely Clell Stanhope. While he'd been gassing, Spurr had heard the thudding of men running around atop the ridge, several pounding down the side, rustling brush and cracking branches. Desperation hammered him. Even with Ryan and Plowright gone to Glory, Stanhope must have seven or eight men left.

Seven or eight hungry Vultures—unabashed man killers.

Spurr wished he had another hand or two. Chris Nordegaard had wanted to ride along with him, to back his play, but Spurr had refused. Chris had been a good hand with a shooting iron in his day, but he was even older than Spurr now. And Spurr wasn't about to allow Two Stabs to become a widow on his behalf.

He grabbed a rock and hurled it down the canyon where most of the thrashing was concentrated. When he heard it splash dully in the shallow stream, he took off running farther up canyon. He had nowhere else to go, but he hoped the rock would confuse the Vultures if only slightly.

They were shouting at each other behind him. Water splashed and brush crunched. Someone took a shot—a pinprick flash of stabbing light that Spurr spied out the corner of his eye. The shooter had fired toward the far bank and the trail down which Spurr had ridden.

A germ of optimism sprouted in him. They weren't sure where he was. He could hear Stanhope shouting straight down the ravine behind him, and a couple of others farther down the ravine. Others, however, were making their way toward Spurr, but he could tell from the sounds that they weren't moving very fast.

Wary of an ambush.

Spurr got an idea. He turned into the stream, swung around, and triggered four shots quickly from his hip. The shots echoed, one screeching off a rock, another making a chugging sound in the stream. One evoked a clipped yell, and the old lawman gave a wry grin as he turned and started up the north side of the ravine, opposite the side he'd come down.

He had to find Erin. It was his fault she was here in the first place. He should have told her that her son was dead and sent her back to Sweetwater. She'd have been crazy with grief, but she'd have been alive.

Downstream, the shouting grew louder. Guns barked and flashed. The slugs splashed in the dark water that Spurr had left. Halfway up the bank, feeling as though his heart was in his throat and strangling him, he stopped and hurled two rocks and branches into the creek, a few feet beyond where he'd fired. They'd think he'd run on up the canyon. He hoped they'd left their camp unattended, and that he'd find Erin there.

Alive.

He sucked a long, deep breath, wincing against the stabbing pains in his chest and, pushing off his knee with one hand, holding his rifle in the other, he continued ascending the bank through the brush, moving as quietly as he could in his winded condition. Sweat engulfed him, trickled like ice chunks down his back. While the shooting and shouting continued behind him, he paused at the top of the bank and dropped to a knee.

He sleeved sweat from his brow, drawing painful draughts of air into his lungs that felt little larger than prunes, and saw lights to his right. Lamplit windows shone about sixty yards back the way he'd come.

"Oh, lordy," Spurr wheezed, heaving himself to his feet. "If you're up there, whoever you are—Jehova, Great Father, the Four Winds—I could sure use a hand 'bout now. Know I don't deserve it . . ." He tugged his hat brim down and began jogging toward the cabin, the words bouncing out of him with each clawing breath. "But the woman sure does."

He wouldn't scout the place as thoroughly as he normally would. No time. He only hoped the woman was there, alive and alone. And that the Vultures didn't savvy his ploy. If not, at least he'd take a few of these bastards with him to hell's smoking gates. He hoped Clell was one of them. He owed Dusty and the other murdered lawmen that much.

The cabin looked dilapidated—probably only used by Stanhope. An old ranch house, long abandoned. As Spurr ran to the wall facing him, he looked in a window, saw a mess of saddle gear, strewn trash, an old deal table, several chairs, one leather one that had likely been left by whomever had built the place. There was a small hearth but it wasn't lit; a coffeepot smoked on a monkey stove in the middle of the shabby living area.

Spurr ran around the back of the place, hoping for a back door. He found one hanging off one leather hinge. As he reached for the handle, he glanced toward the corral and

stable flanking the place. His heart lightened. A saddled
horse stood outside the corral, tied to a slat, whipping its
tail up and down and sideways and craning its neck to look
toward Spurr. It had probably been used by one of the Vultures for keeping watch from a ways beyond the hideout.

Spurr pulled the door open, found himself in a dimly lit
hall, with the main area ahead, lit by guttering lamps. He
could hear nothing, no one, except the Vultures continuing
to shout and shoot along the ravine.

Keeping his voice pitched low, Spurr said, "Erin?"

He moved inside, walking down the short hall paneled
with vertical boards, some of which were missing. The stove
must not have been well vented; smoke hung thick, watering
Spurr's eyes. There was a curtained doorway on each side
of the hall. He swept the right curtain aside, saw nothing
but the shadows of a few sticks of haphazardly arranged
furniture. He swept the left curtain away from the frame,
peered into the dark room quickly, then let the curtain drop
back into place. Turning back to the room, he looked in once
more, saw a silhouette on the floor. Aiming his rifle guard-
edly, he stepped into the room and crouched over the woman
lying on her side, facing the far wall.

She was fully clothed but with her wrists and ankles tied.
Spurr recognized the brown serape and the baggy denims
with the leg bottoms rolled. Thick hair hung in loose waves
around Erin's shoulders. Spurr could see by the starlight
pushing through the room's single window that her eyes
were open. They shone like the water had shone at the bottom of the ravine—dully glistening. She didn't move.

Spurr's heart chugged. Dead . . . ?

"Erin?"

He knelt beside her, closed a hand over her shoulder. She
recoiled slightly.

"Erin, it's Spurr." He licked his lips, squeezed her shoulder harder, vaguely surprised by her lack of reaction. "I
come to get you out of here."

"Leave me here, Spurr," she said in a hauntingly dull voice.

Spurr remembered the scream that had drawn him here. She knew about the boy.

"Can't do that." Quickly, glancing at the window and then at the curtained doorway behind him, he leaned his rifle against the wall and drew his bowie knife from the well of his right moccasin. He sawed through the ropes binding the woman's ankles and wrists, then returned the knife to its sheath.

"Can you walk?"

"Please leave me, Spurr." Again, her voice was dull, startlingly lifeless. "I don't want to go with you."

"Look here, damnit, Erin—I rode out here to get you back, and by god I'm gonna do it."

He straightened, grabbed one of her arms, and crouching, pulled her up over his left shoulder. With a grunt, he staggered to the wall, grabbed his rifle, then swung toward the door. He stopped just in front of it. Running footsteps sounded outside the cabin, spurs ringing raucously. Breaths rasped. Then the man was pounding across the porch and into the cabin's front door.

"Senorita?" a man called, breathless but buoyant. His voice, Spanish accented, was pitched high with mockery. "Are you alone, senorita? The old lawman hasn't come for you, has he?" He tittered girlishly.

His boots thumped as he moved forward.

TWENTY-EIGHT

Spurr whispered a curse. Stanhope had sent a man back to check the cabin.

The man's boots thudded slowly, crackling grit on the trash-littered floor, the spurs now ringing faintly, floorboards squeaking under the Mexican's weight. Spurr had already racked a shell into his Winchester's breech. Now, without setting Erin down—she hung limp as laundry over his shoulder—he stepped through the curtain and thumbed back the rifle's hammer.

The Mexican stopped at the end of the hall, silhouetted against the lamp and candlelight. He held a rifle negligently in his left hand, obviously still expecting Spurr to be in the ravine yonder.

His jaw dropped. Spurr gave a cold smile and squeezed the rifle's trigger. The report was like a thunderclap in the close confines. The Mexican yelped as the bullet slammed him up and back. He hit the floor with a bang. He groaned, softly, and moving his legs slightly, painfully, he lifted his hands toward the blood-spewing hole in the middle of his brown-and-red-striped serape.

Erin had jerked with a start at the rifle's report, but now she flopped helplessly down Spurr's back, too wretched even to struggle against his assistance. He wheeled, strode as quickly as he could down the hall and out into the night, angling toward the corral. Eerily, the shooting in the ravine had fallen silent, and only one man was shouting though Spurr couldn't hear what he was saying.

Most likely, the Vultures had heard the shot and were switching course for the cabin. Spurr moved quickly, sort of hobbling as he closed on the saddled horse, which danced away from him and pulled against its tied reins. The other horses trotted around, manes glistening in the starlight.

Spurr leaned his rifle against a corral post, then lifted Erin into the saddle. "Oh, Spurr, leave me."

"The hell I will!" Anger burned in him now—at both her and the Vultures. His anger for Erin was tempered with tenderness, but he had not come all this way to allow her to throw herself to the wolves.

As she leaned sideways in the saddle, threatening to tumble to the ground, he said, "Grab the horn!"

She shook her head weakly and opened her mouth to speak, but he cut her off with an enraged, *"Grab it!"*

She did, sobbing. He grabbed his rifle, then untied the reins and stepped into the saddle behind her. As she lolled back against him, he ground his heels into the horse's flanks and lit off in the direction he'd come. He'd no sooner passed the cabin and saw the furry black gap of the ravine stretching beyond it than guns began thundering and flashing.

"There he is!"

Spurr raised his arms on either side of Erin, shielding her somewhat, and shouted, "Ha-yahh, horse! H-hahhhhh!"

Bullets screeched around him, zinging off the ground on the other side of him, ahead and behind. The horse faltered,

and a cold stone dropped deep in Spurr's belly as he thought
the beast had been hit. But the horse regained its stride and
barreled off into the darkness angling gradually toward the
ravine that was a broad, black line on Spurr's left.

The flashing of the guns drifted off to his left flank, and
then, mercifully, the bullets were falling short, thudding into
the ground twenty, thirty, forty yards back in the direction
of the cabin. Spurr swung the horse directly toward the
ravine and trotted along its bank before finding a game path
down into its murky, inky depths.

When, fifteen minutes later, he climbed up over the opposite bank, the horse blowing and snorting, the woman still
lolling back against him, he stopped the mount. He looked
back at the dark ravine. A menacing silence issued from its
other side, from back in the direction of the Vultures' cabin.

Would they pursue him tonight in the darkness or wait
for morning?

Spurr had to assume they'd come tonight. He rode on out
across the flat a ways, then stuck two fingers between his
lips and whistled. He did not wait but turned the horse and
booted it into a canter to the west, in the direction of South
Pass City. When he and the woman had ridden a quarter
mile, Spurr heard thuds behind him and turned to see the
big roan galloping toward him, snorting and blowing and
rattling the bit in his teeth.

Spurr stopped the outlaws' mount and swung down from
the saddle, turning to Cochise, who stood obediently before
him. "Figured you'd blown the coop after you heard that
lead swap." He really hadn't. The horse was well trained.
The old lawman was just chattering to ease his nerves. He
lifted Erin off the outlaws' mount and set her in his own
saddle on Cochise's back, the horse craning its head to look
her over, as if he'd never seen her before.

"It's her," Spurr told the horse, glancing up at her. "She
just ain't feelin' too well, hoss."

She sat straight-backed in the saddle, her hair sliding

down to nearly cover her face. She stared straight ahead, her face a waxy heart shape in the darkness, her eyes so dark that the sockets seemed empty. She didn't seem to be breathing, and Spurr knew with a chill that she didn't want to be.

Her son was dead. She wanted to join the boy. He couldn't blame her, but he wasn't going to let it happen. Life was a cold-eyed bitch at times, but it had to be lived.

He swung up onto Cochise's back and, leading the spare horse, continued heading west.

Clell Stanhope kept his right hand wrapped around the neck of his sawed-off barn blaster as he mounted the porch's stone steps. He stopped in the doorway, Lester and Magpie Quint flanking him. Inside, Quiet Boon Coffey and Ed Crow were crouched over the still form of Santos Estrada, whom Clell had sent back to the cabin in case the old lawman had headed here.

Which he had.

Estrada lay flat on his back, blood like red pudding staining his serape. Clell strode inside the cabin and Lester and Magpie walked up to either side, all looking around the smoky, messy front room, their gear piled and scattered everywhere amongst empty bottles and airtight tins.

Quiet Boon Coffey, who never said much but let his two silver-chased Bisleys and his Sharps carbine do his speaking for him, looked incredulously up at Clell. "Spurr?"

Clell walked around Coffey and Crow and the dead Estrada and strode down the short hall to the second of the two curtained doorways on the right. The curtain hung tangled. Behind it, the small room was dark and empty, only an airtight tin—the peach tin that Clell himself had left there—shone in the starlight pushing through the unshuttered window.

Clell squeezed the neck of his sawed-off gut-shredder

harder in his sweaty, gloved hands. His pulse throbbed in his fingers, anger rocketing through him. Not just anger—embarrassment. He'd underestimated old Spurr Morgan. He hadn't figured on the man tracking him and the others in the dark, following the woman, then making them all look like bung-headed hillbillies by leading them up the draw yonder and circling around to snatch the woman out of their lair.

Clell had wanted to use the woman to lure Spurr into his trap, all right . . . so Clell could kill the old man slowly just for fun and to show Spurr how old and dried up and useless he was.

Just for fun. So that he and the others could laugh while the old man howled as he died slow.

But the old man—nothing but brittle bones and sinew garbed in ragged buckskins and a grubby hickory shirt—had made Clell look like a damn fool. Him, Clell Stanhope. Leader of the Vultures—the most savage and feared gang to ever prowl this neck of the postwar frontier.

Spurr was likely having himself a good laugh over this right now, wherever he was.

Clell was tensing his jaws so tightly that they ached as he strode back down the short hall and into the main room, where all his remaining men stood in a semicircle, facing him, on the other side of the sprawled carcass of Santos Estrada. The monkey stove ticked; the coffeepot burped.

The men looked grim beneath their hat brims.

Lester sneered. "No way that old badge toter done this, Clell. He must have someone ridin' with him."

"Shut up, Lester," Clell said, walking over to the eating table and splashing whiskey into a tin cup.

Lester scowled indignantly.

Magpie Quint loudly rolled the cylinder of his Buntline Special across his forearm, making a solid, spinning sound in the tense silence. "What're we doin' here, Boss?" he said tightly. "Let's git after him."

Clell's hand shook as he slowly lifted his cup to his lips once more and drank. "Let's not be bigger fools than we already are—okay, Magpie? Is that all right with you?"

The others sort of flinched at Clell's hard glare.

He sagged into a chair and said with toneless menace. "He's headin' for South Pass City. Only place he could be headed with the woman." He sipped from his cup, swallowed, and said even more quietly, flatly as he set the cup back down on the table. "We'll run into him there. Settle this thing."

He set his sawed-off shotgun on the table and stared at it.

Spurr sipped from his steaming coffee cup as he stared across the fire at Erin. She lay curled on her side, facing him and the fire, a blanket pulled up across her shoulders. Her hair lay in a brown tangle across her face. Her eyes were closed.

Spurr raised his quirley to his lips and drew the smoke deep into his lungs. Blowing it out, he turned to look toward the east. The sun was rising, blossoming rose over the shadowy gray hills, a few flat-topped buttes silhouetted against it. A cool breeze blew, foretelling the end of summer at this high altitude.

Spurr figured they were about seven thousand feet above sea level. If he remembered right, South Pass City was around eight thousand. He hadn't visited the town, once a small city, in a while. The last time, there hadn't been much left of it since the Oregon Trail, running ten miles south from east to west, had been rendered obsolete by the transcontinental railroad and the stage lines, and by the gold along the banks of Willow Creek having been mined out.

He hoped for Erin's sake it had a hotel with a soft bed and a good sawbones.

He turned back to her now, humped on the other side of the fire. Her eyes were open, staring at the flames that were growing thin now with the gradually intensifying morning light. She didn't blink for a long time, and when she finally did, she spoke, as well.

"It was when I looked into those cold, leering eyes of Clell Stanhope that I remembered he'd shot him down like some chicken-thieving dog in the street."

Her voice had been toneless, dry, utterly lacking in emotion. As though all her sorrow lay lodged so deep in her soul that there was none near enough the surface to be expressed except for a flat hopelessness in her eyes. Spurr knew there was nothing he could say to ease her misery, so he merely took another sip of his coffee and looked out over the rolling sage-spotted hills, toward the Vultures' cabin that lay about ten miles northeast.

"Best have you a cup of coffee," he said after a time, nodding at the black pot he'd set on one of the stones ringing the fire. It leaned toward the flames, steam curling from its spout. "Then we'd better fog some sage."

She did not move beneath the blanket, but her eyes lifted slightly to regard him dully over the opaque, dancing flames. "Spurr, do you have anyone?"

He pursed his lips, shook his head.

"Neither do I."

"Yeah, but you're young enough to start over."

The thought seemed to disgust her. She dropped her lids slowly, heavily down over her eyes. "I don't want to start over."

"You'll change your mind." Spurr grabbed a leather swatch and used it to lift the coffeepot from the rock and fill an empty cup. He extended it toward her. She didn't even look at it, merely shook her head slightly as she continued to stare at the flames as though trying to decipher some hidden message written amongst them.

He tossed the coffee out and stood. "I know you don't feel up to it, but we'd best get movin', Erin."

"Where are we going, Spurr?"

"South Pass City."

"What's there?"

"A hotel, I hope. Food. I could use a drop of whiskey."

"The Vultures will follow us," she said in that same, chilling monotone.

Spurr emptied his coffeepot on the fire, dousing the flames. Steam hissed and wafted. "Yep, they sure will."

He walked away to fetch the horses.

TWENTY-NINE

South Pass City sat quietly in a bowl amongst the sage-covered hills sheathing Willow Creek, along which gold had been found and carted off several years ago, leaving the shadow of a town in its bustling wake.

Really, the town wasn't even a shadow of its former self anymore. It was a sad ruin that the high desert appeared to be taking back by hook and crook—the sage returning over ancient wheel ruts, tumbleweeds blowing between mostly abandoned shanties and stock pens and business buildings, some blowing straight through via the town's old main drag without anything to interrupt them. Not horses or wagons or the hundreds of rushing prospectors, cardsharps, whores, cold-steel artists, and confidence men who'd once called the town home—at least for a season or two.

Spurr had killed the legendary gunman Lyle Tate here about seven years ago, at the height of the boom. That was when Zachariah Dawson had been the town marshal, boasting four deputies, all gone now. No, not gone, Spurr thought as, riding into the eerily silent town, he glanced over to the town's cemetery on a flat-topped knoll overlooking the creek. The boneyard was a collection of stone and board markers and wooden crosses presided over by a single ragged juniper and a sprawling cottonwood.

Dawson and his deputies had all been killed during an outlaw raid on the town and planted there. A few lawmen had worn the South Pass City badge since then, but, as far as Spurr had heard, they'd merely drifted on because as the gold disappeared and the town died, there was no longer any need for them. Certainly no need now. While most of the buildings were still here, most were boarded up, abandoned, or falling down.

A few horses were tied here and there to hitchracks before the few surviving businesses, but mostly only the tumbleweeds moved, nudged by breezes. The town was now mostly a supply camp for area farms and ranches and the mining camps pocking the Wind Rivers in the northwest. A loose shutter slapped against the old Wind River Hotel and Saloon; it danced in a sudden wind blowing down off the high mountains, tapping and scraping, tapping and scraping in feeble tribute to the cacophony of song and dance and ribald laughter that had once emanated from one of the most lucrative hotels west of Laramie.

Spurr drew up in front of the Overland Trail House. The three-story, wood-frame hotel had never been as prime a destination as the Wind River, but it had done a fine business in its own right, patronized by miners and saddle tramps who partook of its slightly lower grade of whiskey and whores, but which now looked brown and shrunken and just another dusty, sun-weathered ruin despite the OPEN sign hanging in its dusty front window.

Spurr swung down from the leather and looked at Erin, who had taken over her own reins and had obediently followed the old lawman across the rolling foothills—complying with his wishes to stay seated on the outlaw horse, and to follow him, but doing nothing more than that.

Saying nothing. Merely riding. A husk of a woman owning a heartbeat, breath passing in and out of her lungs. But nothing more than that. If she'd had her gun, Spurr was sure that she would have used it on herself long before now.

He would not bother with a silly attempt at best of trying to arrest the Vultures. Things had gone too far for that. He was a lawman, not a vigilante, but sometimes the law had to stop lawbreakers in the only way it could, lest more innocents should perish. There simply were not enough lawmen or judges to stop them without one man—the last lawman north of all-out hell—taking extreme measures.

He would kill Stanhope and the other Vultures for Erin and her murdered boy, if not for Mason and the other lawmen and all the others this bunch had killed in cold blood.

Spurr had little hope of taking them all down, of course. He himself was exhausted, feeling little more than a shell himself. And he would be alone in his stand against the savages. But he'd get Stanhope if none of the others. Maybe, with luck, his ghost would rise up out of South Pass City's boothill and take down the others with their own guns as they slept. Before they could continue their reign of bloody murder and unbridled torment.

Spurr reached up and took the reins out of Erin's hands. She did not look at him but only gazed at the hotel as if trying to figure out what it was, as though she'd never seen such a structure before. Spurr tied their reins around the hitchrack that bulged around the worn spots in its peeled pine crosspole, then helped the woman out of her saddle, setting her gently on the ground before taking her hand, sliding his rifle out of its saddle boot, and leading her up the porch steps. The second step from the top was rotted out, and Spurr stepped over it, then turned to help Erin over it, as well. He led her across the creaky porch littered with old newspapers and tumbleweeds and through the hotel's batwing doors.

He kept the woman behind him as, while the doors slapped, he stopped a few feet from the entrance and looked around, seeing only one customer in the place—the half-breed, sitting at a table on the room's far left. The big, brown-skinned man sat casually, almost insolently kicked back in his chair, his saddle and rifle on the floor beside him, his saddlebags draped across his lap. He was sewing a patch into the back of one of the pouches, the contents of the pouch—an old coffeepot, a tin frying pan, a pouch of Arbuckles, some cartridge boxes—spilled around a mug of frothy beer on the table before him.

When he looked up, his green eyes glowed startlingly in the crisp, clear light from the doors and windows.

"What the hell are you doing here?" Spurr asked the man, annoyed. He was getting tired of the man's unexpected appearances.

Henry looked up while continuing to sew the leather patch into his saddlebag pouch. "Me? Hell, I'm darnin' this old saddlebag. Plum wore out, I reckon."

Spurr snorted. He ran a hand across his mouth and walked over to the bar paneled in dull green wainscoting on the room's right side. He stopped short when he saw a blond woman standing behind the counter, in front of a back bar painted the same dull green, with a cracked, warped, age-spotted mirror behind several green shelves stocked with dusty bottles and glasses.

Spurr felt his jaw hinges loosen as he stared at the woman, a slow smile crawling across his ragged, dusty face. "Well . . . Della Ramsay. You still here?"

"Where else would I go?" the woman said in her sexily raspy voice, leaning forward, hands spread atop the bar.

She held a cigarette in her right hand; the smoke curled up along the right side of her blue-eyed face that was still fine-lined and even-featured and pretty despite her years. She must have been pushing forty, with crow's-feet around her eyes and mouth. But her long, straight hair was as blond as he remembered, with only a few streaks of gray. Her eyes were as clear and frank as those of a twenty-year-old.

Spurr had met Della Ramsay years ago in Leadville, when she had been plying the trade, and had last seen her here in South Pass City, working for percentages again but also dealing faro at the Wind River. He'd never known much about her—aside from that she knew her business right well—but he'd heard that she'd been married a few times, mostly to cardsharps and prospectors, though never for longer than a few months at a time.

She rolled her eyes toward the ceiling, and a childish light danced in them. "Like the new digs?"

"You own this place now?"

"Why not? It was free. Old Handly pulled out last year. Tried to sell it for a dollar. I offered fifty cents, and he just threw up his hands including the deed to the place and rode away." Della chuckled. "So I contracted with the Davis outfit to haul me in a few bottles of whiskey every spring and fall from Rawlins, and I got a business. Not gettin' rich, but I wouldn't know what to do with rich . . ."

She looked at Erin still standing just inside the doorway behind Spurr and frowned dubiously. "Who's . . . your friend, Spurr?"

"Erin Wilde, meet Della Ramsay." Spurr glanced back at Erin, who stood staring uncertainly into the shadows at the rear of the wooden-floored, low-ceiling room. Seeing that she was not going to offer a response, he turned back to Della and said softly, "Vultures."

Della's reaction to the name of the notorious gang, much feared in these parts, was not oblique. She set a hand on her chest, worrying the brooch pinned to a black choker at her throat. "Don't tell me . . ."

"They're behind me, Della."

She cast a nervous glance out the window on both sides of the swinging doors. "I hope you've got someone to back you, Spurr."

"Did have. They're dead. It's just me, Della. I'll be back

down for a drink, but I'd like to get Mrs. Wilde situated in a room."

"No charge, Spurr." Della offered a weak smile. "I figure you'll drink plenty. You always did."

Spurr tossed several gold coins onto the bar. "Not this time. Gotta keep my head about me. Oh, I'll wet my whistle but I don't reckon I'll be fillin' any trash barrels." He plopped one more coin onto the bar. "But I'd admire to have a cork pulled for me when I get back."

Della winked. "Take whichever room . . . or rooms . . . you want. I ain't exactly overburdened just now. Waitin' on the fall roundup, which usually brings a few punchers in. Doors are open."

Spurr glanced again at Henry, who sipped his beer, set his mug back down on the table, then resumed stitching his saddlebag pouch. It was hard to tell if he'd been paying attention to the conversation. His broad, cherry face was as stony as a veteran gambler's. But he likely didn't miss much.

The old lawman walked over and took Erin's hand and led her to the back of the room and up the narrow stairs. He opened the first door he came to on the second floor, led her inside, and opened the curtains over the room's sole window.

"Please, don't," she said.

Spurr glanced back at her. She sat down on the edge of the bed, her hands on her knees. "I'd like it as dark as possible."

Spurr closed the curtains with a sigh and turned to her. "I'll fetch up some food."

She merely looked at him, downturning her mouth in a remonstration.

"You gotta eat something."

"Is my son eating something?"

Even with the casual, gentle way she'd said it, the retort was like a hard slap across his face. What did you say to something like that? Spurr merely walked to her, placed a

hand on her shoulder, squeezed it gently, then walked out
of the room, closing the door behind him. Behind the door,
he heard the bedsprings sigh.

Spurr walked downstairs to see that the half-breed had gone,
taking his gear with him, leaving his empty glass on the
table. The lawman bellied up to the bar on which Della was
laying out a game of solitaire. She'd popped the cork on a
fresh bottle and set a glass beside it. Spurr splashed whiskey
into it and threw it back.

"You got a safe place you can go? A cellar or
somethin'?"

She looked up at him from her game, a sad, fearful cast
to her gaze. "They won't bother me. They know I'm the only
watering hole around."

Spurr refilled his glass. "They got their tails in knots,
Della. More so than usual." He threw back the shot, set the
glass back down on the bar, and grabbed his rifle. "Best find
a place to take cover. I'll be atop the Wind River, should
have a good vantage from up there."

"Spurr, are you *tryin'* to get yourself killed?" Della
straightened and crossed her arms on her breasts. "Ain't no
one here to mourn a fool."

He racked a shell into his Winchester's chamber, off
cocked the hammer, and glanced at Yakima Henry's beer
glass. "Where'd the half-breed go?"

Della hiked a shoulder. "Who knows where they go? Just
a drifter. Been through here before; he'll likely ride through
again." A strange, pensive, faintly longing expression shaped
itself around her blue eyes and her red mouth as she stared
at the half-breed's table. "A tumbleweed, that one."

Spurr gave a wry snort and went out.

THIRTY

Spurr discovered three other businesses still in operation in South Pass City—the Grover H. M. Henry Hardware and Dry Goods, a harness shop, and the livery barn once owned by Wild Bill Harriman but now operated by an old cowboy named Melvin Lilly, who lived in a cabin behind the place with his consumptive wife, Rose.

Spurr stabled his horses with Lilly, whom he informed of the Vultures' threat and suggested the man spread the word to Henry and Harriman, adding that they all should consider staying low until the storm had passed. Spurr didn't appreciate the dark, worried look the old cowboy gave him after the lawman left the livery barn with his Winchester, but he could understand the man's skepticism.

He wouldn't want him protecting his town from the Vultures, either.

He limped up the street to the tallest building in town—the Wind River Hotel and Saloon. The windows were boarded up, but it wasn't hard to pry off one of the boards and step through the gap. As he moved through the dark, musty bowels of the place, he felt ghosts staring out at him from every dark nook and cranny, remembering all the revelry that had once taken place here, all the chips and gold dust won and lost at the roulette wheels and poker tables.

He continued up to the broad, creaky stairs, rats squawking indignantly, bats mewling and flapping somewhere unseen, to the fourth story and strode through one of the east-facing rooms. After kicking out another couple of planks from over the door to the balcony, he stepped out and looked around at the sprawling, dilapidated collection of buildings appearing forlorn under the lens-clear, high-country sun.

There was little movement except what the light wind blew. Peering off to the east, Spurr saw little movement out there, either. And, when he'd peered off another balcony on the building's opposite side, he spied nothing in the other directions. The Wind Rivers were like giant anvils, tall and sprawling and snow-capped to the northeast, their slopes and foothills sliced with canyons through which the Vultures might ride toward the town, staying out of sight to within a mile or so.

But Spurr didn't think so. They knew he was only one man alone. Even if he'd equaled their number, it was their custom to ride in roughshod and to squeeze as much terror out of their victims as possible before they started blasting away with their guns.

He dragged a chair out onto the balcony that faced east and sagged wearily into it, his bones creaking almost as loudly as the chair's dry wood. He leaned his gun against the wall behind him, sat back in the chair, and keeping an eye skinned to the east, slowly built a quirley.

He'd built and smoked the quirley and was wanting another one, and still nothing moved in the east. There were only the rolling hills of sage, juniper, and cedar, with occasional bluffs and escarpments jutting against the horizon.

Spurr leaned forward, elbows on his knees, blue eyes

carefully scanning each fold, every tree and rock and shallow gulley—anywhere a man might hide. "Where the hell are you?" he heard himself growl, not liking the fatigue he heard in his voice.

The sun arced slowly across the sky and dropped quickly in the west. Shadows turned, lengthened, thinned. A gray veil dropped over South Pass City. Footsteps sounded in the street, and he stood and looked down to see Della Ramsay moving toward him holding a round wooden tray and a plate covered with a red towel. When she saw Spurr, she stopped, her blond hair and the shawl she'd drawn over her shoulders buffeting in the chill breeze whispering over the mountains.

"Spurr, you gotta eat," she said.

It wasn't like him, but he wasn't hungry. Or maybe he just hadn't realized he was.

"Don't come in here, Della," he said, not wanting her to negotiate the hazards of the dark, dilapidated building. "I'll come down."

Inside, darkness had settled thickly over the hotel's ruined husk. He found a candle, lit it, and used it to light his way down to the broad front porch. Della stood just outside the boarded-up doors, holding the tray from which the rich, succulent smell of a hot steak emanated. Spurr's gut gurgled, twisted. He was hungry, after all.

"Just fried one for myself and Mrs. Wilde and remembered that hollow leg of yours." Della smiled. Two bottles stood on the tray—one with amber liquid, one with clear. "Whiskey and water," she explained.

"Don't know how to thank you, Della."

She narrowed one eye as the breeze rustled her freshly brushed hair, bangs hanging over her brows. "How 'bout keepin' yourself alive? I could use someone to share a drink and a game of cards with. Gets quiet around here between roundups."

Spurr accepted the tray from her. "I'm gonna give it my best shot."

"Any sign of 'em?"

He glanced to the east along the broad, darkening street. "Not yet. They're out there, though. I can smell 'em."

"Might be an overfilled privy on the windward side of town." Della gave a disgusted expression. "What'd this territory ever do to rate those devils?" She reached up and placed a hand against the side of his face, caressing his ragged, dusty beard and leathery cheek. "You're one of the good ones, Spurr. You be careful."

"Best get inside now, Della. No tellin' when they'll show."

She caressed him an instant longer, offered him a brittle smile, then turned and, holding her skirts above her feet, walked down the hotel's rotting steps. Spurr watched until she was safely back inside the Overland Trail, then ducked through the gap between the boards over a window, relit his candle, and headed back upstairs. He sat back down in his chair on the balcony, tray on his knees, and dug into the succulent steak, smiling. Della had remembered how he liked it done.

He drank the whiskey mixed with water so as to keep him head about him, and ate the steak and fried potatoes and two large chunks of crusty, buttered wheat bread. When he'd swabbed the last of the steak juice off the plate with a last scrap of bread, he gave a belch and set the tray on the floor. He used his knife to sharpen a match, picked his teeth clean, then tossed the pick over the balcony into the street below and grabbed his rifle.

He looked around carefully. Near darkness had fallen, though small, dull streaks of red and gold flashed occasionally as the sun continued sinking behind the far western ridges. Stars kindled like lamps of a distant town. He raked his gaze carefully up and down the street, but seeing nothing there he retured his scrutiny to the east. The skin above the bridge of his nose creased.

He narrowed his eyes, felt his weak ticker increase its